I0724369

To Die For
VIRTUE
SCARLETT FINN

Also by Scarlett Finn

GO NOVELS
GO WITH IT
GO IT ALONE
GO ALL OUT
GO ALL IN
GO FULL CIRCLE

EXILE
HIDE & SEEK
KISS CHASE

WRECK & RUIN
RUIN ME
RUIN HIM

THE BRANDED SERIES
BRANDED
SCARRED
MARKED

FORBIDDEN PREQUEL DUET
ALL. ONLY.
ONLY YOURS

TO DIE FOR...
TO DIE FOR TRUTH
TO DIE FOR HONOR
TO DIE FOR VIRTUE
TO DIE FOR DUTY
TO DIE FOR LOVE

LOVE AGAINST THE ODDS STANDALONE COLLECTION
SWEET SEAS
HEIR'S AFFAIR
RESCUED
MAESTRO'S MUSE
GETTING TRICKY
THIRTEEN
REMEMBER WHEN...
RELUCTANT SUSPICION
XY FACTOR

NOTHING TO...
NOTHING TO HIDE
NOTHING TO LOSE
NOTHING TO DECLARE
NOTHING TO US
NOTHING TO SAY
NOTHING TO GAIN
NOTHING TO YOU
NOTHING TO THIS
NOTHING TO DO

THE FORBIDDEN NOVELS
FORBIDDEN DESIRE
FORBIDDEN WANT
FORBIDDEN WISH
FORBIDDEN NEED
FORBIDDEN BOND

KINDRED SERIES
RAVEN
SWALLOW
CUCKOO
SWIFT
FALCON
FINCH

THE EXPLICIT SERIES
EXPLICIT INSTRUCTION
EXPLICIT DETAIL
EXPLICIT MEMORY

MISTAKE DUET
MISTAKE ME NOT
SLEIGHT MISTAKE

RISQUÉ & HARROW INTERTWINED
TAKE A RISK
FIGHTING FATE
RISK IT ALL
FIGHTING BACK
GAME OF RISK

LOST & FOUND
LOST
FOUND

ONE

WHEN IN THE AIR on the way to London, the miles had stretched between her and Daire. Those miles didn't feel any shorter on the bus ride to Miami.

Leaving him in the Beast, giving him permission to follow his gut, was the least she could do. The guy dealt with an overwhelming sense of responsibility. Since birth, it had been drummed into him that Olympus was his everything.

Given the explosion, the potential devastation, of course he should be with his people. His Olympus comrades were his family, or the closest he had. That didn't change just because they had feelings for each other. Daire's priority was Olympus. His life was Olympus.

The television news mentioned fatalities. Any number of Daire's underlings could've been killed in the blast. And his superior, his mentor, the man he looked up to as a father, who also happened to be her biological father, whether he'd kept his life was still unknown too.

For her, in their relationship, her Heart said he wanted to be uncomplicated. Tess wanted to be his freedom. Whatever he had to do, whatever was right, her love would endure.

The Sunshine State was beautiful, shrouded in

glorious light. Just like she remembered. It hadn't been so long ago that she and Daire enjoyed it together. Well, her and Danny.

From her current angle, it didn't look quite the same, yet it was so welcoming, comforting. All her memories of being there with him were positive. Even the not so positive ones. In Miami, the truth of her mother's death hit her hard. It was in Danny's arms she'd found solace.

Danny, Daire, one and the same. Almost.

A lot of time was spent thinking about her past. About their past too. Daire had taken over her life. No, he'd taken over her heart. Her soul. Her breath. Her being.

Running away together sounded romantic, though it wasn't really an accurate description. After freeing her from the thug escorting her for Zeus, rather than letting her go on the run alone, Daire hitched his travel-trailer to his truck and fled with her.

They'd been less than five hundred miles from their destination when they learned about the desert house explosion on the TV. In a convenience store. While they were making out.

Damn. Hadn't she told him she wouldn't compromise his integrity? She'd tried to be strict. Well, she'd said the words they should be strict about being platonic, because he belonged to Olympus, not her. In theory.

If that was true, she wouldn't be so worried. Her father, Harry, also known as Hades, may have been caught in the Vegas blast. Her father could be dead. She'd known him for less than two months and might have lost him already.

All her life she'd been with her mother. Only her mother. They moved from town to town, city to city, trying to escape the Olympus shadow. Not that she'd known it at the time. They were running from some unknown something, that was all she'd known.

By complete accident, after her mother's unexpected death, she'd found a stash of letters. Love letters she later learned were from Harry. Written in vague terms with coded references, making immediate sense of them was impossible. Those letters started her on the path of discovery, determined to find out about the writer and the ominous specter in her wake.

As part of that mission, she'd gone to a junkyard to search the remains of the car her mother died in. It was there she met Danny Winger. Hauling Danny's trailer, they traveled across the country and back again, pursuing her mission.

In the end, it turned out Danny was dropping the breadcrumbs she was gobbling up, believing that they were making progress. But it was all a lie. A con. A double-cross. He wasn't Danny Winger at all, he was Daire Canon. Protégé to her father.

His ruse ended at the Olympus Beta site, where he'd been raised to be the perfect operative. Elite expert and the supreme agent, Daire was the pinnacle of a lifetime of constant training. Thrust together by tragedy, Harry fulfilled the role of tutor and parent, and the ward dedicated his life to winning his surrogate father's approval.

She'd learned so much in such a short time. Six influential and affluent individuals from different areas of government, crime, and business created Olympus. They recruited three young soldiers to be trained as the principal agents. Hades, her father, was one of those three principals. Poseidon, James Garrick, was another.

The third principal, Zeus, was a man named Ulysses Sherwood. Heading up the strategic section, he was the overarching leader.

Overarching and overbearing.

Ideas above his station led to the benefactors, known as the Six, bringing Operation Zulu to Harry. Its aim? To eliminate Zeus and restructure Olympus. Of course, the plan was secret. Top secret. Classified. The process was slow; the timing had to be perfect. As the months went on, Harry brought in individual subordinates to inform them of Operation Zulu, so as to minimize disruption after the assassination.

Except it never happened.

Lowell, the only remaining original member of the Six benefactors, informed Zeus of the plot. Harry only just managed to send an alert to his men, saving their lives by telling them to flee.

Long story short, the Exodus happened. The principals and agents disappeared in the wind.

Daire hadn't been aware Zulu was on. While Styx, Daire's surrogate brother, was chosen as the assassin and had been the first person Harry told.

Just like any family, they had their issues.

The brothers hadn't seen each other since at least the Exodus, just over a year ago. Harry hadn't seen Styx since then either, or maybe even before that. Where was Styx when it all went down?

She'd have a chance to ask him. Soon.

Back to the Danny/Daire duplicity. She'd discovered that in the Olympus Beta control room when Daire tricked her into meeting her father. The men faced off in there, any of them could've been killed in a snap. Daire's feelings for her and acceptance of his father's apology prevented him from following through. Whether her father knew about her and Daire's intimacy was still a mystery. They'd never been blatant about it, and he'd never asked.

Sort of by accident, the three of them met up with Poseidon. Through the Zone project, he'd gathered some of the Olympus agents. At the time of the Exodus, most of the agents were taking part in an experimental process that infused them with some kind of synthetic isotope. That isotope was traceable within a certain radius of the control unit.

Garrick had taken a couple of operatives into the field to try tracing others. As far as she knew, they were still out there. If that intel was accurate, they wouldn't have been around during the explosion.

The explosion.

It was so fantastic, in the most horrific way, that she almost couldn't wrap her head around it.

Zeus sent her to the desert house to retrieve the keys he needed to revive Minotaur, the Olympus mainframe. They weren't there, Tess knew that, but she'd gone anyway. Just as she knew her running away would piss off Zeus.

But she couldn't have imagined…

Clinging tighter to the bag on her lap, she stopped looking at what was outside and stared into nothingness. They didn't know for sure what or who caused the explosion. If it was Zeus, it was on her. The man was used to being on top, used to dealing with disciplined, obedient agents who respected his authority. That wasn't Tess. Her attitude tended to center around acting in the moment without a lot of consideration for the future.

Except this time, it was possible her impulse had cost lives.

Olympus might be intrinsically linked with her existence, that didn't mean she wanted it to rule her life. Funny that a big part of the reason she'd started down the rabbit hole was to free herself from the looming threat. Getting away wasn't so easy. The more time went on, the deeper she got pulled into the mess.

All she wanted was Daire's happiness. If that meant Olympus, then she planned to deliver for him. Hence Miami. For her rendezvous with Styx. The brother Daire didn't know she'd allied herself with while in London.

In the busy, fast-moving European city, Styx tracked her down and they got to know each other a little. At the same time, they'd hatched a plot to steal the two keys in Zeus's possession and meet again in Miami.

One of Styx's conditions for helping her was keeping their association a secret. She had, which meant it probably wasn't such a bad thing she'd left Daire behind.

Presenting the brothers to each other without warning could be a disaster.

Fox Den. That was the name of the club where they were meant to regroup. Inside, across the bridge, past the seating and through the curtain. Easy as pie. Other than knowing the club was in Miami, she wasn't sure of its exact location… or what kind of club it was.

People began to move around as the bus approached the terminal. It wasn't super busy, so she didn't have anyone next to her. Still, she'd kept her carpet bag in her lap as opposed to stowing it or even putting it on the seat next to her. It contained most of what she'd had in London and some of her Vegas clothes. In it would be something club suitable to wear, and maybe some makeup, enough that she'd be able to fit in.

She'd get a cab and change in the back. There was no point finding a motel or setting herself up anywhere until she'd seen Styx. Perhaps he wouldn't be there at all. Maybe he'd had an involuntary detour of his own. If he was there, she'd get the keys and… What next? She'd really intended to give them to Daire, except he wasn't with her, and his people were in a precarious position. If she put those keys in his palm, there was a good chance he'd hand them straight over to Zeus to protect what remained of his men.

Everything she and Styx had done would be for nothing. Ultimately, it was Daire's choice, but she didn't want him to regret it. Didn't want him to be manipulated by a man who didn't understand the meaning of honor.

The explosion.

Images from the TV news flashed in her mind's eye. Her father could be dead. Zeus might have killed a man who'd been in his life for decades, since they were basically kids. And to kill his own men. Bodies had been taken out of the smoldering mess. The news reporter said they were unidentified. Who could they be?

Harry had no reason to set charges. Despite not being close or knowing each other well, she couldn't imagine her father, who'd dedicated his life to rearing agents for Olympus, would execute the men he'd nurtured.

Putting it out of her mind wasn't so easy. Except she had to. Would Styx know? He'd have seen the news. That was a reprieve. She didn't want to be the one to tell him his fellow operatives could be dead.

The bus pulled in and came to a stop. People got up to retrieve bags and organize themselves as others filtered down the aisle. She didn't leap up but was in no mood to loiter either.

Slipping into the aisle in front of a guy who gestured for her to go first, she offered a smile in thanks. Without being too pushy, she excused herself around those blocking the way and eventually got to the front.

Tossing her rebellious hair from her eyes, she went down the stairs and jumped onto the asphalt, only to turn toward the sidewalk and stop.

There, leaning against a pole, was a man she recognized. Arms folded, ankles crossed, he was waiting… for her.

TWO

WHILE STANDING FROZEN, holding up others, gaping at the familiar man, people split from behind her to go around and on their way. She didn't even think to kick herself out of her shock until he boosted his shoulder off the pole and came over to take the bag from her.

"Good to go?"

His arm curved around her shoulders to draw her away from the bus.

"What…" she stuttered, stumbling along, being led by the man she'd left behind just hours before. "Daire! What are you doing here?"

"You said Miami. Didn't take much detective work."

Stopping, she turned to face him, prompting him to stop too. "Why didn't you go home?"

"I did," he said, brushing the hair from her face. "Driving in the opposite direction to you wasn't ever gonna be right. You go, I go."

"Daire," she exhaled, her hands relaxing on his torso. "Harry… your men."

"If they're gone, they're gone," he said. "Me rushing over there won't change that. I said never again, and I meant it. Whatever we are to each other, whatever our future is or isn't…" He scooped both hands under her hair to cup her jaw, tipping her face up toward his. "I can't have you out of my eyeline."

Speechless, she couldn't figure out how to show him what his choice meant to her. Olympus was his purpose. Harry the closest thing he had to family. Yet, he'd walked away from both to be by her side.

When she blinked, a loose line of moisture escaped the corner of her eye.

Daire dipped to kiss it away. "You want me to leave, I'll leave," he said, trailing his lips to hers. Though he didn't actually kiss her, the promise was there as his breath merged with hers. "You are my meaning and my reason."

His curse, but not his salvation.

Sealing her lips, she restrained a yelp of emotion that wanted to escape. Her fingers curled around the edges of his jacket, clinging to him. She could force him to leave. Olympus was supposed to be his primary focus. Distracting him could backfire. Taking him away from his unit could lead to resentment, especially because it was her fault he hadn't been there at the time of the explosion.

Except he was there, with her, by choice. No one compelled him to be there. He'd been free to go back and deal with the fallout. Liberating him from any guilt or fear of repercussions in the Beast, she'd given him back to the cause that had driven him since he was a child.

While she was still processing, he stepped back and bent to pick up the bag at their feet. She hadn't even felt him drop it. That was what being so close to him did to her.

"You got the truck?"

"No," he said. "Got a cab, didn't know your plan. Figured it was best not to be hindered… or to show potential enemies our ride."

"Why do you think I brought you here?" she asked, taking his hand to pull him through the people and concrete, seeking somewhere she might find a cab. "We're not here for a fight."

"Shame," he said. "I could use one."

Her lips curled as she peeked over her shoulder.

"Keep that unvented tension for me later. You came all this way, least I can do is be your pressure valve. It's my absolute favorite thing in the world to be."

Spotting a line of cabs, she headed for the first one and was about to jump in when Daire gave her arm a sharp tug, hauling her back behind him. Confused, she watched him open the door and gesture for her to get in. That's what she'd been about to do. Seemed he knew that. Why did he want to open the door?

Once they were both in with the door closed, she slid to the front edge of the seat. "You know a club called Fox Den?" she asked the driver.

"Sure do," he said and got them underway.

Drawing down the side zip of her skirt, she grabbed her carpet bag and slid to the opposite door to put it on the seat between them.

"What's in Fox Den?" Daire asked as she searched around inside her bag.

She frowned at the dress she pulled out. "I don't really know yet."

Deciding it was fine, she dumped it in her lap then crossed her arms to pull her top up over her head.

"Uh, babe…" Daire said, shifting position, shoving the bag around his back to his previous seat while he landed in the center, twisted to face her, blocking her from the driver. "What are you doing?"

"I need to get changed," she said, tossing her top into his lap since he'd put her bag out of reach.

Pushing back, she shimmied out of her skirt and gave him that too.

"I'm not a fan of this plan," he said, planting a hand on the door next to her, doing his best to shield her.

Smiling at him, she sat up, stealing a quick kiss before trying to figure out her dress. "You're adorable," she said. "I doubt he cares and even if he does, you think he'd be fool enough to make a move while you're here?"

"What worries me is this was your plan before you knew I was around," he said as she put her dress on over her head. "And there are people outside too."

"They're even less likely to make a move," she said, raising her hips to straighten out the skirt. "There. All done."

Twisting to put her back to him, she scooped her hair aside and waited for him to pull her zip up. Once done, she slid back to dip under the arm he had braced on the back of the seat.

"What are you doing now?" he asked, trying to see her as she took makeup from the bag.

"Have to sell the picture," she said, opening her lit compact to do what she could in the confines of the cab with few supplies.

"You didn't tell me we had to dress for the occasion."

"I don't know what kind of place it is," she said. "It's better if you don't come in anyway."

He caught her chin to bring her focus to him. "You want me to wait outside?" She said nothing, just blinked at him. "Bambi eyes won't work for you here. They only remind me how important it is to keep you safe."

"I'm not doing Bambi eyes, I'm admiring the man I love."

"That won't work either," he said, tipping her head one way while his went the other.

Tess smiled. "You thinking how much prettier I am with makeup on? You could let me finish."

"I'm thinking I already don't like whoever you're going to this effort for."

"How do you know there's a someone?"

He let her go, so she returned to her makeup.

"Because the thing I thought you wanted to come for, it turns out you already have. We're nowhere near the places we came before, so you're not retracing our steps."

Putting her makeup away, she squeezed under his arm again because he was still caging her into the corner. If it made him feel better, she wouldn't complain. Retrieving her comb and her perfume, she sat up to spray her décolletage and noticed his frown when squirting it on her wrist.

"What?"

"Now I have a hard-on," he said, fixating his grump on the side window.

Poor guy didn't seem happy about it. Laughing, she leaned in and trailed her fingers from his cheek to his chest. "Then you really should wait outside. I don't want to get in a cat fight for your affection."

He didn't say anything, just turned to slouch against the seat, folding his arms. She combed her hair, and used her fingers to boost the volume, twisting to flip it across his lap before flipping it back.

"Now you're doing it on purpose," he said.

"What on purpose?"

"Your little routine meant to drive me nuts."

Leaning in, she held the comb and perfume in her lap, pouting up close to him. "That little routine looks much more like my mouth open and your cock in my throat," she purred.

His jaw relaxed only to clamp shut again as he exhaled. His grump amused her. Maybe it was just because she'd told him he couldn't come into the club. But she liked to think some part of it was down to them being in company.

Living together in the Beast, driving together, they were spoiled by the time they had alone. Sure, it had only been a few days, but it had been enough to remind them what it was to belong to each other with complete unrestricted access.

"Besides," she said, pressing her body into his lap as she deliberately stretched further than needed to put everything back in her bag. Staying there strewn across him, she tilted her focus over her shoulder to find his. "We're platonic, remember?"

The grump dwindled just a little. He laid a hand on her hair, stroking down the length of it and continuing on to her ass. He spanked her so hard she sat bolt upright.

The shock written across her face seemed to erase his bad mood.

His smile quickly became a short laugh. "In Miami, you were mine, Little Red."

No matter where she was on the planet, she was his. Even if she didn't want to be, even if she fought it, not that she would. She couldn't remember not being his and never wanted to. Daire might belong to Olympus, but she definitely belonged to him. Though she'd never put it to him like that, he lived with enough guilt and sense of responsibility. Uncomplicated meant not laying anymore pressure onto his already strained shoulders.

Picking up his arm, she wrapped it around herself and nestled against him, closing her eyes as her head rested on his shoulder.

"I don't know what's going to happen in this place," she said, hoping Styx would be there.

Although she hadn't broken her promise not to tell anyone about him, bringing his brother to his doorstep was really striding deep into a gray area.

"Whatever happens, we'll deal with it together."

Her eyes opened. "Even if we can't be together?"

That wasn't the first time they'd had the discussion. "We will always know the truth."

No matter what, he accepted her, and whatever she needed. Daire accused her of tormenting him with her routine getting ready for the club. But the guy was no saint when it came to tormenting her heart.

The cab pulled to a halt. As she ducked down to try seeing where they were, Daire took money from his jacket to pay the driver. In the shadow of the cab, she hadn't really paid much attention, but something drew her eye downward to a gun in a holster on his waistband under his jacket.

Before she could say anything, Daire grabbed her hand and guided her out of the cab onto the sidewalk. They didn't get far. She tugged his hand to get his attention.

Moving in close, she slipped her hand into his jacket to lay it on the gun grip while searching his eyes. "Why do you need that?" she whispered. "How did you even get it?"

He brushed the hair caught on her gloss away with his thumb. "I have it because you have me walking into an unknown."

"You're not walking in anywhere carrying that," she said, recalling her conversations with Styx in London.

The men might consider each other kin. That didn't mean they wouldn't act against each other in anger. If there was a gun in the mix, Daire could act too quickly. Before he thought through what he really wanted to do. She wasn't ignorant of his ability to kill. That wasn't her problem. Styx believed Daire had the right to take him down for the way things had happened before the Exodus.

She didn't want Daire to kill his brother. Not only because she liked him, but because he'd regret it in the long run.

"Just…" she said, letting go of his hand to step away. "Stay out here. I'll be back."

Leaving him there without giving him a chance to object, she went into the building, toward the pulse of music. Though there were people in the booths and the coat check place, no one stopped her as she strode on to the internal double doors up ahead.

Going inside, she only took a quick second to glance at the clubbers and the lights. Music was the dominating force. Everyone came for the music, for the heat, for the freedom.

Everyone except her.

Following Styx's instructions, she went over the bridge walkway to a seating area filled with tables and booths. The bar was right where he'd said it would be. Between the end of that bar and the empty booth opposite was a curtain with the word "private" above it in stark, glowing white letters. That was her goal.

Everything was as Styx described. The curtain suggested whoever was back there didn't want an audience. Having come so far, a piece of fabric wasn't going to deter her. Confidence got her through the front door, so she let it carry her onward.

Without looking in the direction of the bar, to give the bartender no chance of stopping her, she pushed the curtain aside and stepped around it.

The increased illumination took her by surprise. It wasn't bright, but certainly was lighter back there than it had been in the club. Blinking to adjust her eyes, she found herself under the scrutiny of four men seated around a card table at the far side of the room, next to an opening in the wall that led to a darker… something.

Couches and other tables around the cobbled-together room didn't look like any of the club she'd seen so far.

The men just waited, watching her, so she broke the silence. "I'm a friend of Patch's."

That did something. The four of them looked at each other.

The one who appeared oldest spoke. "He didn't tell us he was expecting anyone," he drawled.

A test. It had to be. She was grateful to her mouth for asking questions. "Maybe because whoever you spoke to wasn't Patch, because Patch is no he."

Again, they glanced at each other before returning to their assessment of her.

"What you need Patch for?" the older guy asked. "Patch only works with the best."

"I'm sure," Tess said. "I'm a friend of Patch's, I didn't say I needed Patch."

"Wrong season," the older guy said. He wasn't old, old, and definitely appeared keen. He'd be handy in a fight. He had that quick, shrewd look about him. "You're looking for a hand-up, you've gotta come in winter and bat those pretty eyes at Dam."

The guys around the table seemed to enjoy that comment. She didn't get it or know who Dam was. How to respond? Styx hadn't told her to mention him and, as far as she knew, that meant his condition of secrecy was still in place.

Before she came up with anything, a voice came from the shadowy opening near the men's table.

"Done playing with her yet?" the male voice rose. She perked up in anticipation, waiting for him to reveal himself. When Styx came into the light, she relaxed. "Took your time, Lady. Deal was for you to come alone."

She frowned, unsure how he'd known. "I did… didn't I?"

Styx wasn't looking at her, he was looking past her to someone she hadn't heard join them. "Hello, brother."

THREE

SHE DIDN'T NEED TO LOOK to know the identity of the person behind her but did anyway. By the curtain, glaring across the room at his brother, was the man she'd left outside. The one meant to stay outside.

Her bag was on the floor a few feet from him. "What are you doing…" she said, though Daire was so focused it was doubtful he heard her. "I asked you to wait outside."

Styx was no less focused. "Golden boy, ignoring orders?" he asked, subtle in his amusement. "The old man will have you running laps for days for insubordination. Lost your tact too. You knocked out three of my guys to get in. Isn't discreet."

Her mouth opened in shock as she twisted to Daire again. Still, he saw nothing except his brother. Given the direction Styx had appeared from and the timing, how did he know what his brother did to get in?

Her Heart's narrow eyes were laser precise on the man in his sights. "They tried to take my gun."

The guys at the table took that revelation as a warning and pushed their chairs away from the table to get closer to the wall.

"Don't worry," Styx said, inching his chin their way.

"My brother is a pretty good shot. If he wants to take me out, one shot'll be enough."

Panic fueled her retreat to Daire. Styx wouldn't put up a fight and her Heart didn't know that. "Daire—"

"What did I tell you about code names in the field, Lady?" Styx asked.

Spinning around to pin her back against Daire, she hoped to prevent him from reaching for his gun. "He doesn't know, Styx. Please don't… Letting him is not the same as provoking him."

"He's trained to take emotion out the equation. He's good at it too. If executing me is his mission, he'll carry it out. What is your purpose here, Ares?"

"None of your goddamn business."

"So it's personal, not professional," Styx said, easing away from the doorframe, showing he held a gun in his concealed hand. "Good. Always said you needed to grow a set."

She gasped but didn't have time to say a word. Somehow, Daire had already put himself in front of her. He'd reacted before she even fully registered the threat.

"Thought guns were for pussies," Daire said, aiming his weapon at his brother.

"I've acquired a taste for them."

Still trying to figure out what was going on, the parallel between her first meeting with her father and this moment was striking. At least this time she wasn't between the firearms. Although either of the men being hurt or killed wouldn't be a win.

Her pulse pounded. Laying her hands on Daire's ribs, she wanted to speak or get in front of him, except any sudden movement could startle the men into action.

"What do you want, Styx?"

"You wandered into my house, brother. Uninvited."

"Please, don't…" she said, trying to go around Daire.

He stepped to the side, blocking her, scooping his other arm around to hold her at his back.

A shot went off. On instinct, she ducked. Daire didn't react at all, he didn't flinch or recoil. The bullet hit the wall behind her, betraying the identity of the shooter. Instead of firing back, as she might expect, Daire's arm sank to his side.

"You need practice," Daire said, stalking across the room toward his brother.

Holding her breath, tension tightened her every muscle. The possibilities were agonizing. She wouldn't be able to bear it if they hurt each other.

One twitch and Styx could put a bullet in Daire. Only she knew he didn't want to. Unless he'd been lying in London. Maybe the plan wasn't to let his brother kill him. If it was a lie, she could be seconds away from losing the most important person in her world.

Styx didn't fire. Daire shoved his gun back into its holster and swept his brother's gun arm aside to get right in close, facing off with the man point blank, toe to toe.

"You always were better up close," Daire snarled. "With your bare hands, right? It's your gift."

"If I wanted to kill you, you'd be dead ten times over," Styx hissed, dropping his gun to shove Daire back.

Her Heart swung, making contact with his brother's jaw, sparking a flurry of movement. Styx swung; Daire blocked. There was a punch and push; the card table tipped over as they crossed the room in combat. Furniture fell and the card-playing men leaped from their seats to get out of the brothers' way. She was frozen to the spot. They were fighting. Actually fighting. Hitting each other, blocking, grabbing, shoving.

Snapping out of her trance of amazement, she dashed across the room. "No," she screeched. "No. No!"

Forcing herself between them, she didn't care about the blood or the panting or the adrenaline racing heart beats firing their testosterone. She wouldn't let them hurt each other. Wouldn't let them turn on each other in that crucial time.

As she ramped up for a lecture, Daire breathed out. He was behind her, his weight bearing down on her back until he began to relax. Styx's lips twitched, he smiled, then the man behind her was laughing and the two of them were slapping their palms together, doing some special handshake.

"You've let yourself go," Styx said.

"Me? Fucker, what was that upper left cross? Weak. You haven't been training."

Styx put a hand to his shoulder and rolled his arm. "Had some fun this year, still getting back up to speed."

"You need an assist?"

"Nah, I was good… Got my ass saved by a beauty with a set of balls and a fuck-me figure."

"Really?" Daire said, the note of interest in his voice teasing. "We get to meet this beauty?"

Styx exhaled a laugh. "Don't think her boyfriend would like that. Boyfriends don't like you."

Lost, she didn't know whether to be shocked or relieved. "What the hell?" she asked. The moment was reminiscent of Daire and Harry burying the hatchet after a simple apology. "You were trying to kill each other!"

"Just for fun," Daire said.

"You get H's message?" Styx asked, talking over her.

Message? What message? Her ignorance was irrelevant.

Daire answered. "Yeah."

When was the message sent? Received? What did it say?

"Get proof of life?" Styx asked.

"Not yet," Daire said. "Tomorrow… This your SP?"

"Nah, just friendlies," Styx said. "Got something serious yet?"

"As per instructions, yeah."

Tipping his head in a backward nod, Styx backed away. "Come upstairs, I'll grab my shit."

He disappeared back into the shadowy doorway. Daire's hands landed on her shoulders to push her after him. They went up some stairs into a hallway that was like going through a time warp. Styx led them into a bedroom with a pink rug, bare floorboards and not a stick of furniture that matched.

"Take a seat, Lady," Styx said without turning around.

Daire urged her toward the bed while keeping his own post by the closed door.

"This isn't Olympus," Daire said.

"Encyclopedia would know," Styx said, grabbing a familiar bag from the floor by the other side of the dresser nearest the window.

"You wanna give me a report?"

"We're not on a mission, bro," Styx said, taking things from the top drawer to put them in his bag. "And no one is coming for us here… Even after all the shit that's gone down, you're loyal to the core… It's the orders, isn't it? You're going nuts without a specified objective."

"How do you know?" Daire asked.

Styx paused to look at his brother. "Twenty-one years, that's how I know. The old man's fine and you know it, he's made of steel."

Just like his word in the letter. These men were raised by her father. Losing him would be a blow. It had to be on Daire's mind, maybe Styx's too.

"We've gotta keep it together," Daire said.

"Yeah, 'cause Z just blew it to shit… I'm gonna bet it's 'cause someone didn't hit her mark." Styx turned to her. "You missed your flight," he said, coming over to angle her chin toward the light. "Your mouth get you into trouble?"

"Maybe," she said. Before giving him any kind of update, there was something more important to clear up. "You have something of mine."

"Yep," he said, returning to his bag to unzip an inner pocket.

When Styx next faced her way, he held up his hand and opened it to let the bullet drop on its chain. Ecstatic to see it swinging, she'd missed it more than words could express.

Pouncing to her feet, she dashed over to snatch it from him. "Thank you," she said, putting it over her head and sweeping her hair out of the chain.

Holding it in a fist, she closed her eyes and exhaled in relief.

"Feel better?" he asked, then returned to his conversation with his brother. "We won't get to Z."

He spoke as though her involvement in the moment

hadn't happened at all. The men clearly shared a mindset and followed the same train of thought.

"No," Daire said. "I'll bet he's already burrowing in deep."

"We have to send a message."

"Your favorite way to send a message is to gift wrap a corpse."

Styx shrugged. "What's wrong with that? I know where the Six are."

A ripple of trepidation crossed Daire's shoulders. "Where?"

"Fourteen."

Her Heart exhaled disbelief. "I should be surprised, but I'm not… You need a go order for a move like that."

"So get me one."

Obviously, Styx didn't think that was going to happen.

"Beta site's in lockdown," Daire said. "I was there but couldn't get into the armory… Guess now we know why H was so adamant about us training without equipment. What I'd do for a field rig right now…"

Styx's hand disappeared into his bag and a moment later, he held up the black box she'd seen in London. "Got a Gizmo."

Daire straightened up, clearly not expecting to see it. "How did you…? Shit, you were in the field when the Exodus went down."

"Yeah," Styx said, putting it down on the dresser. Daire started toward him… or it. "For all the good it will do you with Minotaur offline."

"We can ping H's base unit," Daire said, turning it toward himself.

"Maybe," Styx said, going to his brother's side. "Will he know it's us?"

"We can open comms… if we're careful."

"Can't verify the clearance with Mino offline."

"Then we bypass Mino," Daire said, surprising her by pressing something on the device to bring up a glowing image of a keyboard on the lower portion of the perpendicular device.

She couldn't see it very well, bobbing back and forth to peek between the brothers. The unit hadn't physically changed; the lines were just vague light in an otherwise unremarkable space. What else could it do?

"You have the clearance for that?" Styx asked.

Daire crooked a brow at his brother. "I have H's clearance."

"We're gonna use his clearance to contact him? How the hell does that work? He can't be in two places at once."

Her Heart was working furiously on the glowing keyboard, the screen filling with letters, numbers, and symbols as he went. "With Minotaur offline, we could get away with it. Gizmo won't code through the system; I'll have to reach out to the base unit direct."

"For a guy so set on following the rules, how come you always know a way around them?" Styx asked, putting a glimmer of a smile on his brother's face. "We don't wanna do that when we don't know where he is or who's watching."

Closing the unit, Daire laid a hand on it. "Yeah, we should be stable, prepped and ready."

"He expects a battle," Styx said. "You sure you're ready for this?"

"More ready than you. We have to get you in shape before H sees you again."

"That could be a while," Styx said, putting the thing he'd called Gizmo into his bag before zipping it up and throwing the strap over his head, across his body.

"You got a ride?"

"Out back. Follow me."

FOUR

THEY DROVE THROUGH the dark streets of Miami. Daire in the driving seat, as he knew where they were going. At least, that was her assumed reason for him driving Styx's car.

She expected them to arrive at the Beast. For Daire to take his brother back to the place he'd been calling home. Instead, they ended up in a shady area. The kind of neighborhood no woman would be comfortable walking through in the daytime, let alone in the dark. Glancing around at the spray-painted gang signs and dilapidated buildings, she couldn't believe it when Daire drove down an alley into a shadowy parking area and switched off the engine.

Styx seemed to get that they were at their destination and got out to retrieve his bag from the trunk, his brother not far behind him.

No stranger to shady areas, there were rules about places at the lower end of the economic scale. Walk at a consistent pace, don't look around, keep a key in hand to be used as a weapon if anyone approached. Sometimes she got hassle but didn't have any problem telling people where to get off. Showing confidence was usually more effective than appearing afraid.

Her mind was working. The brothers had referenced a message. She wanted to know more. What did it say? Who sent it if they didn't know for sure that Harry was alive? Daire said he wouldn't get proof of life until the following day. Was that proof of Harry's life? She didn't get it.

The side door opened, startling her.

"Get moving, Lady. No time to take in the scenery."

That wasn't the hold up. She hadn't believed that was their destination. How had Daire managed to find the place, wherever they were, and still be at the bus waiting for her? Sure, a bus took longer, but even she had to marvel at his efficiency… though the why still made little sense.

Climbing out of the car, she took her bag from Styx and went over to where Daire was holding a door open at the top of two steep stairs. He didn't say a word as they went inside, along a short hallway and up stairs that were mostly unlit.

They ascended to an apartment on the fourth floor. Daire unlocked the door like he owned the place and went inside first. She was about to follow when Styx caught her arm and held her back. She expected him to say something, but he wasn't even looking at her. Waiting, she was about to ask what was going on when Daire returned to open the door fully.

"Clear," he said, taking her bag out of her hands and going inside.

Styx prodded her back, forcing her to go after him into a dark living room. It wasn't the homeliest of spaces. Furnished with fabrics and woods that had seen better days, she saw only a narrow galley kitchen to the left and a bunch of other doors, three of them in an alcove at the back of the space. It wasn't home and it didn't make sense why they were there. Was Miami their base now? Where was the Beast?

"Vantage points from three sides," Daire said, going to the right to slide open a glass door that led to a balcony. She guessed anyway. A fine curtain fell over the space as Daire stepped away, so she didn't get a good look. "Three bed, one bath. The master is dual aspect."

"Then that's where we setup," Styx said, checking the front door was locked before crossing the room with his brother to disappear into another.

What was she supposed to do? She didn't want to stay in a dingy apartment in a crappy neighborhood for no reason. Obviously, there was a reason, probably something to do with Harry's enigmatic message.

After standing alone for a couple of minutes, she went after the guys. When she opened the door, both men looked up from the bags they were searching. Something was on the bed. With the low lighting, details weren't easy to pick out.

"You're sleeping across the way," Daire said, grabbing her bag and leaving his brother. "I'll show you."

She was sleeping on her own? Yeah, that made sense. They were supposed to be platonic. It wasn't so easy to play when they had a witness who couldn't know about them.

Daire came over and took her arm to lead her out of that room. "The bathroom's there," he said, pointing to the door on their left at the end of the shallow space.

He took her across the small hallway to a door diagonally opposite. Letting her go when they crossed the threshold, he put her bag on the end of the bed and turned like maybe he intended to stride right on out.

Tess was quick to hop into his way. "Why are we here?"

Laying a hand on her arm, he tried to be gentle about easing her aside. "I don't have time to explain."

Blocking him was the only way to keep him there. "Make time."

The impatience in his eyes didn't linger. Eventually, he exhaled. "We're here because Harry told us to be here."

"How did he tell us that?" she asked. "This message? Can I see it?"

"You won't understand it."

"Because I'm too stupid?"

"Because it's coded," he said.

His hand rose toward her face, but it stopped, and his fingers curled into a fist. Red alert. He'd stopped himself from touching her. Something he'd done before when Harry was around. That time, rather than encourage him to touch, her attention fell to the marks on his knuckles.

"I can't believe you hit Styx," she said, grazing the swelling with a fingertip. "He'd have let you kill him, you know."

"Fucker doesn't get away that easy," he said, lowering his hand from her reach. "I've got work to do."

"That's it?" she asked, swaying to the side to prevent him from opening the door. "I need more than that. Is Harry alive?"

"I don't know."

"How can you not know if he sent you a message?"

"The message could've been setup days ago, I just picked it up today."

"If he's dead, why are you following his instructions?"

Frustration seeped into him again. "We assume he's alive until we get word otherwise."

"When will you get word?"

"I replied to his message. All being well, we'll know tomorrow."

"He could be injured or in hiding."

"Yeah," Daire said without elaborating. "You don't have to worry about anything. Like Styx said, Harry's made of steel. I'm sure he's fine."

"How sure?"

"How worried are you?"

His tension wasn't encouraging. Usually, even when he was stressed, he'd let her past his defenses. In that room, it felt like a wall stood between them, thick and high, impenetrable.

Things hadn't been strained in the cab on the way to Fox Den. Seeing his brother again must have changed something. Except, thinking back on it, things hadn't been quite the same as normal when they met at the bus. He hadn't kissed her, hadn't touched her, not like her Heart would. Right then, if she wasn't wrong, he was avoiding looking her in the eye.

"Kiss me," she said, testing a theory.

"What?" he asked in a low volume. "No. Not here."

"Daire," she said, moving right up close until her body touched his. "Kiss me right now." He met her eye, progress… except the fierce, almost anger she read wasn't positive. "When did you get Harry's message?"

No reply. Taking her time about licking her lips, she wanted to distract his mind and began unbuckling his belt. Before she got as far as taking the leather from the metal, he retreated and pushed it back in.

"What are you doing?" he asked as though she hadn't undressed him a zillion times in the past.

"You came back for me," she said, advancing in a seductive strut, lowering her voice to sultry. "And we're all alone."

Daire continued to back away. "We're not alone. Styx is in the next room."

If being overheard was the only thing worrying him, he'd make some comment about her inability to promise silence when they were together. What she saw wasn't an aroused man pained to refuse her. The prey before her was much more tense, much more angry… much more guilty.

"He doesn't care," she said. Daire came up against the bed and looked around for a way out. "I'm sure he can keep a secret."

"No," he said, snatching her wrist when she reached for him again. "Stop this."

"But you love me," she said, blinking in innocence. "You came back for me." The set of his brow and the clamp of his jaw confirmed her suspicion. "You'd just let me go right on believing that, wouldn't you?"

"Tess—"

"When did you get Harry's message?" she demanded, yanking her arm from his grip. "When?"

His jaw moved, highlighting his reluctance. She wouldn't let him leave without answering. It wasn't like she missed the fact that he wanted to keep the information secret, she just wasn't going to make it that easy for him.

"I can shout if that will make it easier for you—"

"After you left," he admitted.

"Before you decided to come after me," she said,

angry at herself for being so gullible. "Goddamnit. You really would've just let me go on believing you came for me, wouldn't you? This message, Harry's message, it told you to come to Miami, didn't it? Because he still thinks the Scepter is here… or are you going to pretend you haven't told him I have it?"

"I haven't told him any damn thing," he said, bowing to get closer as he spoke in a quiet hiss. "Everything we are is in confidence."

"Yeah, right," she said, tossing her hair from her eyes. "Why bother with all the *'driving in the opposite direction wasn't ever gonna be right.' 'You go, I go'* crap?"

"It's not crap," he said, without raising his voice, though he managed to convey his annoyance. "I do fucking love you, but what the hell am I supposed to do? I got an order from my superior—"

"I don't have a problem with you following orders. I never did. I have a problem that you came to the bus terminal, that you followed me to Fox Den. You and Olympus are back together, I'm so happy for you," she said, ladling on the sarcasm. "But you did not have to drag me back!"

"Would you lower your fucking voice?" he growled.

Reminding her of the shame of their relationship didn't do him any favors. "I'm so sorry that I actually have emotions, that I can be hurt and angry, and know how to express myself. I think I have a right after you fed me a bunch of bull and let me humiliate myself all for your amusement. You could've carried on your damn mission without coming anywhere near me and I wouldn't have been any the wiser." Instead of answering, he closed his mouth. The way his gaze slipped to the side was enough to bring doubt to her statement. "Unless you couldn't…" Easing back a step, another wave of hurt hit. "I am your damn mission," she breathed out the words. "You came for me because he told you to."

"No," he said, adamant in his conviction. "No, I came because what you're doing is dangerous. Because you are in danger."

"That's why he wanted you here. When Zeus figured

out I was gone, he went to the house for me or somehow told Harry to return me. Harry knew I was there. Knew we left together." Concentrating on the window, he didn't show he was listening, but he was. He always was. "So Harry told you to stick with me and come to Miami. The fact I was coming here anyway wasn't even part of the equation."

"Tess—"

"Don't," she said, putting her hands up to back away. "Don't bother." She grabbed her bag from the end of the bed. "Styx has your beloved keys by the way…" She kept on going backwards towards the door. "I hope you'll all be very happy together."

"I won't let you walk out of here."

"Then put a bullet in me," she said. "Because that's what it will take to keep me here."

Spinning around, she crossed the last few feet to reach for the door, but he was already at her side, reaching over her to slam it when she tried to open it.

"What choice did I have?" he hissed above her ear.

"You had the choice to be honest," she said without taking her fingers from the door handle. "You had the choice to tell me Harry ordered you to be with me."

"No one has to order me to be with you," he said. Her eyes closed when his mouth descended to her hair. "Little Red."

"No," she said, facing him, putting a hand on his chest to separate them. "You can't do it to me again. You can't use what I feel against me, it's not fair."

"You think any of this is fair?"

Maybe it wasn't. Whether it was wrong or right, she expected more from him. And that, right there, was her mistake. In falling in love with him, she'd developed expectations of him, something she'd promised never to do.

Going around him, she needed space. "If he hadn't made me your mission, you'd be on your way to Vegas right now."

He shook his head. "You don't know that. I don't even know that."

She smiled, not because she was happy, but because

the truth was obvious. "I always accepted Olympus came first for you." Those were her father's words. At the time, she hadn't understood the depth of their truth or how they would affect her. "I told you I gave you up because Olympus needed you. It was easy to forget that when we were apart or Olympus was in limbo. We made a mistake."

"No," he said, shaking his head again as he advanced on her.

"We should never have crossed that line again after Beta. We shouldn't have done it."

"Don't undo everything that's happened since then," he said, stern yet beseeching. "Don't undo everything we are."

He didn't get it. How he'd hurt her. After promising herself not to be a pawn, the man she loved had manipulated her emotions for Olympus's benefit... again.

"I'll let you do your job," she said, dropping her bag. "But don't talk to me like I'm anything more than that."

"Temptress—"

"Pandora," she said, meeting his severe gaze. "That's who I am. That's all I am. Once you get your proof of life, tell him I want to leave. Keeping me here is your role and I'm not dumb enough to think I can fight my way past you... To be honest, I can't think of anything worse than having your hands on me right now." Despising her own weakness, she turned away while swiping a tear from the corner of her eye. "Tell your superior your mission was a success... But your asset, or your mark, whatever I am, I want my freedom."

"Tess—"

"If there's a problem with using my code name or your objectivity, I'd suggest your colleague be the one to deal with prisoner interaction."

"You're not—"

"I'd like to be alone now," she said, wrapping her arms around herself. "Please."

Silence lingered with the tension in the air. He might want to say more, but she couldn't hear it. She didn't realize, didn't have a clue, just how much it could hollow her out to be hurt by the one person, the only person, she'd trusted. That was her mistake.

The only signal he'd gone was the closing of the door. She wouldn't be dramatic, couldn't be for fear Styx would overhear and figure them out. So she'd stay put and hope Ares passed on her request to his superior.

Objectivity. Daire had been trained to have it. She would fake it until they let her go. If they let her go.

FIVE

TESS DIDN'T SLEEP. At all. Which was a nightmare. Acknowledging Daire's motivation wasn't devotion, as he'd led her to believe, was bad enough. The last thing she wanted was to hear him and Styx moving around the apartment all night.

Neither of them came into her room and they weren't exactly rowdy, but every once in a while, she'd hear a raised voice or a laugh. They were bonding. Finding their normal again. Good for them.

Feeling sorry for herself didn't exactly identify what kept her awake. Sure, she didn't enjoy admitting how easily she'd accepted Daire's reasoning. Considering how being his mission made her feel wasn't fun either. But as she lay there, staring at the ceiling, she fought to come to terms with her own lack of belonging.

Daire always had a purpose. Styx had found his in Harry at a young age. Olympus gave those who were a part of it meaning.

What did she want?

Freedom. For her life to be her own. Why? In gifting her the boutique, Hugo was the first person to offer her stability. Given that his house was now a crater, it didn't seem likely that opportunity was still available.

Such a beautiful home, gone. Trading it in for the dive apartment in a shitty neighborhood was some step down. Daire delivered what Harry wanted. She'd never doubt that. No one who knew the truth ever could. Her father would have his reason for the move, and it was beyond her to figure it out. Hazarding a guess would only end in embarrassment.

She waited until the sun rose before getting up to slip out of her bedroom and into the shower without seeing the guys. Once changed and ready for the day, she was determined to shirk her melancholy.

She departed her bedroom only to stop short at the sight of Styx sitting at a folding table near the mouth of the kitchen.

"What are you doing?" she asked, fixing the chain around her neck to tuck the bullet beneath her shirt.

"Eating breakfast. What are you doing?"

Bending sideways at the waist, she examined the empty table, then crooked a brow at him. "I'm going out."

After only one step, he asked, "What for?"

"For fun," she said, wondering how he liked the explanation they'd given her for their fight the previous day. "And to get coffee."

"There's coffee here," Styx said.

"Not the coffee I like," she said, gliding closer to the door. "I like it to come from actual beans." Just at that, an arm appeared from inside the kitchen, holding up a bag of beans. Daire. Grabbing the front door handle, she scowled at it. "With coconut milk."

It didn't surprise her when he spun away from whatever he was doing to open the fridge and produce the carton in the other hand. Damn him for his training and efficiency.

Styx laughed. "Looks like you're out of excuses, Lady."

"I don't need excuses. If I want to go out, I can go out."

"London teach you nothing?" Styx asked, swinging on his chair. "Who knows what kind of weirdos could approach you out here?"

"The weirdos out here don't worry me, Prince," she said. "Weirdos in America are apple pie and ice-cream, a refreshing taste of home."

He dropped the chair back onto four legs and stood up. "You wanna go out for coffee? We'll go out for coffee."

She bounced backwards, waving a palm at him. "No, I don't want you to come with me."

"It's okay," he said, advancing on her. "I'll give you time to get changed."

She glanced down at her denim cutoffs and tank under a thin white shirt. "What's wrong with what I'm wearing?"

"Nothing," he said. "If you want to get hit on every twenty-five seconds."

She thrust her chin up. "Maybe I do."

"Cool, then you're going about it the right way. Those legs, babe, what the hell?"

The smirk on his face just confused her.

"You armed?" came the call from the kitchen.

"Long as I have my hands, I'm armed," Styx said. "She's shorter and skinnier than me. I can take her down if she gets rowdy."

He was teasing and she resented him for it. Lifting her foul mood would be impossible while he was making it worse.

"Are you having fun?" she asked. Styx just shrugged, slipping his hands into his pockets as he moseyed closer. "Good. Stay here and have some more because I'm going out alone." Except when she tried to leave, the door wouldn't budge. "Where are the keys?"

Styx was all innocence as he twisted toward the kitchen. "I don't know. Ares, you know where the keys are?"

"Nope," he called out.

Keeping his distance was a good idea, especially when the brothers' antics were only souring her mood further. "Are you kidding me?" she asked, setting a hand on her hip. "Is this what we're doing now? Juvenile games?"

"I don't think it's juvenile," Styx said, nonplussed by her obvious annoyance. "Just good sense. If we can't get out, the bad guys can't get in."

She wasn't so sure that she wasn't looking at the bad guys. Mischief didn't equal benevolence.

"Even in London I was allowed to go out."

"Yeah, and look what happened there," Styx said, coming over to take her hand from her hip to loosen her fingers from their fist. "You met me and we hatched a plan to screw over the guy holding you. We won't make the same mistake."

Then, more than ever, she really needed her space. "Have you spoken to Harry?"

"We got proof of life, which is something," Styx said, trying to draw her forward.

Resisting, she took her hand back. "I will not live my life cooped up in this place with you two. I need to do something. To be busy. To get air."

Accepting that he wasn't going to tempt her further into the apartment, he switched tack, turning her around the other way to urge her over to the balcony. The key was in that lock. Styx turned it and slid open the door. Instead of letting her go outside, he pushed the curtain over the space he'd just created.

"There's your air," he said.

She laid a glare on him. "Are you kidding me?"

"You weren't so high maintenance in London."

"It wasn't ninety degrees in London."

The fact it was early and hadn't reached that temperature yet didn't mean that it wouldn't.

"If that's the problem, we'll get you a fan."

"Styx," she warned.

"Here," Daire said, appearing from the kitchen. He tossed something across the room, which Styx caught with little effort. "Take her out."

"Oh, I'm being granted permission," she said, folding her arms. "How magnanimous of him."

"He's right there," Styx said, pointing back over his shoulder. "Aim the attitude at him, if he's the one it's for."

Yeah, he had a point. Refusing to even look at Daire as he disappeared back into the kitchen was hardly discreet.

"Let's just go," she said on a sigh, walking past Styx to stop at the door, waiting for him to unlock it.

The moment he did, she yanked it open and strode down the hallway. Sitting inside stifled, being around Daire, was suffocating her. She didn't know what to do or what to think. Their relationship was a rollercoaster of extremes. Even if she wanted to talk to him about Harry's orders and her hurt, she couldn't. Styx was there to witness their every encounter.

She went down the stairs and was about to turn and stride to the largest door at the front.

From behind, Styx snagged her arm and spun her toward a narrower side door. "We're going out back."

"Why?" she asked, with no choice except to go with him because he had hold of her arm. "I want air."

And from what she remembered of where they'd parked, there wasn't much space, which meant little light or air.

Her explanation came when he continued around the car and opened the front passenger door for her.

"We're driving?"

He nodded once. "We're driving. Get in."

Going out for air didn't mean going for a drive. It might seem ridiculous, but she really despised being dictated to. Not just that she was told what to do, but that they didn't give her any consideration or option for input.

Still, getting into the car, she didn't feel like fighting another battle. Styx got in and backed them out of the alleyway. She put on the air conditioning and considered switching on the radio to prevent the need for conversation. The truth was, she didn't need any more voices in her head.

"He's never had trouble with women," Styx said after a couple of blocks. She didn't even care what he was talking about and slipped off her shoes to slouch deeper into the seat. "I mean that's how it looks from the outside. That he's never had any trouble with anything. Everything comes easy to him. He's good at everything. It looks that way, but it isn't like that. He works at everything; he works hard."

"Do we have to talk?" she asked on a sigh and shaded her eyes from the sun when they turned a corner to head toward the sea.

"I'm saying it wouldn't be such a bad idea to cut him some slack," Styx said. "He's been through a lot of shit this year."

"Mm hmm."

In her peripheral vision, she noted his double take. "You don't give a shit?" he asked. "The guy's gonna keep you alive."

"I didn't ask anyone to do anything," she said. "I'm sort of sick of men coming into my life explaining how they're going to make everything all better for me. I don't need to be saved."

"You think?" he said. "You told Ares about the keys."

Her jaw moved forward. She was grateful to have her hand near her face to conceal her irritation.

"The whole point of getting the keys was to give him a way to make Olympus what he wanted it to be," she said. "So give him the keys, I really don't care. It wasn't a power play for me."

Though if Daire wanted the Scepter, he'd have to tell her where he left the Beast and the truck. Although he'd told his brother about the keys, she didn't know what he'd told Styx about them and where they'd been staying since leaving Vegas.

"The keys are safe. They're not the primary concern."

Her curiosity piqued. "They're safe?" she asked. "Where?"

"Not here, that's for damn sure."

She sat up quickly. "You didn't bring them here? Where the hell are they?"

"Safe," he said. "I knew Zeus would notice them missing. I hoped it would be after your ass was on a plane back to the States, but it worked out. He could've had contacts here intercept you when you landed, so you'd have ended up back in his control anyway."

"I didn't have the keys. What did it matter if I was in his control?"

"You don't think H has his reasons for wanting you

alive?" Styx said. "I read his message. It was clear. You are to be protected at all costs."

Because her blood was important to the cause. Somehow, that information stuck in the back of her mind. Despite Daire's diverted loyalty and misdirection, she was happy to have revealed the blood thing. If his reaction was honest and he hadn't known, then he could tell Harry she knew and deal with that conversation.

Styx was proving himself to be a loyal Olympus agent too. Not that she'd expected him to be a rebel or fight her corner. But, just like Daire, he had a mission, to keep her safe, and he was carrying it out.

As far as she knew, he wasn't aware of the why, but it didn't matter. A mission was a mission. An order, an order. That was the only reason he needed.

SIX

"I DIDN'T ASK TO BE PROTECTED," Tess said.

In the driver's seat, Styx frowned. "You're acting like this is some kind of hardship. That it's a game."

"You know what?" she snapped, twisting her whole self toward him. "Olympus is your choice. It was Harry's. It was Daire's. And yes, I'm using everyone's real name because I am not a super-agent. I didn't ask to be involved in this. My whole life, since the day I was born, I have been treated like an asset or vulnerability to be exploited. Why the hell would I choose to have any part in this? I am never treated with respect, never treated like a human being. I am a thing for all of you to fight over. Not because anyone cares about me, no, because I'm an easy mark."

Because she could be used against her mom, against her dad. Even now, although it went unsaid, she wasn't being protected because her father loved her or cared that much. If Daire was right, Zeus needed her blood to move JARR. That meant Harry needed it for the same reason. Daire needed it because his superior did. Whether Styx knew or not, that was why he'd been tasked with keeping her safe.

Until living it, no one could know what it was to be nothing more than cells in a body. That was why these men were fighting over her. Why they were determined to keep her close to them rather than let their opposition get their hands on her. Having her meant having an advantage over the others. Her blood was taken without permission to be part of their plot. That was what they were really battling over. If it didn't need to be living, Zeus would've just bled her dry and let her die. She wasn't so sure her father's instinct wouldn't have been to do the same.

The one person she'd believed might see her, might care about more than just some biological factor, had used her feelings against her. At the bus station, Daire's return meant the world to her, though it had confused her too. When she thought for that brief moment he'd chosen her over Olympus, for the first time she'd really felt valuable to another human being. He'd let her believe that.

Instead of being honest and admitting Harry's message brought them back together, Daire used her love, her weakness, to gain competitive advantage.

If he'd asked her to comply, told her the truth, explained why they couldn't be intimate while she was his mission, she wouldn't have liked it, but at least he'd have given her some dignity rather than letting her embarrass herself.

Styx took them to a coffee place and parked right outside. He went inside with her and cut her off to say they wanted takeout when she considered whether to sit in. Being there would kill some time. What was there to rush back to her newest prison for?

In too little time, they were back in the car, driving again.

"H doesn't like people feeling sorry for themselves," Styx said.

"You know what? I don't give a damn what H likes. It really pisses me off that I'm supposed to make concessions for him, for you, for fucking Olympus, when all I want is to be left alone. None of you have to deal with me. None of you ever have to even see me again, let alone think about me. Just let me go and it'll be done. I'll be gone."

"Can't do that."

Yeah, she'd figured that out. Wouldn't stop her

reinforcing her desire to be given the right to make her own choices, rather than just dragged along with everyone else's.

"If H is so hard-done-by having to endure my presence, if you and Daire are so damn tired of cajoling and manipulating me, why is that any less you feeling sorry for yourselves than what I'm saying?"

"It isn't," he said, relaxing further, though he hadn't started tense. "I'm warning you not to expect him to be any different, any more open even when he gets here."

She'd sort of known seeing him would be inevitable, though had avoided thinking about it. "And when will that be?"

"Don't know. We got proof of life, that's it. Ares won't post a response until he's tried to get the Gizmo connected to H's base unit. A direct conversation, if it's secure, would be preferable. If we can pick up his messages, others can too. Zeus might be underground, but he could be watching, waiting for his moment."

More drama and intrigue, exactly what she wanted no part of. "You know, I was sort of surprised when I found out Harry wished I'd never been born. Now I see his point."

"It's not so bad, you know," he said, adjusting his shoulders in the seat. "The Olympus life. Sure, it takes over everything, but at least you have something to do… and they teach you how to take care of yourself."

"Something I doubt you ever needed to learn," she said. If he'd killed his father before meeting Harry, Styx had never been a slouch when it came to protecting himself. "Though it wouldn't teach me anything, Harry already ruled that out."

"You asked him to train you?"

"I made an off-hand comment, not a serious request," she said. Just as she'd said to Daire, she wasn't ignorant of how terrible a soldier she'd be. "He has no interest in me being a part of it, which is just fine by me."

"Even so," Styx said. "Living on the compound, you'd be protected."

"Do you really think there's going to be a compound after this?" she asked, checking out his profile. "Do any of you? I don't see how you can go from kidnapping and betrayal to explosions and murder only to turn around and play happy families again."

Styx shrugged, sliding both hands down to rest his loose fingers at the bottom of the wheel. "If anyone can make it happen, Ares can. And we'll be okay. Whoever wields the God of War wins. Ares is victory." She was sort of sick of hearing that too. The man was apparently so incredible that he could do anything, fix anything, yet he wasn't trusted to make his own choices, to follow through with his own directives. "If we can get Poseidon back on the reservation and put him with Ares between Hades and Zeus, yeah, it could happen."

Sort of incredulous, she couldn't fathom it. "Why would any of you want that? Why would you want to work under Zeus again? How could you ever trust him? He might say he's over it, but how could you ever know that for sure?"

"Not my department."

"You just go where you're told and do what you're told," she said, figuring that helped her understand why the agents couldn't see things from her perspective. "You could be more. Both of you. All of you. Instead of all the backstabbing and maneuvering, you could achieve something so much better if you just went your separate ways."

"H saved my life."

"I know."

"I mean, he's my family, Ares is my family. H would have my balls for saying it, but I don't fight for Olympus. Olympus can go fuck itself for all I care. I go into the field to back up my brother, because my brother needs someone at his six, eyes on the back of his head. That's me. I'm those eyes. His shadow. I do the dirtiest of jobs, the wettest of jobs, so he doesn't have to. Why do you think H picked me for Zulu? Because I was his favorite or he thought I was better than Ares? No, he did it so Ares wouldn't be in the position of having to murder his home. Killing Zeus was a prelude to a bigger restructure. You know that. Olympus, the very fiber of it, would've changed... Whichever way it went, it was better for me and H to be the ones making those changes, making those choices, because Ares always carries more responsibility than he should. For everything."

"I know you love him—"

"Fuck love," Styx said. "It's exactly what I was saying when we got on the road. It looks like he's the perfect agent, like he's impeccable, impervious, focused, but that's not his natural state. He trains every day, beats himself up more than any other guy, because he carries the weight of Olympus around with him more than any other operative. To us, it's a job, it's a way of life, a family. To Ares, it's his entire existence, his universe, the reason for breathing in and out. Him and H went through a lot of shit before I came around. You know some of it was about you and your mom. Everyone else came into this with their eyes open, they made a choice. Yeah, I was a dumb kid, but I could've walked away any time if I wanted to. H wouldn't have forced me to stay. Ares knows nothing else. He needed H and after H lost you and your mom, H needed him too. To say they were codependent would be a massive understatement. Then you have Zeus in the mix, aware of just how good Ares is and how eager he is to please. Ares was another way for him to manipulate H, to get what he wanted, to rule over everyone. He'd never let Ares go any more than he'd walk away from Minotaur."

Which gave her a better understanding of just why Styx had been so eager to kill him. Except…

"If that's true," she said. "Assassinating Zeus would've turned his world upside down."

"Yeah, and he'd have hated me for doing it," he said. "Like I told you in London, it would do the guy a favor. Maybe it wouldn't have seemed like it and he'd have put a bullet in me, but it would be worth it. Without Zeus and the weight of Olympus, Ares could breathe. Can you imagine what the fuck a guy like him could do, could be, if he was just allowed to breathe a minute?"

She didn't have to be told. She knew just how much happier he could be if the breath of Olympus wasn't fogging his neck, bearing down upon him, always expecting more.

"We shouldn't talk about this," she said.

Ares wasn't her responsibility. Olympus wasn't either.

Styx had to make his own choices because he'd be the one living in the situation, with those people, long after she was gone.

"I didn't slaughter Z in London because you told me to get a go order... If I'd ignored you and done it, maybe we wouldn't have lost those guys in Vegas."

"You blame me for their deaths?"

Maybe he was right. She'd stuck her nose in where it didn't belong, believing she was sticking up for Daire. It didn't seem she'd had the right to speak for him then, and she sure didn't have it now.

"I don't know who I blame," he said. "If Z was the one to pull the pin, he's to blame."

"You could've had the keys, Z dead, and already be on your way to Minotaur with H and Ares."

"Or you were right and Ares would've put a bullet in me the second we came face to face," Styx said. "We don't know anything. Not yet. Not until we get a direct line with H... Could be he's the one who wants to take me down."

"Why would he?" she asked. "He chose you for Zulu and told you first because he trusted you."

"He hasn't reached out, not since the Exodus alert."

She licked her lips. "Z told him Ares was with him. That he'd chosen Z's side." Maybe it wasn't her place to clue him in, but it wasn't like she had anything to lose. "H left you to Ares. He thought you were together, you were in contact or something."

"He didn't want to make it harder for Ares," Styx said, tightening his grip on the wheel. "He was gonna bow out..." A few seconds went by, then Styx exhaled in frustration. "If that doesn't show you how he values Ares, nothing will. He was willing to take the heat, the blame for everything that went down, and to let Ares and me join with Z, just so Ares could keep Olympus."

His head was shaking, yet the frown on his face didn't seem surprised. Tess wasn't either. She'd known Daire for a tiny blip of time compared to how long Harry had known him. His dedication to Olympus was undeniable. He kept proving that over and over again.

"He belongs with Olympus," she said. "I don't think anyone could ever doubt that. He and Harry put the past in the past for the good of the organization."

"Everything he does is for the good of the organization."

Her attention drifted to the side window. "I know."

He'd come to Miami because Harry told him to. He'd waited for her bus to arrive because his mission was to keep her safe. Harry needed her blood for JARR. Everything was Olympus. Daire valued himself less than any mission, less than the company. Why shouldn't he value her and their relationship less too?

What she'd said to him was right. They had made a mistake. After discovering the truth of Daire's connection to her father and to Olympus, she should never have allowed their intimacy to continue, on a physical or emotional level.

How could she be mad at him for something she'd known since the day of that discovery? But she could protect herself. He was an agent of Olympus. Her father's protégé and trusted advisor. In contrast, she was a tool. A prop. Something they needed to achieve a goal.

They needed her blood. So she needed to talk to Daire. If she complied and didn't offer any resistance, she'd let them take what they needed from her on one simple condition. Afterwards, she would never see or hear of Olympus, or any of its operatives, ever again.

SEVEN

WHEN THEY GOT BACK to the apartment, the balcony door was closed. All the internal doors were. Maybe because Daire was on his feet by the folding table, looking down at the flat Gizmo.

Styx locked the front door after them and carried the iced coffee over to the table to set it down.

"Yeah," Daire said, though she didn't know to who.

"Boy," came the disembodied voice from the Gizmo, a voice that made her blink and move closer. Harry. "You've been up to some shit."

"Missed you too, Stratego," Styx said, taking two coffees from the cardboard tray to hand one to Daire. "What's your ETA?"

Daire put the coffee back on the table. Before his brother could drink his own, Daire took the cup right out of Styx's hand to put it down too.

"Tomorrow," Harry said, a little harried. "Can't say when, I have a stop to make." A stop she'd made with Danny before they met. "Anything to report?"

"All's quiet," Styx said, turning around to look at her. "Wanna tell him you're alive?"

"I wasn't the one almost blown up," Tess said. "Glad

you're alive, Harry."

"You got yourself in some mess, Light-Sprite," he said.

Drawing in a breath, she cocked a hip as her arms folded, though her coffee stayed in her grip. "I think this mess is yours. All of yours. I didn't cook up any plan to murder anyone or kidnap myself, so…"

"You have to stay put," he said.

Assuming Daire had submitted her request, she glanced at him. But the proficient agent maintained his focus on the device. No reason he should ever look anywhere else.

Was it a good idea to be forthcoming? There was only one way to get what she wanted, and that was to be honest.

"I know why Z wants me," she said, ignoring the two men as she approached the table. "Why you want me… It doesn't matter why it happened, I don't care. If I give you what you want, will you let me leave?"

"It's not as simple as that. Z will—"

"Once you have JARR, the rest doesn't matter," she said, feeling the tension increase. "I will give you it. Between the four of us, we have everything we need to extract it. I'll comply if we just do it and get it over with."

"Ares? You talk to him?" Styx asked before she got an answer. "About what we discussed last night?"

"We're not talking any more about that with an audience," Harry said, without answering her or giving Styx the time to receive one. "You have your orders. Carry them out. I'll get to you as soon as I can. Hades out."

And just like that, he was gone. She didn't know how the men knew he was no longer on the line. Nothing on the Gizmo changed. Daire curled his fingers around the back of the folding chair, pushing his shoulders up on straight arms as his body bowed.

Styx picked up his coffee. Once again, Daire plucked it straight out of his hand.

"I'm not allowed to drink coffee now?"

Daire took the other cup too. "You heard me say Omega, right?"

He went into the kitchen with both cups; she heard

the liquid disappear down the drain. His dedication was admirable, though it was easy for her to say that while sipping her iced coconut mocha.

When Daire reappeared, Styx opened his arms. "One coffee was going to make a difference?"

"You're out of practice," Daire said, clearing away the Gizmo, then removing the cardboard tray, presumably to put it in the kitchen trash. "After a year off, you need to get back in the mindset."

"The Hades mindset," Styx said. "Because he'll thrash both our asses if I'm not poker straight by the time he arrives. You know he'll put us through the wringer anyway. Always does when he's stressed about the unknowns. What did he say about our operation?"

"Not much."

Folding his arms and widening his stance, Daire faced his brother, the table still between them. Unfortunately for her, that meant she could see every nuance of her ex's position and expression. Ex. It didn't seem like the right term. They'd always avoided putting any kind of label on what they were. Being nothing didn't change that. Seemed her claim to fading away applied to their relationship as well as her life.

"Is he pissed?" Styx asked his brother.

"What do you think?"

"You get him riled enough, he'll let us follow through."

Daire was dubious though rigid. "He has no backstop here. What you're suggesting is so off the charts—"

"What *I'm* suggesting? You were damn adamant about it yourself last night. You brought it up, and you were fucking right... You're always fucking right. One conversation with H and suddenly you're not sure?"

"Because what would be left?" Daire asked. "We do what we want, it feels good for a minute, but that impulse—"

"It's never gonna be the way it was," Styx asserted. "You want it back to how it was before the Exodus, before Zulu was ever floated. We can't have it back. The restructure will happen whether we want it to or not. All you have to decide is what role you want to play."

"Don't lecture me."

"Why? Because that's usually your role?" Styx asked, leaning closer when Daire's arms fell to his sides and he angled away. Her own gaze drifted to the floor. "You've gotta get your shit together, man. I don't know what the fuck is wrong with you. There's nothing you care about more than Olympus. You've never been so… flat about this shit."

"About what shit?" Daire snapped. "You don't think I noticed the whole thing going to crap? You think, what? I'm like two years old and still believe in never-never land? No, it's over, okay. I fucking understand! It's over!"

Something about the way he shouted that brought her eyes up as they blinked. He'd been looking at his brother, but in almost the same moment she blinked, his gaze flicked to her. Although it was just a brief slip, Styx noticed and turned to her.

"Want to give us a minute?" he asked, taking his brother's action as an indication they shouldn't be talking about internal matters in front of an outsider.

Her opinion wouldn't matter anyway, and if Daire was referencing their relationship, she'd already come to the same conclusion. So she began to cross the room, intending to leave.

Daire straightened up. "No," he said. "Stay, Tess."

"You want to hash this out, we hash it out," Styx said. "We can't do it in front of an audience."

The snarl in Daire's gaze as it snapped to his brother was a new kind of angry. "You think this doesn't affect her? You think she doesn't understand it? Fuck, her whole life has been screwed up by Olympus."

"She told me," Styx said, slipping his hands into his pockets. "You think it didn't fuck up your life too?"

"Fuck my life," Daire said. "I had it better than her. At least it taught me how to stop and take a stand. All it taught her was to run and hide. Now you're asking her to do it again."

"I'm not asking shit," Styx said. "You know Harry wouldn't want her involved for her own sake."

"You think any of this is for her sake?" Daire asked with a genuine resignation.

Styx frowned, looking from his brother to her and back. "What is going on here? Nothing Olympus does is for the good of one citizen. Nothing."

"Zeus is a citizen," she said. "Byron and Balfour are citizens. They don't fund it out of altruism; it's self-interest and ego." That was no puzzle. "Orchestrating the demise of Byron Senior's VP wasn't in the interests of national security."

Styx took a step toward her. "How the hell do you know about that?"

"I know a lot of things I probably shouldn't."

"Yeah, like about JARR. How did you know about that?"

The way he peered at her suggested a new high of suspicion. Styx could believe she was some kind of super-agent for the other side, when in truth, all she'd done was listen while men talked.

"It's best for you I do," she said. "Knowing means I can speed this up for everyone. You guys get whatever supplies you need so when Harry gets here, we can leave immediately. We go to Beta, you get what you need, and then I walk."

"You won't be safe," Daire said, staring into the middle distance, his chin slightly down.

"I won't ever be safe no matter how this plays out," she said. "I wandered into the unknown thinking I could free myself from it. That won't ever happen. No matter who gets there first, no matter who triumphs, I'll always be a target for the other side."

"Then why wouldn't you want to stay?" Styx said. "I told you Olympus isn't so bad."

Exhaling an ironic laugh, she smiled. "No, not so bad, it only took everything from me. My childhood, my security, my freedom, my mother, my father, my dignity." Which was a reference to how she'd humiliated herself with Daire. "I stay there, I'm putting myself in prison for the rest of my life. Resigning myself to always being a pawn and never a person. Besides, didn't you just say there is no Olympus? It is no more. Whether Z gets control or H does, they'll dedicate their lives to taking the other down. There is no security, not for anyone who ever even heard of Olympus."

"Regretting it yet?" Styx said. "You should've let me kill him."

"Yeah," she said, nodding. "I should have. I thought I was standing up for a greater good that meant something… But that greater good doesn't exist anymore."

"We'll go, you and me," Daire said, rounding the table to move closer to his brother, forcing her to back away fast. "Soon as Harry gets here."

"We leave Pandora with him and clear the board," Styx said. "I like it." But he shook his head. "Harry will never go for it."

"We'll make him go for it."

"We take out the Six and we're putting it to rest. Obliterating it and putting ourselves on everyone else's hit list. Harry say who made it out?"

"Lowe and Boze are with Garrick, or they were. Can't make contact. Milo and Zip made it out. They have their orders… Albany wasn't so lucky."

The dead man was the one who'd shot her with the tranquilizer dart. Learning of that assault had pissed Daire off, while she understood Albany was following orders.

"You won't hear me arguing that the Six don't deserve it," Styx said. "How in the hell will you convince Harry to burn it down?"

For everyone's talk about how Olympus was Daire's life, it was Harry's too. Always had been. He'd given up a lot for Olympus. To blast the whole thing to shit would disrespect that sacrifice. An argument could be made that it disrespected her and her mother's sacrifice too. Except she couldn't bring herself to fight for an organization that only seemed determined to take.

"We burn it down to rebuild it," Daire said. "Into something better. Something stronger."

"Sounds great, but where do you get the capital?"

"Beta hasn't been demo'd, there's a fortune in there."

"A fortune that won't last long when we're trying to keep up and carry out international missions. We won't be able to pay for intel or recruits."

"So we go private."

"Mercenary work?" Styx said and scoffed. "Not your style, brother."

"What do you suggest? You think we just suck it up and keep on going? You just fucking said there was no going back."

"We take it apart and shut it down," Styx said. "Scale it back. There are wars to fight on home turf too. People who need the help of people like us."

"Thought you were a barehanded killer," she said, raising a brow.

Styx shrugged. "There will always be people who need someone like me. I'll fall on my feet whichever way this goes."

She smiled. It was nice to see the brothers were at least considering other options, options which didn't include shackling themselves to Zeus again.

EIGHT

"PLANNING WHAT'S NEXT IS PREMATURE," Daire said. "We've gotta get down to it. We both agree Six needs to be taken off the board." Styx bobbed his head. "And killing our own is crossing a line. Zeus has taken out too many of ours already. Albany is the last Olympus body we'll let him drop."

"If we can find him," Styx muttered.

"Drawing him out won't be difficult," she said, attracting the attention of both men. "You have everything he wants. If he has his base unit, you must be able to send him a message. Even if he's hidden it somewhere, he'll get it eventually. Styx, you said Zeus could monitor the same communication channels you guys can. So if he could access Harry's message, use the same route to contact Zeus."

"And say what?" Styx asked. "Come get your keys? You think he'll fall for that?"

"I think he's in an impossible situation. He doesn't have access to personnel. The guy he sent me back to Hugo's house with, Daire called an amateur. That's the level he has access too. Maybe Byron can access more, but everyone is in a precarious position. If Byron funds Zeus, which he might because he's still making up for agreeing to Zulu in the first place, then he's effectively picking sides." In her eyes, he already had. Though that was something to do with being kidnapped and taken to another continent. "That's where you're at. Everyone needs to pick sides. You battle it out and whoever is left are the victors."

"She's right," Styx said. "Don't see us staying in our own lanes, living in peace. Harry gets the kids in the divorce. Who will get the house?"

The Olympus personnel who trained under Harry would be loyal to him… Unless any of them resented him for Zulu, which would be nuts in her opinion since it was the Six's idea. The house would be the property, the base and whatever was in it. There couldn't be a polite division of that property. Neither side would want the other to have any kind of advantage.

She breathed out. It wasn't meant to come out as a laugh, but it did, then both men were looking at her again. "Nothing. Sorry. I was just thinking, you're more than a year down the line from the Exodus, two from when Harry accepted Zulu, and you're only just now realizing it won't be possible for everyone to live and work in peace together… Something I've been saying for a very long time."

"Oh, she's so clever," Styx teased. "So you gonna help us or you thinking about playing for the other team?"

"You're assuming there will only be two," she said, sucking her coffee through the straw.

Styx turned a frown on his brother. "She makes a good point. Garrick has as much right as the other principals and he can fuck us on the tech front."

Things weren't looking too great for Zeus's prospects. Harry had manpower. Garrick had his toys. Zeus… so far, he had the money on side, and she guessed that was because they feared him.

"If Ares has Hades' access codes…" she said, again slipping the straw between her lips.

Styx laughed. "Yeah, we could just say fuck the old man and go out on our own." When Daire didn't laugh, Styx's amusement dwindled. "You want to say fuck the old man and go out on our own?"

Though her lips were occupied, they curled upwards. No way would Daire ever think to turn his back on Harry… Although, he kind of had after the Exodus, but it hadn't taken much for Harry to win him back.

"We give him a chance to see it straight," Daire said.

She couldn't believe he was serious. That he was considering splitting from his superior.

Seemed Styx was as incredulous. "The guys will follow you, if we can find them. Shit, man, you're talking mutiny."

"I'm talking about the greater good. Isn't that what it's always been about? While Harry and Zeus are locked in this fucking pissing match, nothing is getting done."

"You hate it when things are missed," Styx muttered. "You think we take this on ourselves and then what? We bring the old man in when it's over?"

"If he wants in," Daire said, folding his arms again. "We've gotta be serious about what we want, about how we want it to play out, before Harry gets here. If we have a plan, if we're sure…"

"What? He'll listen?" Styx said. "I don't fucking think so. He's had nothing but time since that house went up to think and plan his next move. He knows what he wants."

"So far we know he wants us here and Pandora safe," Daire said. "That's it. We know we lost another guy, our numbers are dropping, and Byron is in the north seducing new investors. What are they investing in?"

"Us," Styx said. "Harry always said the men were the backbone and the breath of the organization. Without us, Olympus can't function."

"It's just a pile of bricks."

"Full of fancy guns," Styx said. The men shared a smile, so she figured that was one of her father's lines or something they'd heard somewhere before. "Other than Six underground, what do we want?"

She didn't know Daire was looking at her until the silence stretched. When nothing was said, she sought a reason and found Daire's gaze on her. Styx was frowning at his brother.

"Now you want me to step out?" she asked. "You think I've been a secret super-agent this whole time." In a loose shrug, she retreated a step. "Who would I tell? I don't know where Zeus is any more than either of you do. Since I left Vegas, I've been in the company of one of you the entire time."

"I guess he's thinking we can't determine what we want until we know how complicit you plan to be."

"Kill whoever you like," she said. "I learned my lesson about stepping in on a murder plot. I already told you I'll cooperate with the extraction of JARR. But I'm not the one holding two keys hostage."

"They're not hostage," Styx said. "You saw how quick and easy it was for us to retrieve them. That's arrogance. Zeus's arrogance and I learned from it."

"Did you tell Ares where they are?" she asked.

"No, but he could find them if he wanted to… so could you."

That was unexpected. Where did she know that Daire would know too? The three of them had never been in the same space since the previous day. As far as she knew, Daire didn't even know they were going to meet Styx in Fox Den, and Styx didn't know his brother would be with her.

"I could?"

He smiled. "You know if you fuck us over, I'll kill you."

The sincerity behind his smile took her aback, the threat was unexpected.

"You lay a hand on her and *I'll* kill *you*," Daire growled.

Another surprise, she didn't expect his defense, not against his brother, not in such explicit terms. However unexpected it was for her, it was more unexpected for Styx.

"You'll kill me," Styx said. His expression relaxed as his body grew heavier. "'Cause she's Harry's kid or 'cause you wanna fuck her?"

Startled, she flinched, her mouth opened. Daire didn't react, the guy didn't twitch. Her eyes darted back and forth between the brothers staring each other out.

"Watch that line, Major," Daire muttered.

"Oh, we're pulling rank now?" Styx asked. "You know, it was obvious she was obsessed with you. I saw that in London. But, shit, man, I didn't think you'd be so fucking stupid."

"Leave it alone."

"Does Harry know?" Styx asked, leaving only a beat of silence before continuing. "Course he doesn't, 'cause if he did, he'd never have sent you after her. Talk about amateur. How the hell could you let yourself get involved with an asset?"

"You don't know what you're talking about," she said when it became obvious Daire wasn't going to deny or defend it.

He probably didn't know which path to go down. With her, he was already on shaky ground and, for the time being, at least, he needed her compliance.

"Actually, sweetheart, I know exactly what I'm talking about," Styx said, taking his time in   drawing his eyes from his brother. "Any involvement with third parties outside the realm of a mission is forbidden, which I guess dates back to Harry's mess with your mom."

"My mom wasn't his mission."

"No, she wasn't. What happened between the two of them showed how a man's weakness can fuck the entire company. And speaking from personal experience, that beauty with the fuck-me figure I was talking about? I watched her give herself up to a real evil guy to save the lives of me and her boyfriend… and I watched that boyfriend almost tear himself to pieces to get her back… They were strangers to me and I stood by them, but witnessing it go down firsthand was tough. You think I'm gonna let my brother open himself like that? Weaken himself? Harry would go fucking nuts if any of his guys exposed a vulnerability like that, if they even let themselves have one. He will never let this happen. He will never let Ares go down for a woman."

"He's not going anywhere," she said. "Didn't you hear what I said? I'll give you what you want. After that, I want nothing to do with any of you. With anything Olympus."

"So you'll just go into hiding?" Styx asked. "Run whenever you think there's someone too close behind you." He raised his chin. "Funny, I think I've heard that story before."

"Think all you want. I don't give a damn. I don't care about your judgment, and I don't care about Harry's. I think—"

"How did you know?" Daire asked.

Styx was quick to answer. "You think I didn't notice the tension between the two of you? Guess you had a fight last night, 'cause you were in a cunt of a mood for hours after we last saw her. Then this morning, you won't look at each other... Harry will notice it too."

"He doesn't want to see it," Daire said. "So he doesn't."

"His blind spot," Styx said. "Damn, you're lucky... I'd guess he doesn't want to believe you'd be so stupid as to let yourself be manipulated with sex."

"I'm manipulating him?" she asked, her fingertips touching her cleavage. "Please tell me that's some kind of Olympus joke I don't get because there's no way you're serious."

"I think—"

"No! I have been a damn good sport through all of this," she said, wide-eyed, almost ready to scream. "I let myself be towed around like an ass for weeks by this bastard. I fell for the ploy, believed every lie. Even after he put me in front of my father's gun, I still forgave everything and played nice. I did everything I was told, including getting on a damn plane that took me halfway across the planet. I kept my mouth shut. I didn't cause waves or expose your goddamn precious organization and I did that so he"—she thrust an arm toward Daire, though her attention stayed on Styx—"and his precious Olympus could live happily ever after. I did that right up until the moment your boss sent me, at gunpoint, to retrieve something that I knew you had. I did it without exposing you, without revealing any truth. Only when I knew there was absolutely no way to extricate myself from your lies and his, did I decide to run. I ran to save you and me because I knew if they got their hands on me, I'd have to admit I didn't have the damn keys, that you did, and then you'd have your whole Olympus army chasing you around the map. I have lied to protect him"—her arm straightened to thrust a straight finger Daire's way again—"I accepted my father's rejection for him"—her elbow jerked to emphasize her pointing—"and I was all but ready to nail myself to his cross until I found out the whole crock of shit was a lie! Cooked up to keep my blood warm until it could be used to extract JARR! That's it! That's all I am to every damn one of you. If it's so damn important…" She marched across the room to slam her cup onto the table and turn the inside of both wrists toward Styx. "Take it. Bleed me fucking dry if that's what you need! Go on! Do it!"

"Tess," Daire said.

Her head snapped around. "What did I tell you to call me?"

"Okay," Styx said into the pulsing tension of silence. "You guys have your issues." He stepped away from the table. "And you have to figure them out before Harry gets here or else you have to be ready for him to lay down some strict rules. He can't do this without his lieutenant at his side and he won't leave his daughter in the cold."

"He doesn't give a damn about his daughter," she said. "I don't know how many times I have to say I just want to be left out of this. I didn't get why I was even in it until I found out about the blood. Just because it makes more sense to me doesn't mean I have to accept it. You two plan your war." She swiped her cup from the table and spun to head for the bedroom. "Leave me the hell out of it."

NINE

SLAMMING INTO HER ROOM, she dropped her cup to the dresser and paced, trying to vent some of her rage. Heat built in her eyes. Goddamnit, the tears. Goddamn them. Calling them angry tears would be some consolation though that didn't make her feel any better about herself.

Styx knew there was something between them. He'd sensed it apparently. That didn't mean squat. As far as she was concerned, no one had a damn clue. Even she hadn't known what it was until she had no avenue left but to admit it was nothing. Nothing. That was what existed between them and all that ever would.

"Tess…"

Flipping around, she burned her glare into Daire who'd managed to come into the room without making a sound.

As he began to close the door, she inhaled. "Don't you fucking dare close that door." He paused. "I do not want you in here. I do not want you near me."

"It doesn't matter."

That made her laugh. "Yeah? Good. Well at least you're being honest about it. Yeah. We don't matter. So say goodbye and close the damn door on your way out."

"It doesn't matter if the door stays open," he said, complying with her request not to close it though he didn't leave, he actually got closer. "I can't do it anymore. I won't."

"We cleared that up last night, Ares," she said, spitting out his code name. "Get the hell out of here."

"No," he said, continuing to approach her.

"Get out of my room."

"No," he said again, stopping in front of her. "You walked out the Beast and I did nothing. I stood there for… I don't know how long. I knew I couldn't let you go… I couldn't even bring myself to leave the spot you left me in. I was in shock. Yeah. I didn't expect Zeus to be so heavy-handed or to lose any of my guys."

"I don't want to hear this," she said, shaking her head. "I don't care."

"You wouldn't be so upset if you didn't care. You know that you care just like I know I hurt you."

"Something you've done before," she muttered, folding her arms.

When his finger curled under her chin and his thumb came to rest against it, she tried to pull away, but he pinched it tighter, directing it upward. "Before I saw the message, I knew driving away from you would be impossible. I was stuck… That message gave me the excuse I needed to return to your side." Peering deeper, he searched her. "I am a resource at your disposal. My primary mission hasn't changed. It never will."

"How many times will we have to do this?" she asked, ensnared by the depth of his gaze. "How many times will I have to go through this? Styx is right. I can't be your weakness. I never wanted to be."

"It's too late for that and you know it."

"Stop," she said, raising her chin out of his grasp to back away. "We have to stop."

"You don't doubt everything that happened between us, every word we ever spoke, everything we ever did… You don't doubt that just because I wasn't capable of admitting I wasn't strong enough to walk away on my own."

"Daire—"

"I wasn't strong enough to walk away from you to go back to Olympus. I wasn't strong enough to walk away from them to be with you. Everyone does have to pick sides. You're right about that. And you were right that the trust at Olympus can't be rebuilt. Not after the loss of life Zeus is responsible for."

"You don't know Harry won't want it," she said. "If he can make amends with Zeus—"

"Then good for him, but he'll do it without me."

"You're still raw," she said. "It's survivor's guilt. You feel responsible for Albany's death. It wasn't your fault, it was mine." His brow twitched, so she licked her lips, getting ready to confess. "Styx wanted to kill Zeus, in London. He was ready to follow through on Zulu. I was the one who convinced him not to. I convinced him to wait, that we'd get the keys, and then he could speak to Harry, to confirm the mission was going ahead... I didn't want you to lose the chance of putting Olympus back together. Everyone always says Zeus is Olympus... It was my fault. If I'd let Styx kill him, if I hadn't gotten in the way, he'd be dead and Albany wouldn't."

"Everything you've done has been for me. The way you put it out there, hearing the words... You're here because of me. You respect Olympus for me... Why?"

"I don't want to answer that," she said. The last thing she wanted to do was lie. Actually, second to last, she didn't want to express her feelings for him either. "It doesn't matter, just like you said."

"It matters," he said, planting a hand on the window when her back hit it. "You did it because you love me. I don't need you to say it. I know my Little Red."

She put her hands on his chest. "Daire, don't—"

"From now on, I follow my superior's orders," he murmured. "After I get a go from my Heart."

"Are you kidding?" she said, shaking her head. "I never wanted to be your master."

"Ever since you met Harry and found out the truth, I've been trying to find a way to make up for my deception. I keep screwing it up. Any time I don't have you around to keep my head on straight, I fuck up."

"Which was exactly what we didn't want," she said. "Exactly why we agreed you wouldn't make a choice between me and Olympus. I'm not upset that you followed Harry's order, even though that order brought you to me. I'm upset that you let me believe your presence was something it wasn't."

"You know what we are, Little Red," he murmured, curving an arm around her. His forearm descended as he crouched to bury his mouth in her hair above her ear. "My presence around you is always selfish… Every second near you is a gift."

"Stop," she whispered, but her head was already relaxing on her shoulders, her eyes drifting shut. Easing her back from the gauze curtain, he slid his hand up and down, teasing her with its span, its strength, its security. "Daire."

"You know it's real," he said, his words gentle, quiet velvet. "I'd give it to you for free, Temptress… Command me to fall on my sword and I will."

"Goddamn," she breathed out, trying to turn her face down. "Goddamn it's your voice…" She hadn't clicked until that moment. "My downfall… You do that deep, soft lilt that makes it feel like you're inside me and I can't… God, I can't breathe."

Laying a hand on his chest, she tried to push him back, but he wrapped both arms around her and came lower, trailing his lips through her hair over her ear to her jaw. "You don't have to, my Heart," he said, his mouth drifting closer to hers. "I am your servant."

When his lips grazed hers, some part of her mind held a vague recollection of why it was a bad idea. Not that she could make sense of it. The majority of her, every inch of her, connected with him, called to him. His mouth opened and as he breathed out, she inhaled, consuming his spirit at the same moment their tongues met. They shouldn't be kissing. She shouldn't kiss a liar… Except his conflict was not bred from malice.

Her Heart was torn. Between the man he'd been raised to be and the one obsessed with her, the one who needed her love to survive. Her palms rose to his face, though they didn't stay long. Soon her fingers were in his hair, skimming the back of his neck, her arms coiling themselves around him.

Just as she began to think about the nearby bed, Daire's knees bent with a purpose suggesting they were sharing the thought. It was possible, their bodies were close enough.

Before his hands could finish their expedition to her ass, a voice interrupted them.

"You should leave."

Daire's kiss disappeared as he twisted to look at his brother in the doorway. "Don't you fucking—"

"Both of you," Styx said before his brother could threaten him again. "Both of you should leave. Now. I'll deal with Harry."

"Leave?" she said, slipping an arm around Daire as he pulled her to his side, away from their nook at the window.

"I thought she wanted to fuck you, man. I had no damn idea it was this…" The men, once again, only saw each other. "You're sunk, bro. Finished."

"I know," Daire said, inhaling through his teeth like he was accepting some terrible fate, except when she looked up at him for an explanation, he was smiling.

"He's not done," she snapped, offended by the notion her Heart could ever be conquered. "I don't know what you're talking about, but he's not finished."

Although she tried to walk away from Daire, his arm tightened around her, so she sprang back. "I should look him in the eye myself."

"That won't achieve anything," Styx said with a single shake of his head. "Make tracks now, before he puts a wrench in the works. He'll separate you."

"He'll try," Daire said, clenching the muscles in his arm, clamping her form against his.

"I don't mean break you up, I mean physically separate you," Styx said, wandering into the room. "I'm sorta surprised he hasn't holed her up somewhere already. I'd think that would be his first instinct."

"He tried," Tess said, still as unimpressed with the suggestion as she had been when it was first floated.

"I can't protect her if she's not in my eyeline."

Right then Daire seemed to be attempting to merge her body into his and not in the fun way.

Using her fingernails, she pinched him. "*Her* needs oxygen or she won't make it out of the room."

"Want me to kiss you?" Daire asked with obvious confusion. "Now?"

"I couldn't beg you to do it last night and now you're offering them for free," she said, squeezing her arm from his back to between them. "I need you to let me go."

"No way," Daire said. "It's done."

She didn't quite know what was done and still wouldn't call him finished. "You two need to plan your war…" With a little more struggling, she got herself free from his restrictive half embrace. Until she was actually gone, he didn't seem to realize how tight he'd been holding her. "And I'm supposed to be sulking."

"You didn't let me finish apologizing," Daire said, his fingers snaking under her hair to tickle the back of her neck.

Ducking out of his reach, her glare faded as her head tilted. Damn, he was smiling. Those dimples didn't believe in making life easy for her.

"Why is it always when I decide to be strong and strict about staying away from you that you sense it and slide back in? Why are my defenses so weak and useless?"

His slow blink only reeked of satisfaction. "Because I'm your soul," he said, moseying a step closer. "Your breath… Your being."

As his arms went around her, she laid hers on his chest. "My Heart."

"That's right," he said.

She kissed her fingertips before touching them to his lips.

"This is bad," Styx said, his words thick with dread. "You two are over there all hearts and rainbows… D, you can't fight a war with a woman on your back."

Although he'd heard his brother, she couldn't tell that

from the way he was admiring her. "Tess isn't a weight holding me back. She's the fire in my belly. The fuel that keeps me going… If I'm fighting for her, victory is guaranteed."

"We're not together," she said as he swept her hair from her neck. "We're colleagues." Daire just nodded on his descent to kiss her shoulder. "Platonic."

"Lady, this is about as far from platonic as I've seen," Styx said. She'd almost forgotten he was still watching them. "Which is why you two need to split."

"Leaving won't save us," she said. "It will put us in more danger. Everyone has told me how valuable Daire is to the organization."

"It's an organization that doesn't exist."

A good point that he kept on making. Daire's hand began to slide down her back. That hand wasn't going to stop until it was full with her ass, squeezing her, picking her up, carrying her to the—

"Stop it," she said, stepping away from his roaming hands to march over and grab her coffee from the dresser.

Focus. Make decisions. Drinking through the straw, her attention floated to the bed. If Daire put her on her back, she'd be more focused.

"I wouldn't choose to bail on you, bro," Daire said, closer than where she'd left him.

He was right there, just two feet away, a hand on the corner of the dresser, his straight arm holding him up. Why did he have to be so close? Why was she suddenly uncomfortable with him being so close?

"You choose this woman, you can't stay here."

"Yes, he can," Tess said, catching her forehead, trying to put her thoughts in some sort of order. "This was never supposed to… We're not…" She spun to show Styx her hand. "Can you just forget everything you think you know?"

Daire's hands slid onto her shoulders. "He's not gonna do that. Neither am I. You're gonna make a decision, Little Red."

"What kind of decision?" she asked, raising her chin though that didn't help her see him.

"Whose side we're on," he said. "We'll fight with your

father, with Garrick, with Ulysses. Whoever has your loyalty has mine. That's who we'll fight with. Or if you want to leave right now, I'll dedicate my life to protecting yours. We don't need anyone else if you don't want them. We'll get in the Beast and hit the road… We had a plan last time we were in Miami. We can pick up right from there…"

South America. Just thinking it relaxed her muscles and she sank back, putting all her weight into Daire's capable hands. That sounded like a dream, as it did every time she fantasized about it.

A plan.

"Why do I have to make the decisions?" she asked. "I'm not the super-agent, Agent."

"No," he said, ducking to kiss her head. "But this one only thinks straight when his something is at his back."

Not on his back, at his back. She wasn't sure she understood exactly what was going on, inside herself or with Daire. Something was different. Just admitting their relationship to Styx was a change, and it seemed to be causing some kind of shift.

Being a relationship novice with a relationship novice had never bothered her. It had never been an issue. Until she was standing there in front of her something's brother, trying to figure out what was happening.

"You're putting it on me," she said, absorbing the new reality. "You want me to decide who has your loyalty? That doesn't even make sense."

"I'm gonna give you two a minute," Styx said, raising a finger at both of them. "I hear anything close to sex noises and I don't have any problem strolling straight back in." He laid his conviction on Daire. "We have shit to get straight. I don't get coffee? You don't get sex."

He went out, closing the door behind him. Sex was about the only thing that would make sense. Though Styx was right they had important issues to clear up. Time without Harry was limited. When he joined them, he'd take charge. Daire already said they needed to be clear on what they wanted before that happened.

Clear on what they wanted. That wasn't going to be

easy while she struggled to figure out which way was up.

TEN

TESS WAS STILL TRYING to process when Daire spoke. "Every problem we've had… Since you found out the truth, every problem we've had stemmed from the secret," he said, correcting his start. "I'm done keeping the secret. Our secret. It's time we faced reality."

"I'm trying. I swear to you I am… I'm just having trouble figuring out exactly what that reality is."

With his grip on her shoulders, he turned her to face him. "You gave me to Olympus because you believed it was worth more than the sum of what we were… That's not true anymore, baby. Olympus is gone and we're still here. Still strong. Still together."

"We—"

"I love you, it's as simple as that. Uncomplicated. With Olympus gone, I'm free… Whatever comes next is us. I won't move on to something else without you at my side."

"You can't walk away from Olympus," she said, fighting her selfish urge to claim him. "It's a dangerous time for everyone. As long as Zeus is out there, he'll be coming for you and your men. For Harry. For me."

"What we're facing now is not Olympus. I can't be loyal to something that is no longer what it was."

His whole life was changing, yet he took it in his stride, without any hint of hesitation or grief.

"How can you be okay with putting Olympus to rest? It's all you've ever known."

"No," he said, tracing his thumb beneath her lower lip. "I know you now. You showed me freedom. Gave me freedom. That's what I want. In whatever form it takes… We do this together. We are a unit. You and me. You are my new Olympus. I dedicate myself to you… Ask me to belong only to you and I will."

"I don't want to dictate your life," she said. "I don't want to be the one controlling you. That's not freedom."

It didn't help that she didn't trust herself to know all the players or make the right calls. As much as she'd love supporting him, her experience and skillset were lacking.

"This is new to me too," he said, searching her eyes. "My life has been better with you than it ever has. Making you happy, being with you, it doesn't feel like following rules. If you tell me you don't want me in your future, I'll find a way to accept that. No matter what you decide, there's no Olympus for me to go back to."

"In the Beast," she said. "Before I left you outside Tallahassee. I made your decision for you. I told you to go back to Vegas."

"And I didn't," he said. "Because you think I let Harry's order override yours."

"No," she said, walking away from his caresses. "I'm saying that wasn't the right choice. *I* didn't make the right choice. All along I've thought I was fighting for your best interest. I've tried to do what I think you'd want. Tried to make sure you never have to worry about feeling guilt where I'm concerned, that you won't feel guilty about prioritizing something over me. I'm independent. I'm headstrong. I rush in and open my mouth and—"

"All you're doing is reminding me why I love you," he said. She glanced over her shoulder to him. "You're my wild."

Closing her eyes, she dropped her head. The eight feet of space between them didn't mean anything. He could seduce her body and her heart with very few words. "I didn't ever want to be the one giving you orders. I thought, in the Beast, I was doing the right thing. All I did was make things more difficult for you. I can't be trusted."

"*You* can't be trusted?" he asked, incredulous. "I'm the one who keeps fucking this up. You underestimate yourself, Little Red. You have an incredible way of narrowing your focus. You can turn and drift, adjust fast, but you know your goal. You have that end point in mind and you never waver."

He'd told her that before. The only thing she'd ever been sure of was acting in Daire's best interests. Her quick assumption that their relationship had been his sole motivator for coming to Miami caused damage. Yet, his conflict between prioritizing her or Olympus had been apparent many times. She couldn't doubt their whole relationship because of that blip. She'd forgiven him greater ones.

Still, the future, she hadn't let herself think about that. Not with him. Getting through the moment, the present, had been tough sometimes. To think about some fantasy that she could never have would just be a way of torturing herself.

"There can't be a future until this is resolved," she said. "With Zeus and Olympus. If it never is, then there is no future. I'll be on the run for the rest of my life."

Just as she had been since birth. Her mother might have held the reins until her death, but Tess would pick them up. She'd have to.

"I don't care what kind of future it is," he said. "As long as we're together. If it's your choice to stand and face this now, I'll do whatever it takes to keep you safe. If it doesn't work out, we fail, and have to run for the rest of our lives? We'll run together." Surprise turned her around. As she blinked at him, he smiled. "You didn't want to be alone... I won't let you be alone. Never again."

"Daire, you—"

"What? Can't give up Olympus? It's gone. Even if it wasn't, I was through with it the second I left Vegas with you... It wasn't a conscious choice. There was nothing to debate. I knew I was going the minute you did."

"What?"

Shaking his head, he approached. "I never intended to go back. I left with you. With us. For good. After losing you… during that time you were in London, the reality sank in. When you were taken away from me, I was done with Olympus. Gathering intel in Vegas was the only thing keeping me there. If it hadn't been for that, I'd have got on a plane the second I knew you were gone." He touched her face again. "As long as we were in the same place and not being together was an intellectual argument, I could be complacent about it. Waking up so far from you, without you in reach… Babe, I was never going to survive like that."

"You were… you left Olympus? For me?"

"When I left Vegas, I left Olympus. I was ready to be with you. To dedicate myself to you."

"The explosion changed your mind?"

"About us?" he asked. "No, definitely not. I just… I didn't…"

"You were in shock," she murmured, repeating his words.

He'd planned to be with her. Believing him, or not, didn't really matter.

"Why'd you think I gave your platonic thing zero respect? Why'd you think I was right there to put you on your back after your shower that first night?"

"You were horny," she said because that was the obvious answer.

He was smiling at her again. "Always am with you. If I'd been monitoring you for Olympus or thought I was going back there, I'd have given you space. I didn't need to give you space when I knew I planned to do whatever it took to keep us together, to keep you."

Everything they'd been through since leaving Vegas took on a new hue. Everything they'd said had new meaning.

"If you weren't going back, why be so strict about Omega?"

"Some things just make sense," he said. "At some point, I'll have to defend us. We'll come face to face with someone who wants to hurt us or take you from me. Being in shape, at my peak, ready to protect you… it just makes sense, babe. I want to be the best I can be because it's what you deserve. I don't have an army at my back anymore, no resources, nothing but my brute force and brain… I can't give you Olympus and all the security that comes with it. I can only give you me."

The suggestion was so incredible, it bordered on the surreal. "You want to be with me," she said. "Out in the open."

"Completely out in the open." Unsure what to make of everything, she could only beg his gaze with hers. Slowly, concern lowered his brow. "If you don't want to be with me—"

"I can't see the future. I can't see anything past what's going on. Do I love you? Yes. In an ideal, perfect world, would we be together? Of course we would. If I had my way, you'd only belong to me—"

"I do," he said, bending his knees to come closer to her eye level. "That's what I'm saying, LR. I belong to you. Only to you."

Except Harry would swoop in the following day and everything would go back to how it had been in Hugo's house before she was taken to London.

"They need my blood," she whispered.

Daire caught her chin. "If you don't want them to have it, no one will touch you. I am your servant. I mean it."

"I don't want you to be my servant," she said. He'd spent his whole life in the service of others. In service of the country, of his superiors. Still, having him close… Swallowing her own trepidation, she snagged his pinkie with hers. "I want you to be my partner."

"You mean like life partner, right? Because the colleague thing won't stand up anymore. My cock can't take the uncertainty much longer."

She laughed. "And how many times have I denied you?"

In that moment, she couldn't think of any time he hadn't been able to seduce his way around her objections.

"So happy to hear you say that," he said, scooping a

hand around her hip to her ass.

Quick to catch his other hand before it could do the same on the other side, she linked their fingers. "Your brother is right outside."

"He knows."

"And he asked us not to… We should talk together, come up with a plan."

"A plan?"

"You don't have an army at your back and your brother needs support. We're not going to bail on our responsibilities. What's the point in running away from those who might want the same thing as us? Besides…" she said and leaned closer to whisper. "I happen to know he takes his responsibility to you very seriously."

He breathed out a laugh and let her lead him out into the living room. Styx was seated at the folding table, a rifle in pieces in front of him.

"What are you doing?" she asked.

"What are *you* doing?" Styx asked, swinging on his chair as he cleaned or oiled some component, whatever he was doing. "Amount of training you do, brother, thought you'd have better stamina than that."

Tess let go of Daire's hand to head for the couch. So far, she hadn't even sat down, and it was nice to take a weight off her feet now that one had lifted from her shoulders.

"You told us not to have sex," she said.

Styx snickered. "Didn't think you'd listen to me."

Raising an arm toward his brother, Daire turned to her and let it drop.

All she could do was shrug. "I'm sorry, baby. We can do it now if you want."

He stomped on over to the balcony door to open it and go outside. Something she hadn't been allowed to do. Before she could say that, he came back in.

"He's keeping an eye on things," Styx said in explanation when Daire crossed the width of the room to go into the kitchen. "He doesn't know how to switch it off."

She slipped her feet out of her shoes to raise her legs up onto the table. "Oh, believe me, I know."

Styx was laughing when Daire reappeared, the master in his sights. "What's so funny?" he asked as he passed his brother.

"Your girlfriend," Styx said, his amusement growing. "Not something I ever thought I'd say."

Daire disappeared into the master bedroom, leaving the door open.

A memory of their trip to the Rotunda put a smile on her lips. "We're not that specific."

Styx kept on working. Daire reappeared with a notebook in hand, his brow furrowed in concentration.

"You know it's sorta sick that you used the sister thing on me when all the time you were fucking him," Styx said. "If I'm your brother 'cause Harry's your dad, what the hell do you think that makes him?"

Unashamed, she stretched her arms up over her head, draping them on the back of the couch. "I didn't say you were my brother because Harry is my father. Even at the time, it sounded weird, and I figured out why fast. I called you my brother because some secret subconscious corner of my psyche fantasized about marrying yours."

She arched in a stretch, wondering what the guys might say about seeking out a gym… or a massage. The smirk on Styx's face distracted her from that train of thought.

"What?" she asked.

He tipped his chin his brother's way. "He's thinking about it."

Twisting around to check out the standing man just a couple of feet from the couch, the expression on his face said it all. "You're not." When Daire didn't respond, she lunged over the arm to bump her fist on his leg. "You're not thinking about it."

"Why shouldn't we get married?"

A dozen possible answers flitted across her mind, but she dismissed them just as quickly as they rose. There were only two reasons that two consenting adults shouldn't get married, in her opinion. One was if one or both were married to other people. As far as she knew Daire wasn't already hitched. The second reason would be if they didn't love each other, which they'd already cleared up.

"Still got your passport, Lady?"

"Yeah," she said, disconcerted by how serious Daire appeared.

"Go get it."

It didn't take long for her to retrieve it from her jacket in the bedroom.

When she brought it back, her Heart was in the same spot. He raised an open hand, she put the forgery in it before dropping onto the couch again.

"Halfway there," Styx said. "You've gotta have some kind of ID, bro. Shame you don't actually exist anywhere."

Daire opened the passport to examine it and he didn't look impressed. "You used her real name? What the hell?"

Did the name on the passport matter? "Walbeck," she said not even sure if that was right because she hadn't looked at it in a while.

Daire offered a quick explanation. "It's Harry's last name," he said before addressing his brother. "Why would you do that?"

"I knew it was likely a one-shot deal. I told her that," Styx said. "Zeus gave her ID with his name on it, I figured this was tit for tat."

Suddenly, Tess found herself under the scrutiny of her lover. "What?"

"Z gave you ID with his name on it?"

"Yeah," she said then switched a frown to Styx. "How do you know that?"

He shrugged. "Don't leave your jacket on my bed when you use the restroom."

"God, you men, always up to something."

If it wasn't Daire stealing from her or lying about who he was, it was Hugo plotting to kidnap her, or Styx threatening her life.

"Would be great if we could get up to something today," Styx said. "I have a pick-up this afternoon... I know you'll wanna train—"

"I'd love to," Daire said. "But we can't take the risk."

"Eyes on, right," Styx said as he began to put the

weapon back together.

"Eyes on?" she repeated. "You mean me? You can train, doesn't bother me."

"I bet it doesn't," Styx said, probably amused by the prospect of her drooling over her lover working up a sweat.

Yes, Daire's capability turned her on, though she wasn't used to anyone else acknowledging that. "If I wanted to raise his heart rate, I know a much more fun way to do it… One that is oh-so-very satisfying to us both."

Undeterred, Styx's smirk only brightened. "Oh, I can't wait, this is going to be so much fun."

She didn't really know what he meant and was still trying to figure it out when Daire came around to sit on the couch at her side.

"You got a white dress?"

"We are not getting married," she said. "And I'm no virgin."

"Bet he knows that," Styx muttered. "She's right though, you should wait and talk to Harry."

The suggestion that the choice wasn't hers was offensive. "You think I need my father's permission?"

Styx put the chair back on all its legs. "No, I think he does."

"I won't dance to Harry's tune," Daire said. "I don't need any go order to be with Tess."

"Well, you've gotta tell him, right? About the relationship before you think about getting married."

"We don't," she said, though Daire was quick to follow up.

"We do," he said, bringing her attention around to him. "We have to tell him… I have to tell him."

"I don't need his permission to be with you," she said, pouncing onto her feet to stride on over to Styx who was standing up with his gun. "I have no expectation, my Heart."

Stepping in front of Styx confused him, but when she stuffed her hands into his jeans pockets, his brows rose. "Hello, sister." Her fingers didn't loiter long, they snagged the keys for both car and apartment. "What are you doing?"

Wasting no time, she went over to unlock the front

door. When she opened it, Daire jumped to his feet. As she slipped the key into the other side of the door, she glanced at each of them. "Training time. Let's see who catches me first."

Both men started for the door, so she was quick to close and lock it before darting down the hallway. She didn't really intend to slip from their net, but they'd need to move fast to catch her, especially if she was in a vehicle.

With Harry's arrival on the horizon, their time for fun could be dwindling. There were serious matters at hand but keeping the brothers on their toes would benefit them all. Harry told her that Daire would be her primary instrument for survival. She didn't doubt that. She did doubt Daire's resolve to confess their love would hold up once he was faced with the man he'd considered his superior officer throughout life.

Even if he faltered, she wouldn't judge him. Adding more pressure on his shoulders wouldn't do any of them any good. Harry's approval meant a lot to her Heart. His love was enough for her, well, his love and his honesty. If they had to continue to keep their secret, they would. He was with her and if Zeus had his way, none of them would be with each other for long.

ELEVEN

AS EXPECTED, THE BROTHERS caught up to her. Styx seemed to enjoy the chase; her Heart was less impressed. Once everyone got over the game, they went for a drive.

She stayed in the car with her Heart while Styx went to his pick-up job that took nearly an hour. Despite all the time just sitting around, her lover wouldn't be convinced that making out wouldn't compromise her safety. She took things up a notch by using her toes to massage him through his pants. In the end, she got a foot rub out of the deal, so it wasn't a complete loss.

They ate out late and used that time to firm up their demands. They only really had two: Six and Zeus off the board for good. Daire hadn't hidden his feelings for Six, not from Harry anyway, so that wouldn't be a surprise. Zeus was a more ambiguous target. They acknowledged he couldn't be trusted and that they wouldn't work under him again. Killing him, especially while he had Byron on his side, was risky.

The ex-president, just like the other members of the Six, liked their seats of power and liked having a hand in such a useful agency. They wouldn't appreciate anyone destroying it… There was a chance Harry wouldn't like it either.

They got home in the dark and despite being wiped

by the time they got upstairs, she waited without complaint in the hall with Styx while Daire did his security checks. He must have noticed she was flagging because her Heart didn't even let her walk in alone. After giving the all-clear, he swept her off her feet to carry her into the bedroom.

His motives weren't completely pure, but she didn't mind. After laying her down, he stripped her naked and kissed her everywhere. The soothing caresses might have sent her to sleep if he hadn't gone for the big finish between her thighs. Just making her come wasn't enough. He'd taken his time about making love to her, slipping himself into her slow, maintaining the easy, intimate mood.

He was good at everything. That's what she'd decided as she drifted into slumber, content to be sleeping in his arms again.

When Tess woke up, she was alone.

That might bother her if the bright sun wasn't sneaking into the room around the dark drapes. On a yawn, she got up, taking the sheet they'd slept under with her. Wrapping it around her body, she pushed her wild hair from her face and tiptoed out into the living room.

Both Styx and Daire were there, in the middle of the room, all the furniture pushed out of the way.

"You like your sleep, huh?" Styx asked.

Still groggy, she went over to Daire who bowed to kiss her. "It's almost noon, you hungry?"

"Noon," she said, leaning against him, noting his tee-shirt was damp. "You're sweating." She frowned at Styx. "What were you doing?"

"We're training," Daire said. "Styx is out of shape."

"Oh yeah, it's all me," Styx said.

Leaving them behind, she kicked the sheet out of her way, holding it in a bunch at her cleavage as she went into the kitchen.

"I can cook you something," Daire called out.

She got a glass from the cabinet and took it to the fridge to pour out some of her coconut milk. Sounds of movement drew her to the doorway. Relaxing, her upper arm came to rest on the doorframe. The brothers were fighting.

Not real fighting. Their actions were fast and slick, yet somehow, they didn't hurt each other. There were jabs and blows, the swipe of an arm blocked, only for the attack to come from the other side. It wasn't quite choreographed, but definitely wasn't a brawl either. They were focused, attuned to the moment and to each other, it was sort of mesmerizing.

"I'm going to take a shower," she said, putting her glass on the kitchen counter, forcing herself to move though she could probably have stayed there all day watching them.

"Want company?" Styx asked. She just smiled, but the question was enough to throw Daire off his game, so his brother jabbed him in the ribs. "Like I said, definitely going to be fun. If she's your fuel, use it… You let her take your focus and you'll lose your ability to protect her."

Distracting him had been unintentional. "My Heart," she said to get his attention since the verve of their training was broken anyway. "You can join me."

The shower in the Beast wasn't big enough for two. Experiencing him under the spray was something she'd only imagined.

"I should—"

"Styx will keep watch," she said, loosening the sheet so it fell further down her back. "You need a reminder what you're fighting for."

He'd had that reminder last night, but apparently wasn't averse to another because he left his brother to head her way.

"Oh, yeah, don't mind me," Styx called out after them. "I'll just stay out here and protect your asses while you screw like bunnies."

Daire raised a hand like his brother wasn't being sarcastic. "Thanks, man."

She laughed as he scooped her into the bathroom in front of him. As her Heart locked the door, she dropped the sheet and turned to wrap both arms around his neck.

Before the fabric even settled, he picked her up.

"Baby," she breathed when he squeezed her ass to push her higher, pressing his lips to her throat.

"I missed you," he said, grazing his teeth down her

collarbone. "Damn, you make me crazy."

"You could've come back to bed. I was right there, aching for you."

"You were asleep," he said, a smile in his voice.

"I ache every second you're not inside me."

His grip loosened until she dropped down his body and their eyes aligned. "I want to get married."

Sure he was joking, she laughed. "Harry is arriving today. Did you hear from him?"

"I'm serious, baby. It doesn't have to be today, just tell me we'll do it someday."

She enjoyed kissing him. Maybe a little too much. What started as showing her appreciation for him, didn't take long to become something much hotter. Planting her against the wall, he supported her with one arm as both of them fought to rid him of his clothes. Skin to skin contact aroused her beyond the point of ready.

"Daire," she said, starting in a whisper and rising to a yelp when he plunged into her before she was expecting him.

His lips bowed in a show of feral satisfaction that curled her nails into his shoulders. Digging them in deep, she didn't mind leaving her mark, wanted to leave it. Maybe he wasn't hers yet, maybe he would be, maybe he wouldn't. That hinged on whether Daire told Harry the truth when he showed up.

She wouldn't do it, not out of fear but because Daire's relationship with her biological father meant more to her than her own relationship with him. The two men had a bond, and a long history, it wasn't her place to step in and create friction.

Her place was supporting her man with whatever he needed.

In that moment, what he needed was her. Whenever they were together, she felt him everywhere. Inside her body, in her mind, in her heart. Moving her body, using the wall for leverage, she struggled to restrain her voice after he took her hips to speed their union, using his strength to take control, using her for the pleasure he needed.

"Baby," she whispered, her teeth digging into her lip as a desperate whine escaped her throat. "Oh… my Heart."

So much for shower sex. They were screwing against the wall perpendicular to the door, they hadn't even made it a foot into the room.

He squeezed her tighter, widening her drowsy eyes to match them on his. A man with purpose, she could sense his determination. The day ahead wouldn't be easy. No matter what, he'd disappoint someone. Either the man he'd worshiped as a father figure or the woman he loved. And he did love her, she didn't doubt that.

Laying a hand on his cheek, she wanted to give him everything. His strength awed her. He awed her. The expectation he had of himself was high, too high. Most people would never dream of taking on a well-funded and equipped organization headed by people who wanted those around them dead. Daire didn't flinch. He didn't fear standing up to Zeus or any of the Six. Her love was a stallion, strong and resolute.

"I love you," she panted as her body clamped in a spasm of climax.

The involuntary move of her form didn't stall his. Nothing would stop him. Not when he had her, when he was owning her, when he was branding what was his from the inside. All of her was his. The thump of her heart pounding in her chest spurred overwhelming emotion to cascade through her body. Deciding to fight for each other was easy. Coming out the other side, still together and strong, wouldn't be so simple.

For all her Heart took upon himself, he'd take losing her the hardest, of that she was sure. She had to believe in him, she did believe in him. But she could also be realistic about her own limitations. Not being a super-agent was one thing. She didn't have the skill or the ability to overcome an enemy, certainly not on her own. But there was something she hadn't faced, something that had never been discussed.

She was his weakness. He'd admitted to that.

He was hers.

Tess didn't have physical strength. She'd rely on her emotional strength, on her ability to get through anything with blinders on if the situation called for it. In the past anyway.

Going forward, if the world knew about them, she could be used against him. No one had mentioned how he could be used against her.

Tess would do anything, absolutely anything, to keep him safe. If she had to make a deal or a promise, even with the devil himself, to keep Daire healthy and free, she'd do it.

On the descent of her next orgasm, Daire slammed into her full force, pinning her to the wall with his body, holding himself deep inside her. He didn't back up, he stayed right there, her pelvis locked between his and the wall, and laid a forearm above her as his heartrate climbed back down.

A tear slipped from the corner of her eye. She hadn't known it was going to escape, she was too entranced by the man gazing down at her. As soon as he spotted it, he frowned and brushed it away with his thumb.

"Did I hurt you?"

"No," she said, grabbing for his hips at the first hint of him relaxing them. "No, baby, I love you."

"Right back attcha," he said, the intensity of his concern growing. "Why the tears?"

"I just love you," she said, sliding her hands up and down his chest. "Today is going to be tough."

"Why?"

"You know why," she said, enjoying the feel of his skin beneath her palms. "I want you to know that it's okay. I don't need you to make any confessions. I never needed for you to prostrate yourself to him."

"I never intended to," he said, stepping back to put her on her feet.

Nestling in the corner where two walls met, she watched him turn on the shower and test the temperature of the water.

"We can keep this to ourselves. I think Styx will let us."

Daire picked up their things from the floor and put them on the vanity. "You've always trusted me to deal with Harry."

Trusting him to deal with Harry was easy. Father and daughter didn't have a close or enduring relationship.

"I do trust you to deal with him," she said. "I just don't know if telling him is best for you right now." Folding his arms, he crooked a brow. "All I'm saying is there is enough conflict and hostility. If you want to tell him, tell him. I already told you Harry has less rights to my sex life than he does yours… He has no rights to my sex life, as a matter of fact. I'm your girl. I support you. That's what matters to me here. You are what matters to me. You don't owe me anything, my Heart." Going over, she laid her hands on his folded arms. "I won't be hurt or think less of you if you decide it's best not to split his focus."

"I understand what you're saying." Though his frown didn't scream agreement. "He won't take it well; I know that already. I'm prepared for it."

"You are?" she asked. "How do you do that?"

"I look at you," he said, smoothing a hand over her still rowdy hair. "Tension between him and me, between me and the guys, it could make things more difficult. But I can take them being annoyed. What I can't take is anyone not understanding how far I'd go for you. If I want their trust, I have to be honest. They have to know you are my focus. I need Harry to know, the guys to know; they need to understand I'll prioritize you over everything else. If we're in the field or on a mission to take Zeus down, I won't risk you or your safety."

Narrowing her eyes, she tried to decide if that was a positive or not. "What does that mean?"

"If you're in trouble, I will turn around and walk away from any mission to get to you," he said, plain as day without any apology. "If you're under threat, if Z gets hold of you or the Six want to make a deal for your safety, I'll listen… and whatever it takes to keep you safe—"

"You said you would never walk away from your family…" Her fingers drifted from his arms. "That me and my mom weren't safe out there on our own."

"Babe, I don't know what's going to happen out there. Taking Z down might be simple. Styx won't hesitate if he gets a chance up close and he told you I'm a good shot."

"I don't doubt you," she said, clinging to him again.

"Not for a single heartbeat, my Heart. I don't doubt your ability or your resolve. I just don't want you to… You don't owe me anything. Unconditional, remember? I don't need you to declare your love to the world to know it's true."

"You didn't know it yesterday."

She sighed. "I didn't really doubt your love. I was hurt, that's all. It's like I've said, when we're together, it's easy to believe you… Sometimes it just smacks me in the face that I'm new to all this and you're so practiced… This life is easy for you."

"This is not easy for me," he said. "Damnit, baby, the life I want involves you, me, the Beast, and nothing but open road."

That put a smile on her face. "Who knew you'd get lower maintenance over time? No need for the rubbers and the weed now, huh?"

"You wanna get high, get high," he said, sweeping his hand from her forehead around to her chin before dipping to kiss her. He left his lips on hers. "But there's not a chance I'll put any barrier between my cock and your pussy any time ever again."

"Fine by me," she said, stealing another quick kiss then reaching over to push the shower curtain out of the way. "Do you know what tomorrow is?"

Despite asking the question, she didn't dream for a second he'd actually have the answer. "Three months since we first slept together."

Agog, she blinked at him. "Oh my God, how did you get in my brain like that?"

Mischief warmed his expression as he crouched to wrap both arms around her waist. "I live inside you; you haven't figured that out yet? It's been thirteen weeks, I prefer to count that way." He lifted her over the edge of the tub to put her under the shower before joining her. "And I'd say this is a pretty damn good way to celebrate."

With the sensation of the water running over their bodies, she closed her eyes when his mouth met hers. They might not have a whole lot else to celebrate. Taking advantage of the good times when they came along was the best thing they could do. The only thing.

Being with her man. For this moment. That was the only guarantee there was, she vowed to do her best to remember that as often as possible.

TWELVE

GOING OUT FOR LUNCH was the best plan. Getting out of the apartment meant less chance of her distracting Daire. Out of the apartment meant less chance of removing their clothes at least. She still distracted him and in turn his hands distracted certain corners of her body.

After lunch, they went to a coffee shop where she got her favorite frappe and a muffin. Both of which perturbed Styx.

Dragging his feet as they went up the stairs, Styx kept glaring at her cup. "I don't see why you have a problem with coffee," he said to his brother.

"It's not Omega approved."

"Is there an actual list? In twenty-one years, I don't think I ever saw a list."

"The list is in my head," Daire said. "Right out of Harry's head."

"I didn't fall for that growing up, you think I'm gonna fall for it now? That just means you and Harry make it up as you go along. Who the hell has anything against coffee?"

"It's a vice."

Styx scoffed. "What the hell do you call sex?"

"A biological imperative," she said, snagging Daire's

hand. "To keep those drives satisfied, I think you deserve some this afternoon."

"He deserves some?" Styx asked. "What has he done to deserve more since the last time you gave it up?"

"He bought me coffee," she said, sucking some up through the straw. "And a muffin."

"God forbid we forget the muffin," Styx said, creeping her out by peering at her. "You bastard."

"You're saying that to me?" she asked. "I'm a bastard?"

"He gets coffee when he kisses you."

Huh. Good point. It didn't take long for her lips to react. "I'm a lot more than his coffee fix."

"You tell him, baby," Daire said, distracted, slowing halfway along their corridor. "Wait here."

His tone was different, curious and serious. As he took his hand from hers, he made eye contact with Styx. Something passed between them, and Styx got in front of her, backing her slowly to the wall. If she didn't know her own man so well and recognize that something had piqued his interest, she'd probably swear and shove Styx away.

Except she knew, from the way Daire crept up the hallway, that Styx was protecting her, tasked with putting his body between her and danger. That was shocking enough, yet still not as shocking as her man walking toward it. He was walking toward a perceived threat… He definitely deserved more sex.

Could she bear it? An odd combination of adrenaline and fear mingled, building one increment at a time, matching the pace of Daire's steps toward their front door. Anything could happen any second. She trusted him enough to have faith in his instincts. If something in him believed there was someone or something up ahead, it didn't matter that they couldn't see it. It was there, without a shadow of a doubt.

Although still breathing, she was almost afraid to take a full breath. Peeking around Styx's arm, she waited to see what Daire would find. Touching the door, he stayed out of the field of it, shifting without sound to put his back to the wall. There was no key, no unlocking, no turning of the handle, he pushed the door, peeking around the frame and then… He stepped back, shoving the door all the way open and gesturing down the hall at them even though his concentration remained fixed on the inside of the apartment.

Styx freed her from his shield to put a hand between her shoulder blades and shove her forward. Daire went inside, must mean it was safe. Traipsing up the hall, she was propelled along by the hand that stayed on her back. It wasn't like she was going to run away, though after the game the previous day, she couldn't blame Styx for being vigilant.

Although she kind of expected it, there was still a surge of foreboding when rounding the door. Inside, her father and lover were face to face. The tension in the air was palpable; she sort of regretted not taking the chance to run when she'd had it.

"Light-Sprite," her father said at the same time she heard the lock turn behind her. "You've got us all tangled up."

"Your mess, Harry," she said, deliberately not looking at Daire as she got closer to both men. "I'm here. Just as you wanted."

He surprised her by touching her face, something a father might do to appreciate his child. Not something Harry did with her. Obviously, he was pleased her blood was in close proximity. That must give him some sense of hope for retrieving JARR from the beta site.

"I'm happy that you're safe," he said. "We'll keep you safe. You should go back to the bedroom, we have things to talk about out here."

"Out here," she said, drawing in a breath. "Strong, valiant men make a plan to save the world…" Sneaking around her father, she kept her distance. "What would feeble little me do if I heard all those brave, gallant plans?"

"Tess…" Daire said.

"It's okay," she said, holding up her coffee cup while sort of wishing she hadn't eaten the muffin in the car. "I'm fine with my coffee… You boys play nice."

Going into the bedroom, she pushed the door over without closing it all the way. It wasn't that she planned to listen in, but the conversation could take a while. Made sense to give herself an avenue for checking in to see how they were doing and if there was any hint of an end in sight.

After putting her coffee on the dresser, she kicked off her shoes and tried to remember if her book was still in her carpet bag.

Harry's words drifted through to her ears. "Styx, boy, it's good to see you," he said, genuine relief in his tone. "Knew you were up to something out there... You catch up with Ares?"

"Pandora," Styx responded. "I was on Three's tail when he took her to London... She's a handful."

Her brow crinkled as her mouth opened. Asshole could at least say that to her face.

Harry's laugh was brief. "She's Helen's daughter, that's for sure." Because the revered Hades couldn't ever be accused of being spirited outside pre-approved limits. "This place is good, but we have several issues. I checked your current inventory; it's a decent start. We might be able to spend another day or two here, we can't stay much longer. I must track something down. Something important."

"You want to tell us what happened first?" Styx asked. "Vegas was Z, right?"

"We got word he was in town, didn't have Pandora. Made a demand."

"Can't give him something you don't have," Styx said.

That had been her argument for fleeing, though Styx hadn't acknowledged it. In his defense, she'd shouted it at him before storming off. So, yeah, maybe he hadn't really had the chance.

"He didn't like it?"

"Didn't like that we were regrouped, developing plans, making progress."

"Not while he was going backwards," Styx said. "He knew Poseidon was off base?"

"I can only assume. Don't think he'd be stupid enough to kill the guy he needs to put Gamma together."

"What's happening with the site?" Styx asked.

Harry talked for a minute about the security measures they'd put in place to protect the gamma site and how they'd been stepped up after she was taken. Tess didn't care so much about that. She cared that Daire was silent.

Creeping toward the door, she could sense his conflict. Touching her middle finger to the wood frame, she rested her chest on the wall.

"You don't have to do it," she whispered, knowing he wouldn't hear her.

Looking Harry in the eye, standing toe-to-toe with him, the words would be harder to say. That was exactly what she'd been trying to tell her Heart that morning. They needed to be focused. The personal would have to take a backseat to everyone's safety, she understood that.

"We need camping gear," Harry said. "We're gonna be on the road a while. Milo and Zip have a mission, once they complete it, they'll be in touch. That's when we'll get together and form a plan, depending on our numbers."

"What's the mission?"

"To retrieve Lowe and Boze… and whoever else they meet. P did make a discovery; we were supposed to be rolling out when we got word about Z."

She hadn't known that. Did Daire? Had he known the plan was to go to Garrick and the others? Someone would've had to stay behind in Vegas. Him. That made his decision to leave with her all the more humbling. He'd have been just a short time away from taking the Vegas reins from Harry while the latter went into the field to retrieve the men. Beyond that, Daire's next mission would be in D.C. The glimmer of Olympus normality had been right there. And he'd walked away anyway.

"You know who P found?"

"No. We'll stay on the road, keep moving, until they have the cargo. Moving and training… you're favoring your left."

"'Cause your lieutenant pointed out my weakness."

"Why do you have weakness?" Harry asked with concern.

"That's a long story. I'll be back up to speed in no time."

"Good because we have a lot to do. We supply up

here, then we'll need to tour Helen's last few bases… Pandora should help with that."

"Didn't find what you were looking for," Daire said, opening his mouth for the first time.

"No," Harry said. "I didn't… which is disappointing."

"You went to the Rotunda?" Daire asked.

There was a pause. "How do you know about that?"

"I've been there… And I figure that's why you wanted us in Miami."

They'd never told Harry about the last letter. In their defense, so many things had happened there hadn't been time to dedicate to revelations or heart-to-hearts.

"You followed Helen there?"

"No," Daire said. Though Harry could be forgiven for that assumption. He, like her, didn't know how long Daire had been tailing her mom before her death. "Pandora."

Another pause. "She knows?"

"She's not just a pretty face, she pays attention," Daire said. "I know your code and I know you found it empty."

"What is the Rotunda?" Styx asked.

"It's the place Carrie left her letters for Harry."

"Yeah, I just learned about this writing," Styx said. "Guess that's how you hooked up again. Tess had no idea you were sleeping together when she was a teenager."

Harry cleared his throat. "That was ten years ago."

"Went on for a few years."

"What?" Daire said. "Why the fuck am I just learning about this now? You were screwing Carrie ten years ago? Tess would've been, what? Seventeen?"

Styx probably figured she'd filled Daire in. However, her parents' sex life wasn't top of her agenda.

"Started when she was sixteen," Styx said. "I know 'cause I was the one chasing her down when she ran away… while the old man was getting his."

"What a fucking joke," Daire muttered. "Here I am, worried how you'll take the news Tess and I are together, and all the time you're keeping secrets about your own sordid affair."

"There was nothing sordid about…" Harry trailed off, which she guessed meant he'd processed Daire's words. "What did you say?"

"I'm in love with your daughter," Daire said, sure and unapologetic. Wow, he didn't even hesitate. "We've been together a while… three months."

"You've been…"

"Yeah," Daire said. "All over the place, as often as she'll let me."

Her lips quirked.

"You're telling me you…" Harry was ramping up to something. "You put your hands on my child?"

"He's put a lot more than that on her," Styx mumbled, she only just picked up his quiet words.

"This is not a joke, this is… You can't be serious. This is a play. A tactic. What do you want? What's the game?"

"It's no play, old man," Daire said. "We tried to end it. Didn't work. And I won't—"

"You will," Harry said. The rage in those simple words was so hot that she pushed away from the wall, bracing to move. "You will end it. You'll forget every damn thought you ever had about her. You know how many fucking lines you crossed? Rules you broke? Orders you ignored?"

"You never ordered me not to touch her."

"Three months… it started before you brought her to me."

"Yeah," Daire said. "She didn't know the truth then. She knows it now. Knows everything."

"Everything?"

"Yeah. I don't lie to her… I won't lie to her."

"You will do what you are told," Harry asserted. "You will follow orders."

"Only one authorized to lay down rules about my girl is her."

"Your… Your girl? You fucking ungrateful little punk."

She heard the smack of hands on a body.

Throwing open the door, she rushed out, determined not to let the fists fly.

THIRTEEN

"EVERYONE NEEDS TO CALM DOWN," she said, rushing to a halt in the living room.

Harry and Daire were within inches of each other, glaring hard. Neither flinched. Neither willing to give up an inch of ground.

Styx was opposite her, near the other wall, a good eight feet from them. "Let them have at it," he said.

She could slap him herself. "What will that achieve?"

"Best way to express their feelings."

"Oh, yeah," she said. "Blood and bruises are much better than just talking it out."

"Nothing to talk about," Daire said, still staring into Harry. "He knows. It's done."

"Done? You…"

When Harry's fingers curled into a fist at his side, she leaped forward, pushing at her father to get between the men. "Don't you dare lay a finger on him!"

"Is that what kind of man you are?" Harry asked, ignoring her to keep glaring at Daire over her head. "You have my daughter fight your battles for you?"

"If it is, he only learned it from you," she snapped. "Isn't that what you've done his whole life? You don't get to lay a finger on him; I am a thousand times more his than I ever was yours. You don't want me, he does. You don't acknowledge my existence, he does."

That brought his attention down. Though there was less anger in his eyes, he wasn't at peace.

"You're punishing me," Harry said, incredulous. "Of course you're punishing me, and what better way than to go after my boy."

"Yep," she said without an ounce of shame. "I saw how close you two were and thought, 'Hmm, how can I get in and stir this up?' Maybe before we get into that, we should talk about how you and mom found all that time to do the dirty while I never saw your face? Think maybe if instead of getting yourself off, you had a conversation with me, that maybe I wouldn't have run away so much? No, but wait, if I wasn't out the picture, when would mom have found the freedom to tickle your pickle?"

"Tess!"

"No!" she replied, matching his outrage. "You do not get to stand there and play the insulted father like you were ever a feature in my life! You want to get pissed at me for loving your prize student? Your ward? Do it! You get to worry for him! For his career! His well-being! His life! You do not get to punish or judge him for feeling something for me! He loves me more than you ever could, more than you ever did! More than any other person ever did! For the first time in my whole life, I know what love is, what it is to matter to another person. He's given me something that you never did, that mom never did... He's given me security. A belonging I've never had anywhere else."

"You can't be with him," Harry said, his jaw still tight. "You can't be together."

"Says you," she said. "And who are you? His superior officer? Yeah, that might fly if Olympus wasn't circling the drain. You're asking us to sacrifice the only true happiness either of us have found for something on the brink of extinction."

"No," Harry said, his head moving in a slow, shallow shake. "For your lives. You can't be together because it will kill both of you. There's no chance of a future; the security you think you have is an illusion. Too many people will be coming for you. Too many people want Daire's loyalty. If they can get it by hurting you, that's what they'll do."

"You think they'll become you and Carrie," Styx said.

"I won't let that happen," Daire said, his hands sliding onto her shoulders.

Harry spat out his disgust but did back off a couple of steps to throw up an arm. "You think you can control it. You think you can anticipate it. You can't." He pointed at Daire's face. "You will spend every second of the rest of your life terrified for her safety. They will hurt her. They'll do it when they see what it does to you… What you'll do to stop them ever doing it again."

The way his intonation changed saddened her. His anger came from a place of grief. He'd lost his forever when her mom died. With everything that had happened since then, had he had any time to process his loss?

"I won't ever let anyone hurt her," Daire said.

Bowing forward, she surprised everyone by picking up Harry's hand. Her father's shock rocked through him. "We have the benefit of your experience… of your sacrifice."

Again, her father shook his head. "I can't stop them from hurting you. I couldn't do it for your mom. I can't do it for you, Light-Sprite. I'm sorry."

And she really believed his apology. "What you had with mom wasn't all bad… I read the letters. You loved each other." He didn't answer with words, the pain in his eyes told its own story. "PK found love. He has a future. And the only part of him that's owned now is the part that belongs to me." She tried to smile. "In your letters, you were mad… The Darkness is Olympus, right? Zeus. You were mad for what they did to you and mom. The letters started after you made the deal to secure mine and mom's release from Olympus… You were mad and wanted to take them down."

"It was complicated."

Licking her lips, she understood he wouldn't want to say anything that might upset Daire, with regards to their past anyway. There were times he thought of Daire as the efficient, supreme Olympus agent capable of anything. Other times he only saw the little boy he'd left in a corridor with Garrick when he went to join his baby and the woman he loved.

"I know," she said, not wanting to push Harry more than they were already pushing. It was a precarious time. They could embrace their similarities and work together, or the revelation could create a gulf that would never heal. "You wanted to hurt Zeus. He made you feel powerless. Took something from you that he had no right to take."

More than one thing in her opinion. Not only his child and the woman he loved, but his dignity and masculinity in impeding his ability to protect and provide.

"He took from me too," Daire said, surprising her with the low, rumbling words. "Never again."

A new light tinged Harry's eyes when they rose to his protégé again. "London," he murmured. After a pause, he breathed out his incredulity and raised a hand to his forehead, turning away from her. "Now I know why you were climbing the damn walls." Spinning around, he fixated on Daire. "You were in love with her."

"Am in love with her," Daire said, correcting his mentor.

"Yeah, and if it wasn't for him, I'd have walked off the reservation ten times over," Tess argued. "I was ready to walk away and never look back after our fun conversation in the wine cellar."

"Shit," Harry said, rubbing his forehead again. "You went after her."

"Yeah."

"Damnit, I put you in charge of her safety! I put you in her room!"

"I didn't touch her those nights," Daire said. "I followed orders."

Tess sighed. "He always follows orders."

Some of Harry's annoyance was back. "If that was true, he wouldn't have fucked my daughter in the first place."

Inhaling, she closed her mouth ready to accept her responsibility for their inception. "I seduced him the first time," she said, without looking any of them in the eye. "I didn't know who he was, but, yeah, I seduced him."

"With a condom," Daire said, squeezing her shoulders.

"At least you're being safe," Harry muttered, though he didn't seem to enjoy the details. "That's something."

"What we are is mutual and always has been," Daire said. "Once she found out the truth, we ended it…" Not that they'd specifically had a break-up, though they'd never put labels on what they were, not back then anyway. "Then it just sort of… happened."

In the Beast, after he gave her the present nestled in her cleavage.

Clarity tipped her head his way. "I kissed you that time too."

"Little instigator," Styx said, strolling closer. "Are we gonna put this to bed? Accept that it's going on and move past it?"

"No," Harry snapped. "I need to know why I wasn't told."

"You didn't ask," Daire said. "You knew I got her to Beta somehow."

"And I did suspect you'd lured her there with false promises. Even if she was enraptured with you, I believed you were stronger than to give in to baser urges… I thought you had more respect for me."

"I was mad," Daire said. "Zulu, the Exodus, everything went to shit."

"I apologized for my role in that."

"I don't need you to apologize again," Daire said. "Tess wasn't even my original target. Carrie was the one I wanted to put in front of you… The accident changed that. I saw an opportunity and I took it. I didn't go into it expecting to fall in love with her. After I was there, I couldn't… You can't take that back."

"I'd think you would understand that," she said to her father. "We know it's dangerous. And you have to know that I am not interested in taking him away from you or causing any rift. I know there are priorities more important than our relationship."

"Why tell me now?" he asked, looking from her to Daire and back. "You told him to tell me."

She shook her head. "The opposite. I told him he didn't have to. Disappointing you hurts his confidence. I didn't want his eye anywhere but on the ball. He has something about honesty and trust though, he doesn't like duplicity, not with people he loves. You two never say it, but it's obvious to anyone who's seen you together for more than a minute, you do love each other. The three of you do."

An uncomfortable ripple of tension went through the air that made her smile. Used to being in such a masculine environment, the trio were more likely to throw a punch at each other than verbalize how much they cared.

"Thanks for that, Lady," Styx murmured.

She laughed. "Sometimes the three of you need your heads knocked together," she said, dropping her cheek to the back of Daire's hand before leaving him to go to the folding table and chairs propped on the wall. "And like it or not, the three of you need each other right now. Someone has to deal with Zeus, to deal with the whole mess."

After unfolding the chairs, she eased the table from the wall, trying to figure out how to put it up. Daire was already at her shoulder, reaching over to take the issue out of her hands.

"You want me to source camping gear?" Styx asked. "You got coordinates? What's the altitude?"

"Altitude?" she asked, startled. "Does on the road mean mountaineering? I love the cold, the snow, all that stuff... from inside, next to a blazing fire."

Daire put the table on its legs next to her and began to put the chairs around it. "I have the Beast."

"The Beast?" Styx asked.

His question amused her. "What we call the Airstream."

"Couldn't see inside that damn thing."

She linked her hands at her back to tiptoe his way. "You should be grateful for that."

He screwed his face up. "Good point. Knowing what I know now."

"I never thanked you for that properly," she said, going closer. "In London... meant the world to me to see him."

"Yeah, you need to work on your poker face."

"I used up all my poker face time during the damn video calls with Zeus."

"Seeing me?" Daire asked in the background.

Styx scratched the back of his head. "The feedback flare that got you up in the middle of the night... Yeah, that was us."

"Us?" she said, releasing her hands when Daire came over to drape his heavy arm across her shoulders. "You. It was you." She raised her chin to look up at the man holding her to his side. "I just did the swooning after you were awake."

Breathing out a smile, he dropped his lips to her forehead. "You're allowed, LR... I knew something was up that night."

"It was me, drooling," she said, amusing both the brothers.

"You were patched into our feed?" Daire asked Styx who nodded. He squeezed her shoulders. "That's why you kept looking at the camera in the garage."

"I didn't know who was watching us."

A frown took Daire's features when he switched to his brother. "How did you break security remotely? That's a major flaw we have to fix."

"I didn't. My SP was the foreclosed house opposite Three's... I went into your mainframe."

"You were inside," Daire said. Styx's smug shrug fooled no one. "Why didn't you join ranks?"

"That's what I said," Tess said, resting her head on Daire.

"'Cause I didn't trust Three... turned out I was right. I wasn't watching you. I was watching them. Pandora showing up was a surprise... you and Harry appearing the day after was a coup."

"Sit still long enough and what you're looking for will cross your path."

"Just put yourself where they'll be," Styx said.

Daire extended a hand to his brother. Tess didn't have a clue why. Neither did the frowning Styx as he put his hand in Daire's to shake. "Never said thank you for protecting my girl."

"I did nothing," Styx said. "She doesn't need looking after, luck is always on her side… We should probably thank her for putting us back together." Before she could get any ideas of being proud of herself, he set a stern look on her. "But you've gotta learn to be more careful. You trusted me too easy."

"I didn't trust you," she said, surprised he would accuse her of that. She laid a hand on Daire's abdomen. "I trusted this guy. I knew who you were. I knew what you were to him. I trusted what he told me, how he felt about you. If you'd been anyone else, anyone I didn't know, anyone Daire didn't trust, I would've got up and left you on that bench alone."

"Talked about me?" Styx asked Daire, narrowing his eyes. "Now we know you're whispering sweet nothings to each other, we've gotta wonder what else you two talk about in the dead of night."

"You told her about JARR."

Harry's solemn words came from behind, forcing the three of them to turn.

"I told her it existed," Daire said.

The disappointment in Harry's head shake put her on the defensive. "He told me JARR existed—"

"I taught you better than that," Harry barked. "Better than to share intel in exchange for getting your rocks off."

Offended, she stepped in front of Daire again. "I got my rocks off that day, he didn't," she argued. "And he might have told me about JARR, but I learned about the blood in London. I learned about Michael Lloyd in London." Shock hit Harry. "I learned the truth about Chester Buford there too."

Her father's mouth opened as he came a step closer. "Ulysses," he exhaled.

"Yeah."

Something about Harry's wide eyes piqued her curiosity. Anger or surprise was to be expected, but he didn't look either.

Worry colored his demeanor. "He told you about Chester Buford?"

She nodded, wondering why he was doing such a terrible job of hiding his panic. "You care more about that than Michael Lloyd?"

"I don't give two shits about Michael Lloyd, I never did," Harry said, blanking his expression. "Ares, you have to find yourself a base. Somewhere off the grid. You need to be completely gone."

"Why?" Daire asked. "Where does Buford feature in any of this?"

"He doesn't," Harry said, shrugging off his telling reaction to her revelation. "You have to keep your head down. Styx and I will deal with Zeus."

"Wait," Daire said, stepping around her. "You're benching me?"

"You've been compromised."

"Because of Chester fucking Buford? Former VP, right? He's dead, isn't he?"

"Yes," Harry said, meeting her eye again. "Definitely dead… Buford isn't the problem. The problem is in your pants. We can't have you distracted in the field. You're useless to me now."

"Because of me?" Tess asked. "I haven't compromised him."

"Tess focuses me," Daire said. "I won't sit on the sidelines and let someone else take responsibility for protecting what I love. He took her from me; I'll be the one to make him pay for that."

Frustration closed Harry's eyes for a moment. "You don't know what you're doing—what it is to be in the field while the woman you love is in danger."

"I tolerated her being in London with him without blowing my stack, didn't I?"

"Before you'd acknowledged her. Admitting the truth weakens you and it weakens her. Once they know where to squeeze, they'll never stop."

"Neither will I," Daire said, burning with

determination. "I won't stop until every threat to her has been eliminated."

FOURTEEN

"HOW WILL YOU DO THAT? Hmm?" Harry asked. "Alone? Because we can't work together anymore."

"You won't fight with him?" she asked, outraged and heartbroken in equal measures. "He's your family, Harry. Just because he's fucking a woman on a regular basis doesn't mean you should disown him."

"It's alright," Daire said, putting a soothing hand on her shoulder.

Without turning, she shrugged it off to march closer to Harry. "He gave you his life. Trusted you. You're the only father he's ever known. He worshiped you, dedicated his life to pleasing you, and this is how you repay that? He fought your wars for you!"

"I am not disowning him," Harry said, managing to maintain his calm even in the face of the tears warming her eyes. "It has been my honor to fight at his side all these years. He will always be my boy… That is why I will not take the risk with his safety, any more than I'd take the risk with yours."

"You expect me to tuck tail too? What happens if you fail?"

"Then your life will never be safe."

"I won't do nothing," Daire said, coming to her side. "I don't need your permission to take him on."

"Which is exactly what worries me," Harry said, matching Daire's fierce tone with his own. "You've never worked in the field without structure, without the hierarchy. Damn, you couldn't even keep your training up when you were on your own after the Exodus. I don't want you out there going rogue."

"You're the one casting me out," Daire said. "I'm willing to work together. For our ranks to stay tight. For our unit to achieve together. We were always best as a team."

Proud of him, she grazed his pinkie with her own.

"There is nowhere we can put Tess that she will be safe," Harry said. "Not right now. With only three of us, we can't afford to release anyone to protect her full-time."

"We protect her full-time," Daire said. "She stays with us. I wouldn't send her off anywhere alone and I wouldn't trust anyone else to keep her safe… You can choose to exile me, that's your call… but what do you think happens with Tess if you try that? Where do you think she goes? You think she stays with you?"

Daire stepped back to turn side on, both him and Harry focused on her. "What?" she asked, her eyes flicking back and forth between them. "Why are you both looking at me? I'm not going to be stuck away in some hidey hole by myself, I already told you that."

"And if I ask Daire to leave?" Harry asked.

"Asking Daire to leave is the same as asking me to leave. He goes, I go," she said, confused as to why there was even the hint of a question over that. "And he's not going to disappear quietly. If we have to take down Zeus just him and I, we'll do that."

"He can't do it alone," Harry said. "Especially not if he is solely responsible for your life at the same time."

"Then don't exile him," she said. "You're talking about changing things. No one else is. We're willing to respect the hierarchy. Daire trusts you not to endanger him. Trust is going to war sure that those with you will give as much as you." Though she noticed Daire's half smile in her peripheral vision, she stayed on Harry. "This is war. It shouldn't be given any less reverence than that."

"You will show it that consideration and respect?" Harry asked. Giving the right answer was important, she nodded once. "It won't be easy. It won't be fun. It will be grueling, and you won't like every play."

Remaining somber, she didn't want Harry to doubt her or for Daire to lose his commander.

"We can do this, Harry," Daire said. "We'll do whatever it takes. But if you're not willing to lead—"

"It's always been my honor to lead you and the men," Harry said. "Until now, it didn't occur to me for a second that I might have to doubt your commitment to my orders."

Daire's guilt over disrespecting Harry would already be high. There was something sad about Harry's words that tugged at her heart. Coming between the men, causing any kind of division, had never been her intention. It seemed she was the one who swanned in and got the best of both worlds. If she could shoulder the negatives, the burden, the guilt then she would. Unfortunately, it wasn't as easy as just being sorry.

"I didn't choose to love her," Daire said, for the first time allowing a hint of contrition to slip into his tone. "I knew it wasn't smart. I fought it… but it happened anyway."

Harry's shoulders sank just before a sigh slipped from his lips. "I know exactly what that's like."

The forlorn breath of those words gave her some hope. Being the source of conflict between them hadn't been her intention. Ignorant to the process, she hadn't had any sort of plan for falling in love or avoiding it. Like he'd said, it happened anyway, regardless of good sense or intention.

With Harry's admission came the idea that maybe the men could become closer. They'd been through something, decades apart, that the other could identify with. Harry had a right to be shocked. Not at her. But Daire was his protégé. All his life, he'd followed orders. Choosing love as the first real rule to break wasn't a gentle approach, he'd gone right off the deep end.

"Okay, now that news time is over with," Styx said, injecting himself at the right moment. "Let's get to the planning. Milo and Zip retrieve the guys, what about Garrick?"

"They're under instruction to let him choose," Harry said. As he went to seat himself at the table, the other two men followed to do the same. "If he wants to join us, he's welcome. There are going to be clear factions here. We didn't want it, but it's here anyway. Everyone has to pick sides."

Both Styx and Daire looked at her, so she offered a finger wave and spun around to head for the bedroom.

"Hey," Daire called out. Catching the doorframe before she went inside, she twisted to see what he wanted. "This involves you too."

"I know, but my coffee is in there. Can I go grab it?"

"Never heard her ask your permission for anything," Styx said.

Despite asking, she didn't wait for a reply and went in to snag the cup from the dresser. The men were still discussing her when she returned.

"…know what's going on," Daire said.

"The details will overwhelm her," Harry said. "We have to protect her."

"You don't have to worry about my ears," she said. "They can take it and I know how to keep a secret. Just ask your boys."

"Yeah," Daire said, setting his brother in his sights. "Yeah, that reminds me, you told her not to tell me about you two meeting in London?"

"Doesn't matter, she did anyway. It's not like I knew you were fucking when I said that."

"You trusted her," Daire said. "You wouldn't have planned an op with her if you didn't. And, for the record, she didn't tell me. I followed her. Even then, she told me to wait outside and I ignored her."

"Yeah," Tess said, sinking down onto the couch. "Thanks for trusting me by the way."

"I was protecting you," Daire said. "You knew I would follow you."

She shrugged and bit her straw. Him coming after her was always a possibility, hence her worry about the gun.

"I could trust her because it was obvious she was hung up on you," Styx said. "Women don't turn on men they're panting after."

"Panting," she scoffed. "I don't pant…" When Daire sought her gaze, she smiled. "Not all the time."

His confident dimple showed he was beginning to relax and feel more like himself. "It's mutual, baby," he said and winked. "You know it."

"This was exactly my concern," Harry asserted. "Already the three of you are distracted."

"We're in home territory," Daire said. "Any reason to believe anyone followed you or knows exactly where we are? Zeus doesn't have an army. The guy he sent back to Three's with Tess was a goddamn mindless drone. I spotted him casing the place in the morning, then an hour later, he's driving up and down again with our cargo in the front seat."

"I'm cargo now?"

"You're not our target or our mark."

"She's gonna be Zeus's target," Styx said. "She played him in London and again in Vegas. He won't like that."

"He didn't like me in the first place."

"Everyone needs to focus," Harry said. "Since the Exodus everything has gone to shit. It's time to pull it back. Get some discipline about you."

Tess smiled. It was easy for her to watch her father crack the whip and would be interesting to witness Daire and Styx working together. She'd seen Daire training under her father, not for long, though long enough to know he was a different person to the one who seduced her in the night.

Her smile dropped. Just a second later, Styx laughed, startling them all.

It was her he pointed at. "I just witnessed the moment she realized her sex life is over."

Unimpressed by his amusement, she scowled at him. "Least I got some today, when was the last time you got laid?"

"Today?" Harry said. "Ares, you claim not to be distracted? You should be on Omega."

Styx raised a hand toward the center of the table. "I am on Omega… Sort of against my will, but I'm on it." He slapped his hand to Daire's shoulder. "Knew sex wasn't allowed on Omega. Get ready for a dry spell."

"It's exercise," Tess argued. "Rigorous exercise is Omega… I've been helping him out. I always make sure he hydrates."

She couldn't see Harry's face but guessed he was pondering.

"Sex isn't expressly forbidden on Omega," her Heart said. "Am I wrong?"

"Sex isn't," Styx said. "But coffee is?"

"Coffee is definitely forbidden," Harry said. "It's a stimulant."

"And sex isn't?"

The conversation was reminiscent of the one they'd had in the hall not long ago.

"Ares isn't wrong," Harry said, though he didn't sound happy to admit it. "It isn't expressly forbidden."

Pushing back in his seat, Daire opened his arms. "Thank you."

"Though I will say it wouldn't have been considered an issue given that fraternizing without orders is against basic SOP."

"SOP?"

"Standard operating procedure," Daire answered fast before replying to Harry. "I slept with her for my mission."

"You weren't on Omega then," Styx said. "And if that's a mission we're allowed to give ourselves, I'm going out tonight."

"You achieved your mission when you brought her to Beta and confronted me in the control room," Harry said. "Your mission is over. Is today the first day you've been intimate since then?"

Some of Daire's bluster dwindled. His reply was humble in comparison to his previous exclamations. "No."

"Between then and London, how many times did you break protocol?"

"Actually break it or consider breaking it?"

"Oh my God," Tess said, scooching closer to the arm of the couch. "There can't be protocols for thoughts. How often we do or don't have sex is our business."

Drawing in a breath, Harry twisted around in his seat to address her. "If you're going to be with us, a part of this, and expect to maintain your relationship, you will have to respect the rules. Others will be joining us eventually and if there's insubordination higher in the ranks, the lower ranks won't be confident in their leadership. They'll hesitate. They won't have trust."

"I respect the rules," she said. "You just said yourself that Omega didn't forbid intimacy. We didn't mean to break any rules. And I can attest that he's stuck to it in every other way, and I have never asked him not to."

"I appreciate that this lifestyle isn't what you're used to," Harry said. "Having one of my people in a relationship, with the object of that relationship in our midst, it's new for me."

"Olympus is done," Daire said. "It wasn't easy for me to admit that, but it is. Whatever we're doing now, whatever is next, it's something new. Something we'll make ourselves."

"I agree that some rules will have to be relaxed, we may do things in a different way," Harry said to him. "But you have to trust me when I tell you what's best."

"I wouldn't be here if I didn't trust you," Daire said. "If I wasn't sure you would get us through this, I wouldn't take the risk with Tess's life."

As Harry rotated more toward his protégé, Daire's expression became more serious. "I know what it is to love a woman more than the air you breathe. If this is a novelty, if it's not real—"

"It's real," Daire growled.

"I'll know is what I'm saying," Harry said. "I'll see the truth in the way you are with her… and if I think for a second that you're not what's best for her, if you can't take care of her, one day you'll wake up and she'll be gone. We'll be gone, her and me. You won't ever see her again. You'll never even hear her name."

Unsure what to do, Tess didn't want to get between them again. Some things they had to work out on their own. She still didn't fully understand their dynamic. Styx was braced too, watching, ready, but hanging back.

"Think a lot of yourself if you believe there's a chance I'd let any man take her from me," Daire said. "London was enough, and I only stayed put because *she* wouldn't let me go to her. If I got even a hint she wanted me there, I'd have left you and Olympus in the dust."

Harry's chin rose. "That's encouraging." He flipped around in his seat to look at her again. "That goes for you too, Light-Sprite. He's a serious man with serious responsibilities, to something much bigger than you and your relationship."

"Which is exactly why I told him that I'd never make him choose. I know the mission is more important."

Her father seemed satisfied. "Good."

"But don't underestimate his will," she said before he could turn away. "Sometimes it doesn't matter what I say, he'll do what he thinks is best anyway… I told him not to come with me. I didn't ask him to leave Vegas."

"That wasn't even a question," Daire said. "I'd have hogtied you and left you in the Beast before I let you walk out into the cold alone."

She presented a hand his way. "See."

"Your relationship creates uncomfortable variables," Harry said. "Daire, you'll have to be ready for the men to doubt you."

"I'll deal with problems when they come up. I won't create them."

"You've created them here," Harry said, breathing out at something of a loss. "I can't believe this… I can't believe you would let—"

"You can't control feelings, Harry," Tess said, appreciating that he'd need time to absorb what he'd learned. "You're focusing on the negatives rather than the positives. Doesn't it mean something to you that the boy you raised knows love like you did?"

"Daire's upbringing left him lacking a lot of experiences… I didn't want him to be only a soldier."

"And he's not," she said. "He's a son, a brother, a friend, and a boyfriend, though that doesn't really cover what he is to me." Despite not focusing on her Heart, from the corner of her eye, she noticed a smile creep to his lips. "What?"

"I don't regret telling him," he said, probably as a way of telling her she'd been wrong that morning in the bathroom. "This is better."

"Because I'm saying nice things about you?" she asked. "I say nice things about you all the time… to you all the time."

"We're not usually this far apart when that happens."

And her brain would be fogged by his proximity and whatever they were doing.

They were just admiring each other from afar when Harry sat up straighter and dropped a hand to the table. "No more distractions. Both of you need to go out and find what we need. Plan for the whole team to be back together at some point. Don't source everything from one place."

"We know the routine," Daire said, rising in sync with Styx. "Could take a while."

"Take whatever time you need. Tess and I have things to talk about."

"I'm not going with?" she asked, picking her legs from the floor to fold them under her. Daire was already coming her way, so she tipped her head back to make eye contact. "Want me to cook dinner?"

"No," he said too fast, though the follow up smirk betrayed it was deliberate. "You left your panic button in the Beast."

"I did leave my panic button in the Beast."

He put a hand on the back of the couch to bow over her. "I'll bring it back for you."

"I won't need it," she said, accepting his light kiss, though she was quick to grab for his arm to stop him standing up. "I would like to know where the Beast is."

He came a little lower. "If I tell you that, you'll move back in."

"Would that be so bad?"

"This is our SP. You have to stay with the group."

"I'll stay with the group."

"Do that and I'll bring back coffee for you," he said,

grazing a crooked finger down her chin. "You need anything else?"

She just smiled. "Nothing you want me to mention in front of my father."

"Right," he said, kissing her forehead before standing up to turn to his brother. "You good?"

"Hey, I was ready five minutes ago," Styx said, heading for the door.

Because it was too tempting to ignore, she smacked Daire's ass just before he got moving. He didn't respond or turn back, but Styx's amusement betrayed his brother's.

"Play nice together," she called out as they exited.

Too soon, the door closed, and they were gone. Being relaxed and playful was easier when she wasn't the sole person under the scrutiny of the still severe Harry. After delaying a while and waiting for the air to thicken with unresolved issues, she forced herself to look his way.

It was him who broke the silence. "We have a lot to talk about."

FIFTEEN

"WHAT DO WE HAVE TO TALK ABOUT?" Tess asked her father, watching him turn his chair to face her.

Harry propped an elbow on the table next to him. "About your mom, about London… About Chester Buford."

The first two things were expected. She didn't expect him to bring up the former VP, though given his earlier reaction, she probably should have.

"You panicked," she said. "When you heard Zeus told me about him."

"How much did he tell you?"

"I don't know," she said on a shrug, then curled both hands around her intersecting legs. "I know he was framed for something he wasn't guilty of… I know about Kaiya and Richard Merrill."

Harry's expression became more severe. "You can't tell him."

"Daire," she said. "That's why you panicked, isn't it? Because if I know, there's nothing to stop me telling him. Wow." The silence confirmed what she'd said. "How does he not know?"

"Records of the Buford operation were destroyed in the Alpha disintegration." Something that Buford was responsible for. "Not long after we lost the alpha site and Kaiya, Buford died."

"And if you expect me to believe that was suicide, you're crazy," she said. "But I go back to my original question, how does he not know?"

"Daire knows he was born during the alpha site's destruction. He knows that his mother died there too. He's also aware that the destruction was precipitated by someone who had beef with Olympus. We tightened our security, worked on new ways to conceal ourselves. The organization was still new then, in relative terms. We learned a lot from what happened with Buford."

"He wasn't wrong," she said. "You ruined an innocent man's life, you ruined it for a training mission."

"A training mission that gave Byron senior what he wanted."

She licked her lips. "Yeah, I worked out all on my own that the training thing was bullshit. You sent Kaiya in there, an agent who trusted you, to win the trust of a man who would allow you to ruin Buford's credibility... or was it just that he didn't like him? What are you worried about Daire finding out? Who his father is or what his mother died for?"

"Kaiya wasn't the only agent we lost that day."

"The agent who meant the most to Daire," she said. "And the one involved in that mission. Jesus, you asked a woman to use her body to further a political agenda. It wasn't to save anyone's life or grant anyone's liberty, you prostituted her for politics."

"I don't make the calls," Harry said, shoving out of his seat.

"Is that how you justify it to yourself? I always thought working under Zeus must have been torture for you, but maybe you liked that separation of powers. You could tell yourself that you were sending your people in to do despicable things without having to take responsibility for the orders you gave."

"That was a different time," he said, crossing to the balcony.

The doors were closed and the window covered, so

he couldn't see out. The point was not to look at her, at least that's what she assumed.

"Before you met mom. Before you and Zeus fell out of step with each other."

"We were never close," he said, clasping his hands at his back. "Sometimes people assume that the three of us were brothers, thought of each other like brothers. Sometimes for the men, for peace and harmony, we allowed them to believe there was unity."

"But there wasn't," she said, maintaining her focus on him. "If you didn't like him before mom, why stay? What was keeping you there?"

"I was young. I didn't always realize what the wider world could offer. I thought I was doing something important… There was a sense of duty and achieving objectives was a worthy cause… most of the time."

"Most of the time?"

"At first, I didn't know the long-term play with Buford. I didn't like that the mission required Kaiya to get physical with her mark. But Merrill wasn't unattractive, and she didn't put up any objections."

"As the first female agent, I'm going to guess that showing weakness or reluctance would've sealed her fate."

She couldn't speak for Kaiya Canon directly; the woman was a generation removed and long dead. But, as a woman, one who'd spent time with the Olympus men, limited time and a small number of them, the predicament was obvious. Kaiya would've understood the value of accepting every mission, no matter how depraved.

Her son was the same way. Most of the time. He'd found his voice to protect his father-figure when he refused the Zulu mission.

Some Olympus missions involved the male agents getting close to women. If they didn't flinch at that task, Kaiya must have felt obligated to undertake her orders with the same unrelenting determination.

"It's done now," Harry said. "The mission was finished long ago."

"Yeah, but we're talking about it now. You never told

Daire who his father was?"

"He never asked," Harry said, turning around to look her way. "I know he must have been curious, and I would assume he has his suspicions."

"About Merrill's identity?"

"No, about how his conception came about. Before Carrie and I there were occasions when agents were allowed to do what they wished with their limited free time. I suspect that's what Daire leads himself to believe, that his mother got pregnant during one of those occasions."

"If that was true, he would've asked," she said. "JARR might not have been a thing back then, maybe not in its current form, but if you vetted potential recruits and their families, you wouldn't have let the identity of Daire's father go unchecked."

"I said that's what he leads himself to believe," Harry said. "But, you're right, he's smarter than that. Some part of him suspects his conception was mission related... I assume anyway, he's never brought it to me. He's also smart enough not to ask a question he doesn't want the answer to. If he wanted to know, he'd ask me."

"Would you tell him?"

He wandered in her direction. "I spent some time worrying about that as he approached his teen years. There was a time that I thought our relationship may not survive."

"May not survive what happened with me and mom," she said. "Maybe because after we left Olympus, you made him live alone in the wilderness for a year."

Surprise flashed on his face. "He told you about that?"

"Don't be surprised if I know more than you think," she said, without correcting him.

Styx had been the one to tell her about the wilderness. A brief flicker of a possibility sparked in her mind. That story hadn't been completely necessary. Offering more information than required shouldn't be any agent's go-to. Maybe Styx had told her for a reason. Something she, Daire, and he would know.

"After you left, it was difficult. For me. For him... If

I'd been able to free him of Olympus, I would've done it. I tried to do it by including him in the deal meant to free you and Carrie. Daire wouldn't go. He loved his home; it was all he knew."

"And you," she said. "He loved you."

Standing at the other side of the low coffee table, he bobbed his head. "Not enough to leave with me when I left Olympus to be with you and your mother."

"He was six years old and scared. His whole life he'd been told to follow orders. His primary mission was to return to base. Then suddenly, from nowhere, you were telling him that you had to go. Forever. He didn't have any time to think about it, any time to prepare."

"I had a mission, I was gone," Harry said. "And he was so young, I couldn't put the responsibility of keeping such a secret on his shoulders. I didn't even know I was going to leave until I was out on that mission. Separated from all of you, from you, your mother, Daire, I had a near miss. It struck me that one day I could disappear from your lives and you wouldn't know why. I didn't want to live my life like that. I didn't want to abandon any of you."

"It was difficult," she said, acknowledging his impossible position. "For everyone. Nothing about it was ideal."

"And then I come back here today," he said, gesturing toward her and the empty room. "And find out the same thing is happening all over again."

"It won't be like that with us," she said, but he didn't appear convinced. "Olympus is finished, and we will take out the man responsible for doing to you what he did. Zeus was the one to put those restrictions on you and the others. He was the one responsible for taking me and for forcing you into the deal."

"He didn't force me," Harry said. "I would've done anything to keep you and your mother safe."

"Whatever comes next, like Daire said, it will be something that you build. You and him and Styx, you can learn from the mistakes of Olympus."

"Assassinating Zeus is no guarantee. The Six still see

the need for the organization. We cannot be sure that they won't rebuild."

"They can do that if they want," she said, thinking about Daire and Styx's discussion.

The Six were a threat. Still, taking them out wasn't as straightforward as murdering Zeus, a man who'd lived a covert life for decades.

"Their first goal will be to recruit experienced agents."

"You're worried they could take your men from under you?"

"If Olympus is truly done and if Daire wants us to build something new, we won't have the resources of Olympus. He doesn't understand just how much the organization, and the Six, did to support us. We can't afford to look after our own people. We won't be able to stop them going over to the Six's scheme, whatever it is. In fact, if we have any kind of conscience, we should encourage their defection. We trained them how to live this life, with nothing and no one. If we can't support them, it is our duty to ensure they have a safety net, a way to look after themselves."

Daire's sense of responsibility featured a lot in her thoughts. She didn't think so much about her father's. While he and Daire were close because they'd been together all of the latter's life, Harry had still known and cared for the other soldiers under him since they were teenagers.

The divorce analogy wasn't so inaccurate. Even if Harry wanted to keep all the kids, he'd be left with no home, no money, no support system.

"They have the right to make their own choices," she said. "If they want to join whatever new organization the Six come up with then, you're right, you shouldn't stop them from pursuing that path."

"Which might mean coming face to face with them in future," he said, identifying another problem.

The Six's objectives might not complement Harry and Daire's endeavors. In fact, it was likely they wouldn't. Without someone like Harry at the helm, the men would be at the mercy of whoever became their new commanding officer.

Could Harry, Daire, and Styx come face to face with their former comrades? Would they be forced to hurt each other? Kill each other?

"I'm sorry about Albany," she said. "I heard he didn't make it."

Running a hand through his hair, Harry came around the table to sit on the other end of the couch. "Losing anyone is difficult. To know they were lost at Zeus's hand is even more sickening… And, of course, Daire was right that this is my fault. Accepting Zulu caused all of this."

"The Six instigated that. Two came up with the idea, he sold it to them."

"And he paid for that with his life," Harry said, resigned in the way he looked at her. "We should pay for our crimes."

"You did not commit a crime," she said, unfolding her legs to bounce a little closer. "No more than Daire or Styx or any of the men did any time they followed an order. You were respecting the hierarchy."

"Daire said no. He understood the larger scheme at play. I recognized the possibility, maybe I couldn't see past my own desire for vengeance."

His eyes wandered until she pushed closer still and laid a hand over his. "You promised mom vengeance."

"And it almost got everyone killed," Harry said, his attention on their point of contact. "If it was me, only me, I'd take Zeus and all of the Six down in a heartbeat. I have nothing else to lose… But it's not just me. I must think about the men under me. They will need a home."

"If you kill Zeus, or let Styx do it," she said. "Zulu will be complete. Maybe the Six will let you rebuild."

"What happens after he's gone can't be anticipated. We also can't assume taking him down will be easy."

Because he'd be more entrenched than ever. In London, she'd persuaded Styx not to murder Zeus, believing it was the best thing for Daire. Believing her love wanted to put the Olympus pieces back together. Every time it came up, it became more difficult to accept how so many of their problems would be solved if she'd just let Styx follow through.

"So is that the plan? Taking Zeus down?"

"As I said, we'll regroup when Milo and Zip return with Lowe and Boze. If they bring Garrick, we'll have to listen to his perspective."

"Are you sure you can trust him?" she asked. "You don't know if he's had contact with Zeus."

"No, we don't," Harry said. "Which is why we won't stay in any obvious place while we're waiting for them to come back. Planning the op will be easier when we know how many men we have."

"Yes," she said. "Because you don't know who Garrick found."

"In this frustrating time, it might not matter. Lowe and Boze are there, which is a positive, but we don't know the mindset of whoever they're approaching."

Just like it was stated in the video call. Sneaking up on agents who had been on the run for more than a year was risky. They wouldn't know who to trust. Would they hurt men they'd once fought alongside? Even if they didn't cause any physical damage, they could choose not to return. Maybe they had new lives. Maybe they just wanted out. Or lack of trust could keep them away.

"Where do you think Zeus is?"

"Holed up," Harry said. "But in contact with One. Power and resource lies with him. Three would've wanted to know what happened to his house."

"They're together," she said. "The Six."

"All of them?"

She nodded. "I think so. I don't know exactly. One and Three were in London with me and Zeus until they left to recruit the new Two and Five. Six was there too. Styx says he knows where they are. No one mentioned Four."

That she could remember. Four had been enigmatic. Few people spoke of him; he didn't seem to be as much of a threat as the others. Though assuming that could be dangerous, so she'd ask Daire later.

Already she couldn't wait to be alone in the dark with him. Everything was so much simpler in his arms. And now that Harry knew about their romantic relationship, there was one less obstacle between them, one less thing to cause stress.

"I suppose Styx wants to confront them," Harry said. She just shrugged. "If the Six don't have the support of Garrick or Ulysses, storming the place would be easy. Their people will be easy to overcome. Dealing with the fall out will be more difficult. The death of an ex-president will garner attention. Federal agencies will investigate and without the Olympus resources at our disposal, it won't be easy to divert them from the truth."

"Your men know how not to leave evidence," she said, knowing that Daire could be particular. "If there's nothing linking them to the crime, no one can be prosecuted."

"Prosecuted is the least of our worries," Harry said. "Exposure is the biggest issue we have to be concerned about."

"But Olympus doesn't exist," she said, unsure why it would matter who knew about a defunct organization. "Isn't that what we've been saying?"

"Maybe, but its history isn't gone. The things we have done, been responsible for, if that were to come to the public's attention…"

Good point. That truth gave her a better understanding of why they'd made JARR so inaccessible.

A long period of reflection stretched between them.

She sighed and sank back, her hand drifting away from his. "It's such a mess."

"Life isn't simple, Light-Sprite." Especially not for those associated with a secret organization. "The key is to face what's in front of you."

"Yeah?" she asked, shifting her head on the backrest to look at him. "And what's in front of us?"

"The first thing we need is supplies. Ares and Styx have made a good dent in that. The next thing we need is leverage."

Her. Tess was leverage. But she recalled what he'd said about touring her mother's last few bases. "The keys," she said. As far as she knew, Harry had no idea where any of the keys were. "You want the keys."

"Whoever controls Minotaur and JARR has the

strongest position. We need them. We need all three."

All three keys. Tess knew that, she'd known that, just like Styx had in London. Her father would have some explaining to do and some questions to ask. Whatever came next was going to be interesting.

SIXTEEN

"WHOEVER HAS THE KEYS HAS THE POWER," Tess murmured. "Zeus must have thought the same thing. That would be why he took Garrick's key."

Harry nodded. "What I'll need you to do…" He got off the couch and went to a backpack in the corner that hadn't been there that morning. Picking it up, he dumped it on the table and opened an inner pocket. "Come over here."

Curious, she left the couch to go to the table.

Her father put a notepad and pencil down in front of one of the seats.

"What?" she asked, glancing from it to him. "What do you need me to do?"

"Sit down and write as much as you can remember about wherever you and your mom stayed in the last year and a half."

"Year and a half?"

He nodded. "Since January of last year."

For a few seconds, she thought about it. "That's when you stashed the key."

He frowned. "How do you know I stashed it?"

She breathed out a laugh. "You said you did. I was right there in the Beast when you told Daire you stashed it…

January last year was before the Exodus, months before, why would you stash it then?"

Although he didn't look like he wanted to answer, he relented. "Because I anticipated there could be an issue. The more men who knew, the more likely the secret would get out or Zeus would become suspicious. So I did what I thought was best and gave the Scepter to the one person I trusted. The only person I could trust."

At that point, Daire would've been ignorant of Zulu. Harry handing him the Scepter would've led to questions, maybe in front of Zeus, so Harry, it turned out, opted to give the crucial piece of Olympus to her mom. A woman already on the company's naughty list.

"You gave it to mom," Tess said, trying to think of a time when she and her mother had been separated for long enough that they might have met up for that to happen.

If Harry hand-delivered letters and knew where they were, he could've given the key to her mom any time without her knowing. It wouldn't have taken long to hand one thing over. Though after learning about her mom and Harry's rendezvous when she was a teen, maybe they did more than just a simple handover.

"I left it for your mother," he said. "In a place we both knew… Somewhere I understand you were aware of."

"Not until after the fact," she said. "I figured it out when I was trying to follow what I thought were mom's clues."

"I went there," Harry said. "There's nothing there. She must have picked it up." Yeah, probably when she was leaving the letter that Harry didn't know about. "That's why I need you to write down where you stayed. I assume she must have hidden it somewhere herself." His brow moved in a show of confused concern. "Though I never knew her to go there and not leave anything… which is strange." He shrugged off the thought. "Will you please sit?"

"You'd rather me write down a bunch of locations and traipse around the country searching everywhere mom went than ask me."

Startled, another frown creased his expression. "Ask

you?"

"Yeah," she said, folding her arms. "Do you really believe I'm still two years old or do you do that to put distance between us? Maybe you just think I am a complete idiot."

"Tess, I don't know what you—"

"Ask me if I know," she said. "Ask me if maybe I might know something that you don't." He still didn't seem to follow. "You're close to Daire because you've been at his side all his life. Though you did have missions apart sometimes. Mom and me didn't have missions apart. It was her and me. Always. So if she had something that was important to her, something that was special, and I was the one who dealt with her things after she died, did it even occur to you that I might know where it is?"

"How could you…" he trailed off. "Even if you found it, you wouldn't have known what it was."

"I knew it was in her room," she said and his eyes widened. "Yeah, I knew it was significant. I had no idea what it was and no idea where she got it, but she wouldn't have kept such a weird thing unless it was important. We traveled light. Mom didn't carry around anything unnecessary."

"Oh my God," he murmured. "Why didn't you say anything? What on earth—all this time you've known where it was and you didn't say anything?"

"Why would I say anything to you?" she asked. "The only time we talk, we fight or you dismiss me. Besides, like I said, I didn't know exactly what it was at first. It was just a thing. It didn't mean anything to me."

Harry's chin drifted for a second before his attention snapped back to her. "Daire…"

"Yes," she said, nodding. "I told him."

Even more incredulous, anger tinged his confusion. "He knows you have the Scepter? If he has it, he would've told me—"

"I only told him after we left Vegas," she said. "And he doesn't have it. I do."

"Where is it?" he demanded.

"I'll tell Daire," she said, hitching her chin.

His attention narrowed. "You're using it against

me… You're using him against me."

"No," she said, shaking her head. "I'm showing respect to a person who respects me. Daire trusts me. Why do you think he hasn't harassed me about handing it over? He knows I have it and he knows if it becomes relevant, I'll give it to him. Until it does, it's best not too many people know."

"You don't trust me."

"Why should I?" she asked. "You knew about the blood, my blood, that they'd need for JARR and you didn't tell me. If you didn't trust me to know that, why should I trust you with all our power? You, me, Daire, and Styx, right now it's just the four of us. We have to find a way to trust each other."

"You trusted Styx. You trusted him because the way Daire spoke of him led you to believe he'd look out for your best interests."

"Options in London were limited, but yeah."

"He spoke about his brother," Harry said, intrigued. "What did he say?"

"I'm not going to stand here and recount every conversation me and Daire ever had. It doesn't matter what he told me about Styx. It's worked out so far."

"Except whatever he said about me has led you to the opposite conclusion."

Unable to believe his deduction put the blame on Daire, she shook her head. "You started from a negative position," she said. "Styx had a clean slate."

His head tilted. "Why did I start from a negative position? It was my understanding you knew nothing about Olympus or your father."

"And that," she said, bouncing a pointed finger his way, "is why you started from a negative position. When Daire and me walked into that control room, I had no idea who you were. He knew everything there was to know about you and I knew nothing."

Irony existed in the fact that after discussions with Zeus and Harry, Tess now knew more about Daire's biological father than he did. Telling him the truth would be difficult. They'd never talked much about his mom or his views on how she'd died.

"It was for the best. You were troubled enough as a teenager, we didn't want to—"

"Oh, so it was my fault?" she asked. "You're unbelievable. You didn't want me to know the truth, fine, I didn't know it. But you can't stand here now and ask me to trust you when you've never shown me an ounce of it in return."

"You're cavorting with the man I trained, the boy I raised."

So he wasn't as ready to accept that as he'd tried to make out. "You didn't know that until today," she said. "You can't claim to have trusted me right up until the moment you learned that because you never have. I'm your daughter, biologically. You didn't raise me. You weren't there in my life when I was a kid. We have no loyalty to each other. We're nothing to each other."

"And you like to keep punishing me for that, throwing it in my face. I did what I thought was best for your safety. I won't apologize for that."

"And I won't grant you automatic loyalty and respect because you had sex with my mom twenty-eight years ago."

On a frustrated sort of a groan, he spun around, rubbing his forehead. His hand stayed there even in the silence that followed.

What did he want? For her to act as one of his men would? To defer to him with the same reverence? To follow orders and never ask questions? Why didn't he see it could never be that way? He didn't even treat her as he would one of his men. From what she'd seen of him with Daire, the two men did have respect. But Harry included Daire in his thinking, gave him the right to speak up and ask questions.

Sure, Harry didn't give Daire much of a chance to argue his case when their viewpoints differed, but at least there was an opening. She got nothing. Her father expected her to sit in another room, let the plans be made, and just fit in as told.

She'd grown up being directed and having information withheld. Her mother wouldn't tell her why they were moving, why there was urgency. It didn't matter if she accepted it or argued, her mother got her way. She couldn't let her life be dictated anymore. If her mother had been more honest, more forthcoming, maybe she wouldn't have walked into the Olympus mess blind.

"We can't keep going on like this," Harry murmured, his hand falling from his forehead. "We have to find a middle ground."

"Okay," she said. "What do you suggest?"

Turning around to look at her, his demeanor didn't inspire confidence. "I don't know, Tess… I have no idea how to work with you."

And she didn't know how to work with him. Avoiding each other had been her suggestion in the past. With them in such proximity and her importance to his purpose, she guessed that wasn't much of a long-term solution.

"I know I'm not easy to live with," she said. "Mom and I loved each other, we were the best of friends… some of the time. But it wasn't easy. Both of us infuriated each other at times."

"But you trusted her," Harry said. "You must have. If you didn't, why didn't you leave her as soon as you were old enough? The running away stopped eventually and you chose to stick with her."

"We were all each other had," Tess said. "When I was about nineteen, she went through a bad patch, got really depressed, it was so difficult to reach her. She wouldn't go to work, I had to support both of us. It wasn't easy, but it showed me how much she needed me… I'd never been needed before. I guess it showed me that I had a responsibility to her too. I didn't know what it was, but I knew she'd been carrying some kind of burden all my life. At that point I realized, even not knowing what it was, it was my job to help shoulder some of it."

"And you don't see that I need your help now? That the responsibility all of us have—"

"Our responsibility is murky," she said. "I know what kind of man Daire is. I know his heart. I can trust him to do the right thing, to be a good man no matter what."

"I raised him."

"I know," she said, acknowledging that with a nod. "I'm not saying you're not a good man. I'm saying I don't know. Think about what you're asking, about what you want from me. You want me to hand over the key, which you've just admitted is power, and then what? I say nothing until you make another demand? That's not who I am."

"You don't understand what you're dealing with. As long as you have that key, the danger you face increases."

She shrugged. "Let's not pretend it matters who has the key. I don't know the details, but I know my blood is needed at the beta site. So whatever happens, I'm in danger. And you're just through telling Daire that I'm in danger because people will use me to manipulate him. You want the key because you want the power not because it's best for my safety."

"I want the key because I—"

He was quick to seal his lips. Again, he turned away.

What he'd almost said intrigued her. "What? Why do you want it?"

If she was just right, he wouldn't have said anything. He certainly wouldn't have corrected her in such an abrupt way or cut himself off. Whatever had almost spilled from his mouth was a truth he didn't want to admit.

She heard him draw in a nasal breath. As he turned back to face her, he expelled it. "I don't trust you not to hand it over."

The words filtered in and her opinion shifted, not in any dramatic way, her perspective just realigned. "Why would I do that? If I was going to use it to save myself, I could've offered it to Zeus in London."

She couldn't figure it out. Tess was no super-agent, she'd admitted that. Having never been subjected to torture, she didn't know how she would hold up if someone turned the screws on her. The key would have to be used eventually. By someone. No one was advocating throwing the three of them in the ocean and forgetting about Minotaur and JARR.

"You have a weakness," he said, his words calm, straightforward.

Her father was the expert. He'd reached the same conclusion that she had that morning. It had taken her a long time to get there, he'd taken less than an hour.

"Daire," she whispered.

He nodded once. "Once Zeus finds out how you feel about him, he'll use it against you. He'll use it against both of you."

"So if neither of us have control of it, we can't be exploited against each other."

That worked on the condition Zeus believed them when they said they didn't have access to it.

"Exactly," Harry said.

"Except you have a checkered history on that front," she said. "How many times did Zeus bring up mom to force you into doing something? I know at least once that you agreed and let yourself be manipulated. You made that deal to save her, promising never to have contact with her. What happened in the year we were there? How many dirty jobs did you do for him? Handing the key over to you doesn't ensure it won't be passed onto him. What will you do if he threatens Daire?"

"Daire can look after himself."

"Yeah," she said. "But Zeus isn't beyond killing to achieve what he wants."

"He wouldn't kill Daire," Harry said. "He's too valuable to the future of the organization. Daire wouldn't let him close enough."

Unless Zeus took control of her and forced Daire to surrender. The more she thought about the possibilities, the more she understood Harry's aversion to her and Daire's relationship. But they weren't ignorant of its inconvenience. Falling for a man in such a fraught circumstance was idiotic when looked at from an outsider's perspective. Unfortunately, love didn't care about good sense, and it definitely didn't care about convenience.

Her having the key did make Daire vulnerable. Handing it over to her love would put that vulnerability onto her. She wouldn't trust Harry with it and didn't want to be used against Daire. The smart choice might be to give Styx control of it, except he was the only one who knew for sure where the other two keys were. One person being responsible for all three would be the stupidest course.

"We can't trust each other," she said. "We can't work together."

"We can't go our separate ways either," Harry said. "Whatever you think of me, you have to believe I don't want you hurt."

"If I left, Daire would be put in an impossible situation," she said, her chin descending.

Like Harry said, Daire couldn't fight Zeus and protect her at the same time. It wouldn't be fair to ask him to try when there was a unit available to support him.

"Yes," Harry said. "We are stronger when we're cohesive."

"So I suppose that leaves us avoiding each other," she said on an inhale.

They weren't going to solve their issues in one day and certainly not while they were both so entrenched in their positions.

"It won't be easy."

Accepting the situation, she strolled toward the bedroom. "Nothing about this is easy. Daire is our bond. As long as we both do what's best for him, that's the most important thing to me."

She went into the bedroom and closed the door. The trio of Harry, Daire, and Styx were used to working together no matter the circumstances. They understood how each other worked. She wasn't a part of their band, didn't understand their rhythm. Maybe she was their hindrance, the one who'd ruin everything. Even if she believed that, there was nothing she could do.

Running away, freeing them from the burden of protecting her, was an option. They could forget about her, pretend she didn't exist, that their paths would never cross. Except there was her blood. They needed her blood. No matter what, she'd be pursued.

Tess was trapped. A victim of circumstance. A tiny cog in a machine that started running long before she was even born. Maybe it was inevitable. Whatever *it* was. Someone would win and someone would lose and there was no way to predict who would be the victor.

SEVENTEEN

TESS HAD JUST FINISHED her book when sound carried from beyond the bedroom. Voices, movement… Daire and Styx left hours ago and since coming into the bedroom to give her father space, she'd stayed there.

Someone went into the room opposite, the master, where all the supplies had been stored as far as she knew. Setting her book on the nightstand, she slipped off the bed and went to open the door. She didn't go out, just peeked to see who was there. The master bedroom door was open and she didn't see anyone else.

If they'd gone out and left her, she'd have the place to herself. Though it wasn't exactly like she had big plans to party or go wild.

Another noise came from the master and then Daire appeared with Styx and Harry just behind him.

He paused to look at her. It only took a second for his eyes to narrow like he saw something. "What's wrong?" he asked, moving out of the way of Harry and Styx.

"Nothing," she said, raising her hands to reach for his shoulders as she crossed to meet him. "I'm hungry."

"We're going out for something," he said, bending his knees to wrap both arms around her waist.

As he straightened up, taking her feet from the floor, she traced her lips on his. It was amazing how he could make her feel better, even when their relationship was the cause of so much aggravation in their den.

"That all I'm getting?" he asked of the chaste kiss.

"Did you get the supplies you need?" she asked, ignoring his question.

The square space that served as a hallway to two of the bedrooms and the bathroom was open to the rest of the main room. Although not looking at them, she was aware of Harry and Styx in the living room.

"Everything *we* need. Yes," he said, his brow descending even further as his probing stare intensified. "Talk to me."

"Where are we going to eat? Do I need to dress up?"

"What you see is what you get with us," Styx answered from the living room. Daire was too busy trying to burrow into her mind. "But if you want to put on something short and tight…"

"She should be able to move," Harry said, unimpressed by Styx's suggestion. "Nothing restrictive. Something modest."

"Exactly the opposite of what her boyfriend would want," Styx said.

At least someone was in good spirits.

She pushed on Daire's shoulders. "Put me down, I'll find something."

He did put her on her feet. Despite avoiding his gaze, she could still feel it all over her. Going back into the bedroom, she closed the door, sort of wishing that she hadn't bothered going out.

Closing her eyes, Tess slid her hand onto her forehead. Everything was a mess. She just couldn't shake it. Being so out of control, so at the mercy of others, was an unsettling sensation that was gaining mass.

The door opened, startling her into turning around. She was even more surprised to see Daire closing the door behind him. Not because she wouldn't expect him to come into her room, but because she usually didn't hear him before she felt him.

"What's going on?" he asked. "What happened?"

"Nothing," she said, grabbing her bag from the floor to dump it on the bed.

Daire came over to her side. "Something happened between you and Harry while we were out."

"Nothing important," she said, searching in the bag. "I wouldn't mind a stop at the Beast sometime… I have more clothes there. Should I shower?"

"Don't shut me out, Little Red," he said, a serious warning weighing his words. "No matter what, we have to be honest."

"I'm being honest," she said, yanking out a dress from the mass of clothes, thankful it wasn't made of a material that creased. "Should I shower?"

Wriggling out of her clothes, she ran her fingers into her hair, deciding that she couldn't be bothered with makeup and styling.

The bedroom door opened again. Daire was standing perpendicular to her, blocking her view of the door, so she leaned back to see her father there in the doorway.

"This stays open," he said and then disappeared back into the living room.

It didn't really matter either way, seduction wasn't in the cards. She stepped into her dress, put her arms into the straps, and was zipping it, thinking about her heels, when Daire swept her hair back from her shoulder.

"You wanna get out of here, you say the word," he said, the back of his fingers floating up the side of her neck to her jaw. "You don't want to be alone with him again, just tell me."

"I'm not your master," she said, fixating on the open bag. "You do what's best for you. What you need to do."

Pushing the clothes aside, she found the shoes and took them out, one in each hand.

"You are me, Temptress," he said, edging closer. "I won't let you be unhappy."

As well intentioned as his words were, they didn't help. She tipped her focus up to his. "Too late, Heart."

Leaving him in the bedroom, she went to the living room and tossed her shoes to the floor to step into them.

"Wow, that was the quickest turnaround ever," Styx said. "Guess leaving the door open was a good idea."

Tess crossed to open the front door. "Are we going out or not?"

She went into the hallway, striding away from them all. There wasn't space, wouldn't be space. All she kept thinking about was how she weighed their efficient team down. Without her holding them back, they'd probably have taken Olympus back and rebuilt it on their own already.

She needed to think of something, to be useful, she just didn't have a clue where to start.

****

THEY ENDED UP in a steak and beer type place. A big wooden building with cluttered décor. There was a stage and a large dancefloor at the back of the open-plan space. The four of them were seated in a booth on an upper level, waiting for the food they'd ordered not that long ago.

The music was happy, upbeat, just like the atmosphere of the place. Everywhere but at their table anyway.

"This is fun," Styx said into the awkward nothingness.

He was propped in the corner opposite her. One arm on the table, the other against the fixed padded section stuck to the towering wooden back that separated their booth from the next one.

"We're here for food, not for fun," Harry said. It was some consolation that she wasn't the only one not in the mood for pleasantries. "Ares, go, follow up."

Daire didn't respond, he just got up and left the table, following orders. They hadn't even been waiting that long. Harry was probably thinking that takeout in the apartment would've been a better option. At least then they could've sat in different rooms.

Eating at the same table, even in a restaurant, didn't

align with their avoiding each other plan. It was possible Harry didn't want the brothers to know about that plan. Either that or coming out hadn't been his suggestion.

A few seconds went by, though they felt like days.

She sat up to down the rest of her drink, then shoved to the end of the booth. "I'm going to get more booze."

She didn't wait for permission. If she expected her father to grant it, she'd be waiting a long time. With her glass in hand, Tess wound through tables, went down a half dozen stairs and through a bunch more diners before reaching the bar. She ordered another drink and a couple of tequila shooters just for good measure.

The second was still heating the back of her throat when someone took hold of her waist. Daire. He dropped onto a stool, facing her, and pulled her into the wide vee of his thighs.

"Let's leave," he said, to which she frowned. "Right now, let's just go."

"Go where?"

It wasn't like they had a bunch of options lined up.

"Anywhere you want," he said. "Anywhere in the world. Let's do South America."

Believing he was kidding, she breathed out a laugh. "Sure, let's just sprout wings and fly."

"We have the Beast. We don't need anything else."

She laid a hand on his cheek. "You're sweet."

The bartender came over with her drink and she sipped the sweet liquor.

"You can't tell me you're unhappy and then refuse to let me do something about it," he said, running his palms up and down her sides from her hips to the outer curves of her breasts. "We'll just walk out the door, you and me, right now."

"And you think that would make me happy?" she asked, sliding her drink further along the bar as she turned to face him.

"I think something happened with Harry today that neither of you are talking about. Is it us? He gave you shit about us being together?"

She shook her head and picked up her glass. "It's no

big deal."

"It's a big deal if he hurt you," he said, squeezing her waist. "You need to tell me if he hurt you."

"He didn't… It's really not a big deal. We just both had to face some hard truths is all."

"Hard truths about what? Z?"

"Our relationship, our history, this mission, the future." She exhaled. "There's nothing you can do to fix reality… There's nothing I can do to fix it, so you can't expect to do a better job."

"I don't like seeing you like this," he said, his hand drifting up the front of her body to linger at her cleavage before continuing to her neck. "You are the most beautiful woman I have ever seen."

She just crooked a brow at him. "That's a lie."

"You telling me you've met a guy hotter than me?"

Playing with her was his way of trying to brighten her mood. She wasn't sure how deep it went, but at least he made her smile. "Never anywhere in the world."

"Exactly. Good… Now put a boundary on it for me. What wouldn't you do to make me happy?"

That curled her lips even higher. "If you want me to drop to my knees right here, you better be willing to feed me some other way after we get kicked out."

"You'd blow me at a bar?"

"Course I would," she said, tipping more of her drink onto her tongue then putting the glass down and looping her arms around his neck. "I'd blow you anywhere."

"What about that body?" he asked, his gaze traveling down to her breasts, she pushed them deeper against him. "Would you show me that?"

"Anywhere," she said, decreasing the size of her circled arms to get her mouth nearer his. "But there are a lot of guys in here. I don't think you'd spend much time looking at me if you were busy gouging out their eyes."

Something he'd said he'd do in the past. He hadn't forgotten that conversation either. "And their tongues," he said, brushing his nose across hers. "So you'd get naked and pleasure me, but you won't tell me the truth about your afternoon?"

So much for the anticipated kiss. Relaxing so much that her arms fell away, she turned to the bar and grabbed up her drink.

"We had a conversation," she said, the intimacy of the moment gone. "It ended just like always. We can't work together. We don't trust each other. That's it. That's all it was."

"Then why are you so withdrawn and quiet?"

"Because what the hell am I doing here?" she asked, slamming the drink to the bar, turning toward him again. "I'm useless. Completely useless. All I can do is bleed, that's all I'm good for. That's all Olympus wants from me."

"You're here because I need you to be here," he said, coiling his arms around her again. "Zeus is a threat and you're going to help us take him down."

"I can't do that," she said on a clumsy shrug. "I can't take anyone down…" She scoffed. "No one except the man I love."

When she tried to return to her drink, he tightened his hold to keep her in place. "Is that what it was about? He said you'd take me down?"

"He didn't say anything that we don't already know. He wanted to go on the hunt for the Scepter. He didn't even ask me about it, just assumed I'd be useless." Which wasn't completely out of line given she was facing the truth. "I called him on it, asked if he'd rather traipse around the country than ask me."

"You told him you had it," Daire said and she nodded. "And he wants it." She nodded again. "What did you say?"

"Some version of go to hell," she said and sighed. "Maybe it wasn't fair, I don't know, but I told him I wouldn't hand it over."

"Bet he loved that."

"I assumed he wanted it because he wanted the power."

"Makes sense."

"But that's not why," she said, her arms drifting around his neck again. "He doesn't want me to have it because he thinks I'll fold as soon as Z glares at me." Daire frowned. "It's not like he's wrong. I have no idea what I'll do. I've never been tortured or interrogated."

A steely determination flattened his affect. "And you never will be."

"It doesn't matter," she said, taking one arm from around him to stroke his face. "As Harry pointed out, all Z will have to do is threaten you and I'll give in. We always acknowledged that I was your weakness, we forgot that you are mine."

"Don't worry about me," he said, his hands sliding up and down her spine, from her ass to the back of her neck. "Let him threaten me, I can take care of myself."

"It shouldn't be like that. Everyone keeps saying you can take care of yourself. I want to take care of you, I want to be able to..."

Frustration stole her words as emotion closed her throat.

He took the back of her neck and head in both hands, holding her tight. "I love you, Little Red," he whispered the words. "As long as I have that, I'm invincible."

"But you're not invincible," she said, caressing him. "I want you to be. I want you to be safe and happy... but I can't give you that."

"Do you love me less because I can't give you the same? I told you what I'd do for you, I told you. There's nothing I wouldn't do for you, but it's not enough. I can't make you happy... Goddamnit, baby, I want to make you happy."

"Being with you makes me happy," she said. "Knowing you're mine, that makes me happy... It doesn't do anything for my relationship with Harry."

"You want to fix it?"

"I don't know what I want," she said. "Every time we talk, it ends the same. We're too different. There's too much water under the bridge."

"Nothing is too broken to fix."

"Says you," she said. With him still holding her head, she couldn't move it, but her eyes did descend. "I don't trust him and he doesn't trust me… I can't see any way that will change. As long as that's the case, your unit will be unstable. I'm the unstable element. The three of you work together, you trust each other. I'm just this… variable. A useless variable. And I can't even promise you what I will or won't do because I don't even know. I don't have your experience either, so I could do something and not even know whether it's good or bad. I'll screw up everything. Somehow I will, I just know it."

"Which is why you have me to talk to," he said. "You run everything by me and you can't screw anything up."

She met his eye. "I love you, Daire, but you suck at saying no to me."

He laughed and pulled her closer. "Okay, so you run everything by me and I'll do whatever it takes to keep the train on the tracks… and to keep you safe. That's still my primary mission."

"We're safe," she said and sighed. "I guess that's all we can ask for right now."

Happy wasn't exactly a long way off. It would be further away if she didn't have Daire around to keep her sane. She didn't want to distract him. The implication that sex might distract him was one thing, the last thing he needed was to die because her crappy mood was on his mind.

"You just have to say the word," he said, using his chin to tip hers up. "I'll do whatever you need me to do."

"So much is resting on you, it's not fair."

Everyone was so sure that Daire was safe from Zeus. His physical self might be safe from death, that didn't mean he wouldn't have to endure other forms of torture.

"The universe balances itself out," he said, his mouth just an inch from hers.

The hippie response was unexpected. Her arms stayed tight around him though her head dipped back. "What does that mean?"

"It means…" he said, skimming his hands down to her ass. "I have to earn you. The universe put us together and I never considered that I'd ever find this. That love was an option for me."

"That you'd break ranks and rules for a piece of ass?"

His lips curled and he gave her a squeeze. "An amazing piece of ass."

"I ruined your whole life," she said, pained by the truth of what their relationship had done to him. "Didn't I?"

"You gave me life, baby. Harry was right in his letters. I was manufactured. Owned like a piece of kit. Nothing more than the robot they trained me to be. With you it's okay to be more. It's okay to be me."

"I always want the honest Daire," she said, recalling their conversation in the Beast a zillion years ago. "I know you love me now, that you want to be with me." His eyes closed in a slow blink as he nodded once. "But are you sorry I kissed you in the Beast?"

"I'm never sorry when it comes to us together," he said, squeezing her again. "I mean it, LR. Even in the craziest moments, even when we talk about everything that could go wrong, I never regret being with you. I'm only happy when we're alone. That's when I'm free."

"You gave me a gift and I took advantage of you. I know that you didn't mean—"

"Took advantage of me? Are you nuts?" he said, his smirk approached her lips. "Baby, I want you every second. Sometimes I amaze myself with my restraint. You think I didn't want to kiss you back there? I always want to kiss you. Just takes the nod from you and I'm there."

And if she wasn't aware of the men in the room related to them, she might be dragging him to some back corner or even to the Beast to give him the nod right then.

"It'll be weird."

"What?" he asked.

"Sharing a bed with you while there are others around. The Beast is usually ours… just ours."

"If you don't want them in there, we'll come up with some other plan. Stash the Beast somewhere long-term and come back for it when this is all over… or we can sell it and—"

"No," she said, offended by the suggestion. "The Beast is our home. I don't want to sell it or stash it…" Watching his lips, she licked hers. "I'll just have to learn how to be silent."

His brows wiggled. "Or we get creative."

She laughed. "I have no idea what you're thinking, but I'm game."

"Yeah?"

"With you," she said, brushing her lips across his. "I'm always game."

Without saying another word, he joined their mouths, taking his time about slipping his tongue between her lips.

There was no time to waste feeling sorry for herself. To be useful, she had to take responsibility for what she could do. That included looking after her man. Daire was their ace card. Zeus would kill to have his loyalty and Garrick knew his value.

She didn't care about any of that. Other than being grateful he was capable of fighting for himself, she didn't care about what he could do for Olympus, his training, or his value to the future of something that no longer existed.

She cared about him. About what was inside. His wellbeing and his love. They'd need to be strong for each other and she was ready to stand up for him. Ready to do whatever was required of her.

EIGHTEEN

THE FOOD WAS ON THE TABLE when she and Daire got back there. Everyone ate, Tess had a couple more drinks, and then they were heading home.

She couldn't remember ever looking forward to bed so much in her life. Not just because the day had been tiring, but because lying with Daire would make everything right again, even if it was just for the duration of the night.

Flopping against the wall by the door, she closed her eyes and waited for Daire to finish his check of the apartment. Harry and Styx stayed outside with her too. She'd always assumed Styx stayed outside with her to keep an eye on her in case anyone tried to sneak up on them in the hallway. With Harry a part of their ranks, two people doing the sweep would get it done in half the time. Not that she said anything, she was too tired to face another debate.

Daire came back and opened the door, a sign they were safe to go in.

Groaning, Tess traipsed inside, picking up her feet one at a time to yank off her heels and drop them to the floor. "I'm beat," she said, glancing back to see Daire picking up her shoes.

Styx was locking up. Once he was finished with the front door, he went over to check the balcony. It was likely

Daire had just done that, but ensuring their safety wasn't something she minded being checked and double-checked.

"I'll be through in a minute," Daire said.

Returning to him, she took her shoes, figuring it would be better to put them away than leave a mess for him to clear up. "Don't be long."

Pouting up at him, she didn't have to say anything for him to know she wanted a kiss. As he descended to indulge her, Harry interrupted.

"You won't be sharing a room," her father said.

Daire stopped without giving her a kiss. His scowl mirrored her internal reaction. "We won't?"

Harry shook his head, moving deeper into the room. "Your brother and I were talking about D.C."

"We got the resources for that?" Daire asked.

"That's what we have to talk about."

"Okay," Daire said, sweeping her hair from her face. "Do you want to sleep or stay up with us?"

It didn't really matter when she slept. Tess wouldn't be required to get up and train or source supplies the next day, so she could sleep in. Still, her bones ached and she'd been looking forward to lying down… with her man.

"Tess doesn't need to hear this," Harry said.

Frustration set Daire's expression and he huffed out an exhale. "When are you gonna learn that she's with us not against us?"

"It's not about that."

"No?" Daire asked, turning away from her to face Harry. "Then why don't you trust her?"

"Daire…" she murmured, slipping a hand onto his back.

"No," Daire said, still fixated on his father. "What does she have to do to prove her loyalty to you?"

"You told him about our conversation."

Tess wasn't looking at Harry but didn't need to. The disappointment in his tone could only be meant for one person.

"It wasn't exactly breaking news," she said.

"I told Tess that it's not about trust," Harry said.

"There are things she doesn't need to hear for her own protection. You should want to protect her, not scare her with talk of strategies and missions."

"It scares her more to be in the dark," Daire said. "We tell her the truth or risk all of us losing her trust. We do that and she walks. The only thing keeping her here is her belief that we're doing the right thing, that we don't want her to come to harm."

That and the man she loved was there, but, yeah, she wouldn't argue against his point.

"There are different forms of harm," Harry said, becoming sterner. "She doesn't need to hear the details of what we do."

"Because you're worried she'll think less of you for sending us into dangerous situations? She already knows what we do, what I do. She knows what we're capable of."

"Knowing it and facing it are two different things," Harry said. "She'll look at you differently. After living it, she'll look at you differently."

"Please don't speak for me," Tess said.

Harry didn't respond to her. "And protecting her from the details also protects us. We don't know what Z is planning, what he might do. If he leaks mission details or puts us in the crosshairs of someone who can do us harm, Tess will be first in the interrogation chair. She can't reveal what she doesn't know."

"If there was the possibility of her being hurt in exchange for information," Daire said. "I'd want her to reveal everything she knows to save her life."

"But you're smarter than that," Harry said. "If it's someone official and she tells them everything, she's still looking at life in prison. If it's someone unofficial, they kill her as soon as they're sure she's given up everything."

"Lose, lose," she muttered, breathing out and wandering toward the couch. "Daire will tell me anyway. Whether I'm in the room for the conversation or not."

As if proving her point, Daire turned to her. "There's a facility in D.C. that houses particular kinds of tech. Beyond cutting edge, it's the futuristic type stuff you see in movies.

The things that someone's deemed too dangerous for the public or that the population just isn't ready for yet."

"That's why you need to go to D.C."

"Yes."

"They'll just hand you this thing? Whatever it is you need."

Daire shook his head. "No, we'd have to retrieve it." Which she translated to mean steal it. "It's a specific kind of processor, something that will help Minotaur and JARR run faster and smarter."

Thinking back to when she'd first heard about the mission to D.C. Tess tried to remember details. "You said you'd need two agents."

"Ideally," Daire said. "I'm less concerned about manpower than I am with ordnance."

"We're not gonna blast our way in," Styx said.

"You want subtle, we need tech," Daire said. "I'm guessing you don't want to wait until we hear from Garrick."

Dropping onto the couch, Tess let her hands flop onto the seats at either side of her, letting go of her shoes. Harry's expression was severe, pinned on Daire, and definitely not pleased.

"We can't take the risk of waiting," Harry said. "Your brother has some gear—"

"And there's more in Vegas," Styx said, pointing at Harry.

"So you go by Vegas, get what you need," Harry said. "I'll make sure there's ID waiting for you."

"Florida to Nevada to Virginia," Daire said. "Too much time."

"You need support," Harry said. "If I can't give you the men, I can give you the tools."

Or Styx could, if they were talking about whatever he had left in his Nevada SP.

"You set up Gamma," Styx said, sauntering a few steps closer to his brother. "Think you can get in."

"I know I can," Daire said. "But if you want me to do this job by myself, I need what's in Beta."

Harry shook his head. "We can't get in there without

the three keys."

"We have two of them," Styx said.

"We have three," Daire said.

Harry's chin rose in surprise. He wasn't the only one to be taken aback by the news. Styx was startled too.

With an awkward exhale, Tess opened her hands on the couch. "Uh… My Heart."

"What are we waiting for?" he asked, whipping around to pin her under a frown. "We have the keys. Let's get there and take what we need."

"What do we need from there?" she asked. "You want to get Minotaur and JARR?"

"It's too risky to let Zeus get close," he said, approaching her and hunkering down in front of her. "We go and get them while it's just us."

"And do what with them?" she asked. "Install them at Gamma? Because I don't think you're going to be interested in destroying them."

"Once they're out, they're less secure," Harry said. "Why am I only now learning that all three keys are in our possession?"

"Maybe I'm not the only one with trust issues," she muttered before inhaling. "They're not in our possession. All three are hidden, but safe."

"We can't install anything at Gamma without Titan," Styx said. "We take them out before we have that and it's in the wind. Zeus can take it from us. It's too risky."

Harry's attention narrowed on Daire. "You know that. You know it's too dangerous to release either before we have the means to secure them. You know it's likely Zeus is waiting for us to do just that. We do his work for him and all he has to do is take us down to get what he wants."

"I want to know more about the blood," Tess said.

If Daire wanted to retrieve JARR, he'd need her blood. Some part of her was all for getting it out of the way, as it seemed inevitable that one day she'd be expected to do her duty anyway. It would be good to know what that duty involved before showing up and being forced into doing it.

"The blood?" Styx asked.

Boosting back to his feet, Daire was determined. "It's JARR, isn't it?" he asked. "Z said they needed Tess's blood and that's all I could think. Garrick and Asclepius were screwing around with biological safeguards, they did something when they had her, didn't they?"

"I was on a mission when it happened. I don't know what they did exactly," Harry said. Tess wasn't sure whether to believe him. "But yes, I gather it's something to do with releasing JARR."

"They need my blood," she said. "Which means you need my blood."

If Harry was the decent man he claimed to be, the one who'd raised the man she loved to be a good person, then he should be in charge of JARR. If the whole thing was a ruse, and he was just as power hungry as Zeus, then she and the brothers were making Harry's life easy for him.

Just like with Styx, all Tess could do was trust Daire. Sure, she didn't trust her father on any personal level, but when it came to Olympus, Daire was the man she followed. In that moment, that meant following her father, allying herself with him, so that's what she would do.

"How do we find out?" Daire asked. "I'm not taking the risk of letting Tess walk in there before I'm sure no harm will come to her."

The only thing they knew was that her blood was required. In whatever way that went down, it meant getting hurt. Still, she understood his meaning. A pinprick on her fingertip wasn't the same as opening an artery and emptying herself.

"Garrick will know the details," Harry said. "Your brother is right; Gamma has to be setup before we retrieve Minotaur."

Omitting JARR, though that was obviously on the agenda. It spoke volumes that her father had never bothered to find out how she had been linked to JARR against her will. Either truth wasn't encouraging. Either he knew and wouldn't tell her, or he didn't and hadn't cared.

"No," Daire said, shaking his head. "You install them at Gamma and that's doing Z's work for him. That place won't be secure so long as he's walking around… We need to take him down."

"The longer you let him roam, the more chance he has to make his own progress," Harry said. "We retrieve Titan so he cannot. If Byron is on his side, he has the connections—"

"Then we take them all down."

Harry exhaled. "We are not going through this again."

"Why?" Daire demanded. "I've made my position on this clear. Six has to be eliminated."

For a moment, there was silence. It confused her. The men were on pause, looking at each other, like something was going on between them that she couldn't hear… or they were waiting… for something.

"Retrieve Titan and I'll let you have Lowell."

Lowell was Six. The man who'd betrayed Zulu to Zeus and put all of them in their current positions. Straightening her spine, she waited to see what would happen next. Her Heart had wanted to take Six down since she'd first heard talk of him. Until that moment, Harry always dismissed him.

"You don't let Tess out of your sight," Daire said to her father. "And I won't waste time traveling. We need a chopper."

Styx scoffed. "We don't have the money—"

"We'll find the money," Harry said, marching up to Daire to offer a hand. "I'll protect her life with mine."

"If I didn't believe that, I wouldn't be going anywhere," Daire said. "If she has so much as a scratch on her when I get back, you won't see Titan or the Scepter again, and Six won't be the only one in my crosshairs."

Rather than be angry or upset by the threat, Harry smiled. Daire slapped his hand into his father's and the two men shook hands.

A breath passed and then Harry backed away.

"We'll take the car," Styx said. "Get rid of it on the way out."

Harry nodded. Daire headed straight into the master.

"Comms will be difficult without Minotaur," Harry

said to Styx. "Takes too much time to patch in and secure."

"Which means we're going in alone," Styx said, heading for the master bedroom. "We'll be in the dark."

"If we can't monitor you, they can't either."

Tess sat up, thought for a second, then bounced to the front edge of the couch. They were preparing. A mission. Talking about choppers and cars. They'd gone into the room where all the supplies were kept.

She didn't have time to really face what was happening before Daire, Styx and Harry came marching out of the bedroom. Daire had a backpack in his hands, Styx was stuffing something into one of his own.

"You're not..." Tess stood up. "You're not leaving now... Are you?"

"Quicker we leave, quicker we get back," Daire said, leaving his backpack on the table to walk over to her.

"Don't you need to plan like details and..." He scooped both hands around her jaw to tip her head up. "I thought these op things took weeks to plan?"

He was smiling. "We did all the talking we needed in Vegas while you were in London. We have a plan, a contingency, even a contingency for the contingency." He kissed her. "Four days tops."

She grabbed his tee-shirt in both hands. "Four days?" Distress bled into her exclamation. It hadn't been intentional, but the idea of being away from him for that long was terrifying in so many ways. "You said seventy-two hours!"

In one of his letters to her in London, he'd reassured her it wouldn't take longer than that.

"We have a detour first." Rather than be stressed, Daire smiled. "We'll make it."

"You might," she said. "I won't."

"Harry will protect you," he said. "You don't have to talk to him, just don't try to slip the net, okay? No games. Be good."

Her head began to shake. "I don't like this. It doesn't feel right."

"It never does when we're apart," he said then his brow came down. "Taking you with me would be dangerous.

I don't have to say it, do I? If I could take you with me and keep you safe, I wouldn't hesitate."

Tess would distract him from whatever he had to do. She understood that. It wasn't the mission that worried her, her man was capable. More than that, he was skilled, elite at what he did. The job would be a walk in the park for him, she didn't need the details to be sure of that.

"I know you'll be safer without me," she said, tightening her hold. "I just… could've used a little time to get used to the idea. I woke up with you this morning and now…"

"No wavering," he said, pulling her mouth nearer to his. "We'll find our way back to each other. Always. Remember?"

She nodded. "I love you, My Heart."

His smile rose slowly until his dimples came into view and he rested his mouth on hers. "Right back attcha, LR."

The press of his kiss closed her eyes. Desperate to remember every nuance of him, Tess wanted the moment to last a lifetime. It couldn't. Before she was ready, he let her go and went to grab his pack from the table. Styx opened the door and with purpose shimmering around both of them, they left. The door closed, and then she was alone with her father.

A few minutes ago, she'd been in the hallway, anticipating sinking into Daire's safe arms and spending the night in the security of him. That possibility was gone, right along with him. Until he was back with her, she'd never feel hope like he gave her.

"He'll be okay," Harry said. "Both of them will. I trained them well."

Which was where his confidence came from.

"I have faith in him," she murmured, still fixated on the door. "I just don't like it when we're apart, not with everything that's going on."

"I'll keep you safe, Tess."

Safe didn't mean happy. It didn't mean secure. She didn't despise her father, but his presence didn't make up for Daire's absence.

When she couldn't bear to stare any longer, Tess turned around to retrieve her shoes from the couch. "I'm going to bed," she said, without looking at her father. "Good night."

Sleep wouldn't be easy to come by when with every moment that passed, Daire was getting further and further away. The only hope was to focus on the seconds. Each one was another closer to them being together again.

Whatever Titan was, however it worked, Tess just hoped it was worth it.

NINETEEN

"UP! UP!"

Someone threw the sheet from her body. Tess rolled onto her back and instantly had to cover her eyes when the drapes were flung open to let in the morning light.

"What is going on?" she grumbled, tugging down the end of Daire's tee-shirt that served as her pajamas.

"Get up," Harry declared. "It's time for us to move."

"Time for us to… what?"

"Everything is packed," he said. "Getting it out of here could take a couple of runs."

She was still trying to figure out what was going on when the scent of coffee drifted her way. It tempted her out from beneath her shielding hands. On the nightstand was a travel mug without its lid. Steam rose from the top. Hope, right there wrapped in steel.

Sitting up, she tugged the shirt over her thighs and reached for the drink. "Where are we going?"

"The Beast," he said, standing by her door. "Why do you call it that?"

"I have no idea," she said, but wouldn't really be sure of her own name until the caffeine worked its way into her system. "You won't hear me complaining, but I don't know where he parked it." She raised her attention. "Have you heard from him?"

At least he was nice enough to be solemn. "No, and I won't, not until the job is done. He said the keys were in your bag and you'd know where it was."

"He did?" she asked, frowning at herself. Daire hadn't told her where the Beast was parked, even when she'd asked. "I don't—"

"He said not to try the seafood place without him."

Her lips immediately curled. Of course he'd leave it there. It wasn't that far from where they were and held a lot of good memories.

"I take it from that expression you've worked it out," Harry said. "Grab a shower and I'll call a cab. Be ready to leave in twelve minutes."

He left the room, like he hadn't just made an unreasonable demand. Mouthing at no one, because he was already gone, she was still trying to figure out what was happening. The Beast? Why were they going there and why was he talking about things being packed and moved?

A choice lay before her, she could roll over and go back to sleep or get up and try to make sense of her father's orders. She chose the route that let her keep the coffee and got up to grab a towel from the closet, draping it over the arm that was responsible for her coffee cup too.

In the living room, bags and large plastic bins were stacked by the door.

"What's that?" she asked, stifling a yawn behind her coffee cup.

"Our supplies. Everything Ares and Styx put together for the next leg of our mission."

Everything seemed to be a mission. She drank some more coffee. It wasn't as good as the coffee Daire made.

She eyed the pile of stuff Harry was checking and rechecking. "Why is it out here?"

"We're going to pack it up in the truck," Harry said. "We won't be coming back here."

That shook the last remnants of sleep from her foggy mind. "We won't be…? Daire will be coming back here. I plan to be here when he does."

"Once their mission is over, they'll contact my base unit. You've seen him do that before, right?" Harry asked. "When we had a conversation after Vegas." She nodded. "So you know it's possible, I'm not lying to you."

"Why didn't you tell Daire that you wanted to go somewhere else before he left? Is that why you sent him away, so you can take me somewhere? You can't get JARR, I don't know where all the keys are."

"That's not where we're going," Harry said.

"So where are we going?"

He stopped what he was doing to look at her. "You asked me a question I couldn't answer. If you want to know what is required of you, of your blood, there are only two men who can tell you. Garrick is still in the wind; I haven't heard from my guys. That leaves one option."

"Asclepius."

"Yes."

The man who was or had been the Olympus doctor. Finding him, she'd assumed would be impossible.

"Do you know where he is?" she asked, infused with optimism. "You think he'll talk to us?"

"I think trying is better than sitting here accomplishing nothing for four days. Wouldn't you agree?"

Yes. Hanging around in the apartment, waiting for Daire, with nothing to do but think about missing him and all the things that could go wrong, would be a special kind of torture. Doing something was definitely better. Gathering information counted as something. Intel was the key to survival after all.

Gulping down some more coffee, she put the cup on the low table and returned to the bedroom with purpose. She grabbed her clothes and hopped in the shower. Time would go so much faster with a goal. At least then she'd have something to tell Daire too.

From the sounds of the next stage in Harry's plan, they had to load up the truck with the gathered supplies. Fitting everything in wouldn't be easy, but there was storage in the Beast too. They'd find a way. Providing they traveled north, they'd be narrowing the distance between her and Daire too, reducing the time it would take him to get back to her.

Harry wasn't in the clear. Not by a long shot. But he was proactive, and she couldn't fault him for that.

***

THE CAB TOOK THEM and a few bags to the truck, which was parked next to the Beast exactly where she'd expected it to be. They took the truck back to the apartment and filled it with everything that was left.

Harry did a bit on taking their trash and wiping down the place for prints and other forensics. Teaching her and showing patience weren't things she'd have associated with her father. When they went back to the Beast, he even let her help hitching the truck to the trailer and gave her a few tips about hauling the thing.

He was a good driver, careful and particular. Riding next to him wasn't the same as doing it with Daire though.

"You're worried about him," Harry said after they'd put a few dozen miles between them and Miami.

"Yes," she said.

"You don't have to be. He knows what he's doing."

"That's not why I worry," she said, opening the glove box. "Would you like to listen to music? I don't know your taste. Daire's is… eclectic."

"It's important for him to know music. Just as it's important for him to know details on a range of subjects. We never know what will be important for a mission. The more he knows, the more likely he can extract himself from a difficult situation or ally himself with a key asset."

"He's more than just a collection of parts," she said, searching through the tapes, trying to remember what was on each one. "You talk about him like he's some robot you built."

"In a way, he is."

That he'd admit his role in using Daire didn't sit right. To exploit someone in such an overt way for so long should be shameful, yet those from Olympus accepted their failings… almost proudly.

"It might surprise you to learn that he can laugh," she said. "He's funny. And he can be romantic too, when he wants to be."

His scowl was so quick that it might be amusing, if it wasn't so infuriating. "I don't want to hear about that."

Slamming the glove box, she bounced around to face him. "What is your problem with us? I mean, really? You keep telling me that Daire can look after himself, so you shouldn't be worried about his safety. You wanted him to experience love, now he has. You should be happy."

"You're my little girl."

She shook her head. "No, that doesn't fly either. I wasn't raised by you. You didn't know me as a child, so it's not like you don't understand I'm all grown up."

"I did know you as a child. You just don't remember it. I lived with you after you were born and saw you at Olympus… sometimes. For a lot of your life, that was the only way I could think of you. You're right, you did stay two years old in my head for a long time… And I still remember that two-year-old playing with Daire… he looked at you with such wonder, like he'd never seen anything so fragile, so precious."

Exhaling a scoff of disbelief, she sank back in her seat. "I find it difficult to believe I was ever fragile."

His head tilted. "You were compared to him… You were female… not something he had a lot of experience with at that age."

"Well, he has plenty of experience now."

She put the innuendo in her voice on purpose to see his expression intensify. What was his problem?

"He got over it," Harry said, continuing like her insinuation hadn't happened. "It didn't take him long to get frustrated or annoyed when he was put in charge of you."

A burst of a laugh left her throat. "In charge of me? Wasn't he like eight years old?"

"Yes," he said, glancing at her like he didn't see the problem with that. "But he'd have defended you with his life."

"Some things never change," she muttered. "How can't you see the problem with loading that kind of responsibility onto a kid? You knew his mom. She trained under you. Do you really think that this is the life she wanted for him?"

"Kaiya was a complicated person, but she was dedicated. Thorough. Very focused."

Like a female version of Daire then. "Doesn't answer my question," she said. "You don't think she'd want him to be happy?"

"That's all any parent wants for their child."

Difficult to believe when her own father was so disgusted by the relationship that gave her purpose and the only joy she'd known for a long time.

"Tell me about you and mom," she said, watching his eyes narrow on the road. "You said we would talk about it."

"What do you want to know?"

"How did you meet?" she asked, figuring a good way to judge Zeus's veracity was to get what should be the same story, from a different angle.

"I thought you knew about Michael Lloyd."

"I do," she said.

His next look her way lingered before returning to its duty. "You're testing me."

"Both of you, all of you," she said. "I'm not a good secret-agent. I don't have a problem misleading you, or testing you, or telling you that's what I'm doing."

"I didn't do a bug sweep."

"Daire has that covered," she said, noting his intrigue. "We can't be monitored in here… trust me."

His hands shifted on the wheel as he inhaled. "I was on a mission. Monitoring Michael Lloyd who was funding a candidate with terrorist ties. They weren't obvious ties, of course."

"You were worried about the candidate winning office?"

"To a degree," he said. "But that wasn't my mission. It was my job to uncover Lloyd's purpose. At first, we weren't sure if he was aware of those ties. It didn't take long to uncover that he was… Anyway, long story short, we were closing in on his target, realigning objectives, when he was murdered."

"Murdered?" she asked, calming her suspicions. "By anyone we know?"

"Your mom worked in his office. She didn't know him, but I saw her around. My cover was doing maintenance in the building, she was an administrator... She was so beautiful. Young, vibrant, so open and honest. I used to stare at her... For hours, I could just watch... I'd never known anyone so magnetic... so captivating... "

When he didn't continue, she looked to see why and was surprised to see the lazy smile on his face. "Do you miss her?"

"Oh, every minute," he said without a flicker of hesitation. "But I've been missing her for thirty years... She was working late, I was there working, supposedly, when the murder happened." He glanced at her. "I was with your mom when we heard the shot. Lloyd was dead. She was shaken up, so I took her out of there. There were security cameras and electronic locks. She wasn't safe, wouldn't have been safe. I was proved right about that when she became a target of the same people who'd killed Lloyd."

"You protected her."

"I did. I took down everyone who might hurt her. I eliminated them all and gave her a brand new life. A new identity."

"I'm surprised Zeus was so supportive."

His snicker was ironic. "Not one of his qualities. He hated it. Didn't see the point. Didn't care. Thought it was a waste of resources. But I had nothing to lose back then and plenty of favors to call in. I got her setup."

"She must have known," she said. "Who you were, I mean, what you did."

"I told her the truth," he said, then conceded a half shrug. "To an extent. I didn't want to scare her... We're trained not to be loose lipped, but it never felt like that with her. Sharing with her was just like sharing with an extension of myself. After being tied up in Olympus for so long and dealing with the intrigue, it was nice to just be... me."

"Why did you ever go back to Olympus?" she asked. "If you got her a new life, couldn't you have given yourself one too?"

"Two targets are always easier to track than one," he said. "Besides, I had… commitments."

"Commitments?"

"We snuck around for a couple of years before you were conceived. I'd visit her whenever I could, delay returns, take longer collecting intel. Anything I could to be with her… I didn't know she was pregnant until she was over six months."

"Daire," she murmured, remembering exactly how her father felt when he learned of her existence and what he'd wanted her mom to do. "He was your commitment."

Harry nodded. "I wouldn't leave him. Your mom was amazing, she was the only person I could talk to about him. About fatherhood and the difficulties that came with it, especially in the Olympus setting. I don't know if I'd have gotten through those difficult years without her. When he was a baby, it was easy… easier. He didn't go anywhere I didn't put him, didn't ask questions. Taking care of his needs at Olympus was always a challenge, but I had a squad of men under me."

Midnight diaper runs wouldn't be a problem for a person who could command his people to retrieve whatever he needed.

"He was Olympus's child," she said. "Did you ever think about giving him a different life? Sending him away with mom or putting him in the system?"

"I made Kaiya a promise," he said. "That I wouldn't abandon him. That I'd raise him as my own. She understood the potential problems of him learning about his father… or his father learning about him."

"He doesn't know?" she asked, consumed by shock. "Merrill doesn't know?"

"He knew she was pregnant. He told her to get rid of the child."

Merrill's first reaction to Daire had been the same as Harry's first reaction to her. "She told him she did?"

"After the Alpha site was destroyed, we got word out to him that Kaiya was dead… and her child."

"Why?" she asked in an exhale, wondering what good could come from that. "Merrill might have raised him, given him a different life."

"Kaiya didn't want it. She didn't want her child to be a part of Merrill's world. The man was trying to climb the political ladder, an illegitimate child was less acceptable in those days. He wasn't interested in being a father to her child."

"Did she talk about her plans?" Tess asked. "You must have known what she planned to do when the baby was born."

"She planned to keep him, there at Olympus with her. Putting him out into the world wouldn't make him safe. Anyone who wanted to find her could do so through him. And if he ever came looking…"

She thought about that. About how different life would be for Daire if he'd been given up for adoption or abandoned somewhere. He'd have no clue about Olympus, he'd be as in the dark as she had been when her mother died.

That didn't mean they wouldn't know about him. JARR would know. The system would keep tabs on him, and alert Olympus agents to his threat if he ever tried to find out where he'd come from.

"He was always going to be at risk," she muttered.

"Yes. I wanted to teach him how to look after himself. I didn't want him blindsided by a life he was clueless about coming to look for him. I taught him what he needs to know to protect himself."

Promises to his mother aside, Harry probably cared for the infant on his own because he wanted to. Maybe it was a link to Kaiya that he didn't want to break, or it could be he felt responsible for his agent going down on his watch. Perhaps Harry wanted some love of his own, some family to hold on to. If her math worked, Daire was born before Harry ever met her mother, before they were intimate and long before he had a child of his own.

"But you didn't want that for me or mom."

"If I could've given you the tools to prepare for facing Zeus, I would have. You were fortunate that I'd learned my hard lessons with Daire. When they took you, when Zeus took you, it was a power play. He kept you at the beta compound knowing I'd come get you. When I did, he let me see you, but wouldn't let me take you home to your mother."

"He made you work for him."

"He tried, I refused," he said. She didn't understand having thought her captivity gave Zeus ammunition to manipulate Harry. "At least I tried. Carrie was on the outside, alone. I could come and go, you were stuck. The only way he'd let Carrie in to see you was if I agreed not to see you… I couldn't keep her away from you… Zeus got both of you and complete control of me."

"Why give him what he wanted?"

"You were two years old. Your mother had never been apart from you… I'd have done anything to take away her pain… Agreeing was our only option. Carrie came to Olympus and both of you stayed there. I would train the guys, I had Daire… He was the only one allowed to socialize with you and your mother."

"We could've existed that way for a long time."

"Yeah, but I wouldn't let it go on forever. I already realized I'd put Daire in a prison. I wouldn't do it to you too… When Zeus started to talk about training you… I couldn't do it. I didn't want you to be…"

"Like him," she said. "Like Daire. You saw Olympus as his prison. He saw it as his home."

"It was all he knew and that was on me. Even when I tried to show him there was more, tried to convince him to leave, he never would… Olympus was his life, and I promised his mother I would never abandon him."

That promise. Maybe it was what kept him at Olympus with Daire. But she didn't believe that honor was the only motive at play. It frustrated her that he couldn't be honest. His respect for Daire was obvious, he valued his ward. She didn't know why he couldn't just say it.

Choosing not to start another argument, she turned her attention to the glove box to search for some music that might distract them. Harry loved her mom. Any time she asked, he didn't deny his feelings for her and wasn't self-conscious about them either.

Apparently when it came to his kids, he wasn't so uninhibited.

TWENTY

THEY FOUND A PARK that took travel-trailers and stopped for the night. Harry was a determined driver; they'd made a lot of progress. Without knowing where they were going, she couldn't say how much.

Efficient Daire had emptied the fridge of all perishables, which left them reliant on cans and dry goods. Pasta with sauce wasn't so bad, nothing special, but it filled them up. Harry went out to do some sweep of the trailer and the truck while she washed up their dishes.

As long as there was something to do, she could talk herself through the task, and ignore the niggling voice in her head. Once everything was clean, dry, and put away, it wasn't so easy. While drying her hands, she leaned on the counter, staring up the hallway to the bed.

"Where are you, My Heart," she whispered, desperate for news.

Anything could happen. Anything at all. Even if he was the best agent in the world, he couldn't stop accidents that might befall anyone. Losing him to a mission would tear her to shreds, losing him to some mindless wreck, as she had her mother, would end her. All she needed was to hear his voice. To get some kind of signal that he was still out there, still fighting.

"You can take the bed, I'll sleep out here," Harry said. His voice startled her, she hadn't heard the door open or him come in. But the surprise revealed where Daire got his stealth. When she turned, a daze in her eyes, he stopped to frown at her. "What's the matter?"

"Nothing," she said, quick to shake her head. "I was just…"

She didn't want to admit that her mind had been on Daire again. When they were together, she drew so much strength from him. Being apart made her feel weak… and sort of pathetic.

"He is alive. He'll only reach out after he's completed his mission."

"I know," she said. Had she been that obvious or was he just taking a shot at what was on her mind? "I'm not worried, I just…" Exhaling, Tess surrendered to the inevitable. "I want his head to be in the right place. I don't want him thinking about me. If he needs to blank out the world to get the job done, that's fine."

"But…?" he asked, coming a step closer.

Rolling her lips together, she moistened them. "When we're together, I feel his strength. It holds me up and when we're not… I don't feel that."

"You don't need anyone to hold you up, Tess. You're your mother's daughter. You have strength of your own."

"I know," she said, thinking of all the times Daire told her that too. "I'd never forgive myself if something happened and I wasn't there."

That was the crux of it. Having confessed to Daire that she didn't want to die alone, the possibility of the reverse terrified her too. She'd thanked him for being with her mother in her final moments, offering some comfort, even if there was nothing he could do to save her.

"Styx won't leave him."

Depending on when and where it happened, he wouldn't necessarily have a choice.

"You said Daire has a habit of putting others before himself, even in the field. You keep telling me he's capable.

Even he said that you don't worry about him because you trained him to look after himself…" She pushed away from the counter. "I don't get why neither of you see that isn't comforting. Not for me. All it says is you're complacent. Neither of you acknowledge he's a human being. He has human weaknesses. He's the strongest man I know, but even he can't stop a bullet."

"I taught him how to fire his own. How to deflect. How to move. How to take cover." Tess didn't realize how close they were until he laid his hands on her shoulders. "He will come back."

She sighed. "He doesn't even know where I am."

"He said you'd find your way back to each other. Don't you trust him?"

Startled, her focus leaped to his. "With every part of my soul."

He smiled. The expression was unfamiliar, certainly on her father's face and having it directed her way. "You do love him."

Already aware Harry didn't trust her, she wasn't offended by the statement. "So do you," she said, not surprised when his smile faded. "Why do you find it so hard to admit? It took him a while to admit it to himself, but from the moment Daire knew he loved me, he's never had a problem saying it to me… But you, and Styx, and him, the three of you don't ever say it to each other. You raised them, you trained them, you've spent years together, all three of you. Why is it so hard to let down those walls?"

"In the field, we have to be detached," he said, stern in his demeanor and words. "We can't allow ourselves to be distracted by emotion."

"But you're not in the field with them most of the time… You relax with each other when you're not training. If you can be a father to them, why can't you be honest with them?"

"It's not the way I was raised," he said, his hands falling from her shoulders.

Watching him retreat to the pack he'd left on the recliners, she considered something she'd pretty much ignored so far. "How did you get involved?" she asked. "With Olympus."

He opened the bag and began to take things out of it. "I joined the military as soon as they'd let me sign on the dotted line. I got through basic training and was approached… Apparently there was some test I'd taken and got the highest score. I was asked if I was interested in joining an elite unit. An elite, covert unit."

Which was probably all a young, adrenaline-fueled soldier needed to hear. His country needed him, if that was thrown in, would've sealed the deal.

"What about your family?" she asked. "Your parents and siblings."

"My mom died when I was born, some complication my dad never talked about. He never talked about her… or about anything really. He worked, took care of me, and that was it… until the booze took over."

Putting a hand on the back of the dinette seat, she stepped closer. His back was to her, so he couldn't see her intrigue. Questions filled her mind. Questions about who he was and why he'd chosen to leave his father behind to join Olympus.

"I was sixteen when my old man kicked it." There was her answer. "After that, I didn't care about much. I was on my own. Couldn't stand the system. I met a guy in a shelter. A vet. The way he talked about the army made it seem like a family who'd take me in. It wasn't really a choice. I don't remember being unsure or second-guessing myself."

Staring at him wouldn't achieve anything and she didn't want to be caught gawping, so she went to work removing the dinette cushions to transform the space into a bed.

"You second-guessed yourself about Olympus," she said.

"Not at first. Garrick and me were recruited at the same time. He was some tech savant or something, only a year older than me, but he'd done college and everything. We were trained together. At the same time anyway, our training didn't consist of the same lessons."

No, because Garrick was needed to develop the technology that would put Olympus ahead of those in their game. Harry's specialty was personnel. While her father could be dry, strict and regimented, he was also personable, with his men anyway. She'd seen it at the desert house. He could put them through their paces, thrash them hard until she was sure, if she were them, she'd want to aim her frustration right at him. But straight after, he could show them kindness and concern. He could relax with them, joke with them, treat them as equals.

As well as Harry knew people, he'd missed something major about the man he called son. "It was easy for him to believe you turned your back on him," she said without looking up from her task even when he turned around. "At the Exodus, when he got the alert about leaving and didn't know what was going on… He spent a year angry at you, so angry that he went after the only thing he knew you loved. You believed it was easy for him to switch his allegiance to Zeus. Z told you that truth and you believed him… because you still resent Daire for what he did when he was six." She stopped to put a hand on her hip and make eye contact. "Do you think maybe it was easy for both of you to believe the worst because you've never really told each other the truth about how you feel?"

"It's complicated."

"No, it's not," she said, stepping closer when he tried to turn away. "You talk about Olympus being his home and his family. He talks that way too sometimes, or he has. But the truth is, it was never Olympus. You were his home. His family. And the fact he resisted that when he was six years old only tells me how afraid he was to lose you and the life you had together. He hated me, you know? Hated me for being born, for changing things, for taking his father away. That festered in him because you didn't deny how you felt about your other family, your real family. Even if it was just mom you were in love with, he didn't see that. Daire saw that I had been born and suddenly everything was changing, he was losing everything. And then, after you made the deal to get rid of us, you didn't just embrace him as the family you had left, you took him out of Olympus, put him outside in a scary place, far from everything he knew. I don't care how much you trained him or how unlike other kids he was, did you ever think what it was like for him to lie in the woods alone in the dark, wondering if you'd ever come back for him, wondering if you were going to abandon him just like you did when you came to live with mom and me?"

"I did not abandon him," he asserted, offended by the suggestion. "I wanted him with me. I begged him to come with me. He wouldn't come! What was I supposed to do?"

"Stay," she said, trying to appear non-judgmental by putting a simple smile on her lips. "You were supposed to stay. Don't you see? You didn't choose him. You've never chosen him. He's just the boy that was there. The boy under your care. A soldier just like all the others you trained."

"It was never like that."

"He doesn't know that," she said. "To this day, I don't think he knows that. If he did, you blasted it all to hell with the Exodus."

"I didn't know he'd refused Zulu. I didn't know that they'd—"

"Not because of that," she said, frustrated by both men. "You believed Z. You believed him." Peering into him, she went closer. "Daire would die for you. He'd die to please you. And you believed your enemy over Daire's heart. You believed the enemy over your protégé's loyalty."

"I apologized for my actions."

"I know and he forgave you because it's what he does. He accepts everyone else's treatment of him because since his birth, all he's been to anyone is a tool, a weapon to be wielded..." Her father would need time to process. "There are sheets in the back."

She went to retrieve pillows and sheets for the dinette bed. It was warm, so he probably wouldn't need much, but the Beast still felt like her home, it seemed right to play hostess. He was still standing by the end of the dinette when she returned to begin making up the bed.

"I know I damaged him," Harry said, something humbler in his tone. "I realized that when he was young... I think that was why I was so eager to send him away with you and your mother. Carrie adored him, she would've raised him… and done a better job than I did."

"You are his father," she said, tucking the sheet around the cushions that served as a mattress. "He loved you… and he wouldn't ever dream of abandoning you."

"I always intended to go back for him," Harry said. "As soon as I had you and your mother established somewhere safe. When you were older, a little more aware… I didn't plan to just leave him there forever."

Whether his good intentions were honest or not, she didn't think leaving Daire, an impressionable youth, with Zeus for a considerable time would've encouraged the youngster to rethink his decision to stay. Harry's position had been impossible, she understood that. But Tess had her mother. Leaving Daire left him with no one. It left him alone. Something he'd believed himself to be most of his life. Harry was his CO. Harry was his anchor. But some part of him never believed he had his father's love. Given what had transpired when he was so young, it was easy to see how that happened.

"None of us can change what happened all those years ago," she said, retrieving a bottle of water from the fridge. "We can change what we're doing now. You should tell him the truth… Tell him about his mom, your promise to her, how you felt about leaving him when you came to stay with me and mom. Tell him how it hurt you when he wouldn't leave with you and that you always planned to go back… Tell him how you feel." She opened the bottle, thinking about her mom. "Because one day, one of you won't be around, and neither of you will have a chance to say any of it."

She drank from the bottle, assuming their conversation was over. As she lowered it, Harry spoke.

"How is it you can talk to me about Daire, but you can't talk to me about yourself?"

She shrugged. "There's nothing for me to say. We don't have a relationship that needs to be saved. You don't owe me anything and I don't need anything from you. I can talk about Daire because I know him, I love him. I want what's best for him. I want him to have everything in his life that he deserves and that includes understanding he was more than just a student to you."

"I do owe you something," Harry said. "I'm your father. I owe you an explanation."

She licked her lips and sat her bottle hand on the closest dinette seat back. "The trouble with anything you would say is I wouldn't necessarily believe it. And everything that happened when I was a kid is tainted by what I now feel for Daire. I don't care what it did to me to have you with me before I was abducted." She shrugged. "I don't even really care that I was abducted. Like I said, I had my mom. She was my anchor and she never shied from telling me that she loved me. I was secure in that, even if the lies did frustrate the hell out of me. I was never raised a soldier, drilled and trained and disciplined. I was raised with love... by a determined woman who showed me how important it was for us to stick together. I don't need validation from you. Daire does. He's been waiting for it his whole life. Except he was raised to never let himself show anything less than invincibility. That's the only way he thinks you want him to be."

"I always knew Olympus damaged him, that what we did skewed his perspective on the world." He exhaled. "It's amazing, isn't it? I was there almost every day of his life. I know everything that happened to him, where he was every second... But I still managed to make the same mistakes regular parents make."

"I don't think Kaiya would be disappointed," she said because it wasn't fair to just rag on Harry and lead him to believe he'd done a terrible job. "I know I'm not. Yes, I ache sometimes for what he didn't get as a boy. I want so much for him. But, I guess, that's understandable given how much I love him." She smiled, trying to encourage the downtrodden man in front of her. "But I do love him. I love him so much that there isn't a thing in this world I wouldn't do for him. If he wanted me to go to him, to be with him, even if it meant certain death, I wouldn't hesitate for a second. I love him and he's a good man... You did that, Harry. You made him into the man I want to spend the rest of my life with... Thank you."

Tossing Daire into the system would've led him to be a different person. One who would probably never have crossed her path. She wanted her Heart to have the world, but no matter what, she'd always love him, right on through to his bones.

"We should get some sleep," Harry said, approaching to lay a hand on her arm. "You're a good girl, Tess. Your mother did an excellent job raising you."

Though there was love in her house growing up, it wasn't like she and her mom were without issues. Still, that was nothing to what Daire went through as a child or what Harry did as a parent to him. It must have been difficult to strike a balance. The agents under him, those who were recruited as adults, would respect the distance Harry fostered, understanding it was necessary to have some separation.

Disconnecting from a child wouldn't be so easy. He'd have needed to give Daire enough love and comfort that he didn't feel abused twenty-four seven. At the same time, Harry needed to train his protégé to detach from personal bonds out in the field.

That wasn't an enviable position. She didn't envy her Heart in the field at that moment either. Detaching from his bond with her wouldn't be as easy. Her own connection to him felt as real as ever.

TWENTY-ONE

THEY DROVE FOR A DAY AND A HALF, hauling the Airstream, making their way through the tapes in Daire's glovebox. It had become something of a mission, and maybe a bonding exercise to try to identify the song and the artist, so she could write them down on the notepad Harry provided.

They didn't get through the whole collection, though they were nearly there when Harry grew serious and told her to switch the music off. All she saw on either side were fields. Civilization had dwindled a few miles back. Now they were surrounded by farmland, with only sporadic houses dotted around far from the road.

"Are we there?" she asked, wondering why a doctor would live on a farm. "Why does he live out here? When did he leave Olympus?"

"Asclepius continued to do work for us up until just a few years ago. He was never a full-time Olympus member, he was a pioneer in his field, which was why Zeus wanted him involved. Part of his use came in understanding what was on the cutting edge. That meant being in the world, finding out what the other pioneers were working on."

"So he was a spy?"

"Asclepius is a man of science. His interest in what

Olympus could provide was academic. Almost unlimited funds and resources, and zero oversight."

No worrying about official agencies poking into what he was doing or perhaps chastising him for being unethical.

"What did it involve?" she asked. "If he's a doctor, what was he working on?"

"Various things. Whatever he wanted, or whatever we needed him to work on."

"I don't know if I like the sound of that," she said, a dubious streak of uncertainty trickling down her spine.

"Most of us didn't," Harry said. "We could be accused of being complicit by our willingness to look away and not ask the difficult question. Everyone had their role in Olympus. It wasn't our job to question each other... so we stayed in our own lanes, ignoring anything that we didn't want to face."

The confession didn't assuage her suspicions. "Why did he leave?"

"He and Z got into it."

"About?"

His tongue touched his top lip, maybe as a way to buy time or come up with a nice way to say something unpleasant. As he moistened his lips, his hands slipped back to their correct positions on the wheel.

"One of the first things I teach my men when they're learning about intelligence gathering from an ally or asset is to never ask a question they don't want the answer to. It's a difficult line to tread because it's often assumed that an intelligence agent should want to know everything. The more information, the better, right?"

"Information is power," she said. "Intel is the key to survival."

The brief flash of a half-smile suggested he was pleased to hear his own line parroted back. "Except that's not always the case," he said. "We might want to know where it's being kept... we don't necessarily want to know that those who've been subjected to it are dying a slow, horrible death in the basement."

"Why wouldn't you want to know that?" she asked.

All she could do was show him a frown when he glanced her way. Though he hesitated, like he didn't want to reveal the reason, she didn't let up. "If Daire was here, he'd tell me."

After a loud inhale, he answered her when he breathed out. "Because ignorance is bliss, Light-Sprite. If that agent's mission isn't to liberate those people…"

The truth was ice-cold when it trickled in. "He has to leave them to die… You would really leave people to die?"

"If it isn't our mission, yes," he said. "Olympus isn't about being righteous or even particularly wholesome. It's about getting the job done, the greater good. Sometimes to do that, we have to sacrifice a few individuals."

Unsure how she felt about her father's truth, she understood why he hadn't wanted to admit it. Her judgment probably wasn't a factor in his reluctance, it couldn't be nice to say something so cold and without apology. He knew it was wrong, if he didn't then he wouldn't have been hesitant to say it. Yet, he wasn't sorry. He didn't regret it. She wondered if he regretted anything.

"You switch off the part of you that's human," she said, wrapping her arms around her waist as she stared straight ahead. "It's not only about being detached from those you care about. You switch off your compassion too."

He didn't answer but didn't need to. Her own humanity wailed at the notion of innocent people being used and discarded like pieces on a chess board. Though that wasn't what chilled her through to her core. Selfish as it was, she thought of Daire. Thought of her warm, loving, incredible Heart and how it pained her to think of him being so cut off from that part of himself.

When he was Danny, after they first met, she spent a long time believing that he was easy-going, so laid back that extreme emotions like anger and love weren't really in his repertoire. If what Harry was saying was true, she hadn't been so wrong.

"He is what I made him," Harry said. "If you have to hate anyone for what he's done in the past, I'm the one you hate."

Blame could be assigned all over. It could be Harry's

fault or Kaiya's for getting knocked up in the first place. It could be Merrill's fault for just accepting his child was no more without proof. It could be Daire's for not refusing the orders. Though his training demanded he always be compliant.

It all went back to the original Two, the man who'd envisioned Olympus and recruited the rest of the Six.

"Six betrayed you," she said. "I know you've been through this with Daire and you didn't want him to take revenge, but… Why? Why defend a man who betrayed you?"

"Killing Six opens up new issues and we have enough of those right now."

"What kind of issues?" she asked. "I don't get it. He betrayed you and your agents. He betrayed the other five members of the Six."

It took him a minute to come up with a response. "The Six have always existed inside a sort of protected bubble. They get away with their choices and demand we follow through on them because they gave us Olympus. It exists because of them."

"Because of their money."

"Yes, that," he said. "But they also have connections that give us access to information. They cut the corners for us that need to be cut, deal with red tape. To some extent, they do have skin in the game. Six fears Zeus, there's no denying that, all of them do. Because at the end of the day, it is within his power to ruin any of them, even to hurt them or their families."

"So why doesn't he?"

"You've heard of MAD, right?"

"From the Cold War, Mutually Assured Destruction."

"Right," he said. "That's Olympus and the Six. We work together because we must. Most of the time we resent the shit out of each other. The Six don't understand that sometimes things take time or go wrong. While we resent begging for scraps, asking for handouts. And if, God forbid, we do need them to use their connections, it can be infuriating to wait or deal with their ineptitude."

Because none of them were trained Olympus agents, they wouldn't do things the way the principals would.

"So there's friction."

"I'll say."

"I don't understand how that protects Six. Why you wouldn't want rid of him as much as Daire does."

"Because while we might despise each other, we need each other. We could expose them, sure, but we're the ones who committed the crimes. You know how difficult it can be, especially in a covert organization, to prove what one person knew over another? To be convicted of conspiracy, you first must prove it. They might give us orders sometimes, but when it comes to planning and executing, that's on us."

"You have the power to destroy each other. You're stuck with each other."

"Z hasn't turned on them because he loves Olympus, loves being in charge, having people follow his orders. He likes to feel important." She'd figured that out within minutes of meeting him. "And he has them on the back foot now, he's discovered their betrayal, so they're at his mercy... They owe him."

"And if Daire takes Six down, the only member of the Six who was loyal to Zeus, he might... demand reprisal." Letting her words linger, Harry didn't say anything else while she worked the scenario through to its conclusion. "Which means Daire is at risk."

"Daire is valuable, he's the most trained and experienced man we have. He's spent his life doing this. No one else is like him. No one else even comes close."

Which was why so many people liked to tell her Daire was about the only man safe from Zeus's need for vengeance. "If he kills Six," she said. "Zeus won't offer him that protection anymore."

The idea scared her. She didn't want her Heart to be in pain or at risk from anyone. The more she thought about it, the greater her fear became.

Noticing the smile on Harry's face, anger surged through her. "How the hell can that make you happy?"

"It doesn't make me happy. It's just been... a long

time, since I spent any time with anyone who sees things so clear cut. Your mom was like that. One person makes a mistake, that's the person who should be punished… that's not the way Zeus will see it. He has a better view of the big picture. You remember how he got me back onto the reservation when I tried to follow my own path?"

"He came after me and mom."

"That's right," Harry said. "I was an asset. Valuable to the organization. I had men and experience… You and your mom didn't have that. You weren't valuable to him as anything more than tools to manipulate me. He could send me into the field, give me orders, and never doubt that I would do exactly what I was told."

"Because if you didn't, me and mom would've faced the consequences."

Daire had told her Zeus mentioned her and her mom to Harry even long after they were no longer at Olympus. He had resources and nothing was beyond him.

It didn't take her long to make the leap. "Daire is valuable. Zeus wants him."

"Yes."

"Even if he murders Six, Zeus will still want him."

"If he can be manipulated into doing what Zeus wants him to, yes."

She was beginning to see. "He won't hurt Daire."

"Not physically," Harry said. "But it's incredible what can be inflicted upon us without ever receiving a single wound."

Daire would be manipulated, just like Harry was decades ago. "But you didn't want him to hurt Six even before you knew about me and Daire's relationship."

"Didn't mean you weren't at risk," Harry said. "Zeus could still have used you against me and if I make demands of Daire…" He'd carry them out. "You weren't the only one at risk. As I've said, Daire does have a habit of putting others ahead of himself. Zeus could've threatened anyone in the unit or everyone… He could take hostages, innocent civilians with no ties to Olympus. Daire doesn't have to know a person to feel responsible for them. People dying for the cause is one thing. People dying because he refuses an order… He works hard to keep his people alive, to keep them safe. He never wants to be responsible for any death, not directly… Sometimes I've wondered if…"

She perked up when he didn't finish, turning his way to prompt him on. "Wondered what?"

"If it goes back to his mother… He's never said it, but sometimes I think he feels responsible."

"For her death?" she asked, amazed. "How could he be responsible for her death? He was just a baby."

"And it wasn't childbirth complications that killed her," Harry said. "By the time I found her, she'd already been shot, she survived long enough to give birth to him, but… there was blood loss. Childbirth wouldn't have helped. Maybe if she hadn't been in labor…"

"You blame him?"

"No!" he said, quick to reject her incredulity. "Jesus, no. But who knows what goes through a man's head?"

She folded her arms. "Maybe if you'd asked him how he felt about it, you would know."

"No," he said, doing a double take her way. "You can't bring this up with him."

"Why? Because he might feel some emotion or connected to me? He's in love with me, Harry, he already feels connected."

"Bringing up his mother could lead to discussing his father."

"And you still want me to keep that a secret."

Even though Harry had said it, she'd never really intended not to talk to Daire about his father. There just hadn't been time. With everything else going on, something always took precedence over serious discussion. If they were going to be living in close quarters with Styx and Harry even after the brothers returned, there might not be much chance to talk about it any time soon.

"It's for his own good. Merrill is in the public eye, more so since he made the decision to…"

"Run for the big chair," she said. "Zeus told me."

"It's a gradual process, not something that happens

overnight. He wants the job… and I don't know what it would do to Daire to see that. To have to see his biological father all over the news with his family."

"I don't think Daire will envy that life," she said. "He doesn't care about public adoration and the only father's approval he is interested in is yours."

"Can you say it will make his life better?" Harry asked. "Why would you tell him? To make yourself feel better or because you think it's best for him to know?"

"Both."

"Kaiya didn't want that. She didn't want Merrill anywhere near his life."

"If I keep secrets from him, how can I ask him to be honest with me?" she asked.

"You forgave him. When you met, you didn't know who he was or what he did. You didn't know about his connection to me. That's a lot of lies. You forgave them… And there's no reason for Daire to ever know that you know, he won't ever know about his father. I've made sure of that for thirty-three years."

"I don't want to lie to him. I do know who his father is. I know what happened. I should tell him."

"Did you think about Zeus? About why he told you… You don't think this is what he wanted. If you tell Daire, he'll learn not only what you tell him, but what I've kept from him all his life. Zeus wants there to be a rift. The further he can pull Daire from me, the more likely it is that my boy will go to him."

She shook her head. "Daire won't ever work with Zeus. Not after London. Not after what he did, taking me away."

"You've given Zeus the trump card. You tell Daire about his father, he learns that everyone he's known has been lying to him his whole life, he pulls away from us… And then there's you, the one who told him the truth, the only one he trusts… And the easiest one to use against him."

Her father was manipulating her. Given his line of work, that had to be obvious even to him. Yet he was telling the truth too. Daire knowing the truth would make her feel better because she didn't want to lie to him. Would it be better for him?

"I don't mean to put you in a difficult position," Harry said. "We have to focus. We must focus on our goal. If we can eliminate Zeus, then we can try to salvage something. When we're putting it all back together, everyone will have a chance to offer input."

She couldn't imagine that would be a better time to tell Daire. With everything up in the air, pieces scattered everywhere, what would happen if she revealed then that his father had been lying to him all his life? And her, without knowing how long it would take to carry out the objectives, she could've been withholding for months at that point. Maybe years. Would he forgive her?

"He never asked," Harry said. "Remember what I said about asking questions we don't want the answer to? If he asks, he wants to know, then we're duty bound to tell the truth."

"Is that how you've been justifying it to yourself?"

The somber, yet stern, set of his brows suggested either pity or annoyance at her defiance. "I trained the man. I taught him about gathering intel. If he wanted to know, he would ask. Believe me, he would. Forcing information onto him that he doesn't want won't help anyone."

Harry slowed and turned the car down a dry dirt road.

"Are we here?" she asked, tugging at her seatbelt, sitting up straight.

"We're here."

TWENTY-TWO

THERE WERE SOME TREES UP AHEAD. Once they were hidden among them, Harry pulled over to the side of the road and stopped the truck.

"What are we doing?" she asked, a mixture of scared and exhilarated.

"I haven't seen him in a while," Harry said. "I won't take any chances. Stay here."

Staying there wouldn't get her answers. Harry got out of the truck and started back toward the Beast; she was quick to leap out after him.

"No," she said, falling into step beside him as he passed her door. "I won't just sit here and wait."

"Because you don't trust me," he said, unlocking the Beast to jump up inside. "Do you think I will learn something and withhold it?"

"Yes," she said without any hesitation.

She didn't go inside, just watched Harry open one of the overhead cabinets and reach into the back, behind a box to retrieve a gun. That there were weapons in there didn't surprise her. But watching Harry check the clip and chamber a round did make her uneasy.

"Rushing in on a guy with greater numbers is a recipe

for disaster."

"Because he'll see me and assume I'm a super-agent?" she asked. "I don't think it'll make him feel better that you're carrying a weapon… How do you plan to get answers if you have to shoot him to get in?"

"His problem was with Zeus, not with me," Harry said. "How do you think I knew where to find him?"

"So far I haven't seen anyone," she said, not that she'd know Asclepius even if he fell on her. "You're telling me that you set him up here?"

"I have some experience with giving people new lives," he said, coming over to leap out of the Airstream, forcing her to move aside.

"And Zeus just trusted you to do that," she asked as he locked up again. "He had some issue with the guy, but was happy for you to set him up somewhere he didn't know about?"

"He never asked," Harry said, starting toward the truck while tucking the gun into the back of his pants and covering it with his shirt.

"Why wouldn't he ask? I thought Zeus needed to know everything."

"What they fell out over…" Harry said, pausing by the front passenger door. "It was one of those ignorance is bliss situations. Zeus didn't like what Asclepius was doing. He didn't accept it. Asclepius insisted it was necessary, so the Six continued to fund him."

"He's still Olympus?"

Harry shrugged. "Technically."

"Are you going to tell me what they fell out over?"

He opened the door next to them. "No…" Harry gestured to the inside. "Would you please stay here?"

She shook her head. "Daire would tell me."

"Daire's not here," Harry said, calm in an almost unnerving way. "If he was here, he'd want you to stay away from Asclepius."

"Why bring me all this way if it wasn't to introduce us? You could've left me in Miami."

"I told Daire I would protect you," Harry said. "I

couldn't have left you behind. But if I take you inside to see Asclepius, I can't promise you'll be safe."

Reading into his words, she peered at him. "You don't want to tell Daire you chose to take me to this doctor. I have to tell you that I want to go. You want this, me insisting. That way if things go wrong, you can put it on me." Harry didn't say anything, which didn't make her feel better. "I don't trust you, Harry."

"I know," he said, opening a hand at the front seat again. "That's why I'm telling you to stay here."

"I could stay here and you might never come back," she said. "I could stay here and you could go up there and be murdered, then what? I just sit here and wait until the maniac finds me too?"

"Or I could go up there, talk to the man, and come back to take you somewhere safe."

Except if Asclepius said something distasteful or gave Harry some insider clue he didn't share, she would be an idiot for waiting behind and missing the opportunity for intel. Her lack of trust worked both ways. She didn't trust her father not to lead her into an unsafe environment with a dangerous man, but she also didn't trust him to come back and relay the entire conversation.

The point of coming to the doctor was twofold. First to learn about what was required of her at beta and how she'd ended up connected to JARR. The second reason was to give Daire any tidbits of information she might be able to glean about the man, his honesty, and what else Zeus might expect of them.

Stepping forward, she took the door in both hands and slammed it shut. "I'm coming with you," she said, pointing into his face before he could go anywhere. "But if I get hurt, if you abandon me here, or use me with your doctor friend in anyway, Daire will tear you apart. Who you are won't matter."

After a tense pause, he curled his fingers around her wrist to draw it down. "Your unshakeable faith in him is admirable, humbling even, but you can't accuse me of using him as a tool if you do exactly the same thing." She faltered.

"Threatening people with him only reveals his love for you. You weaken him every time you mention his name in relation to yours… Don't do it again."

He let her go and turned around to start down the road. Mentioning her Heart weakened him, yes, but she was stuck on what he'd said before that. Using him as a tool… She didn't want that, didn't want him to be her tool. Her Heart told her he was a resource at her disposal. She'd never thought much about it, not until that moment. All she wanted from him was love.

Not long after she and Harry met, he'd told her that Daire would be their primary instrument for success. He'd told her that she wouldn't ever need to shoot a gun so long as he was around. Was she just as bad as the principals? As every other person at Olympus who used Daire for his skills?

Harry was a good twenty feet ahead by the time she snapped out of her daze and raced after him. Walking at his side, she kept up his punishing pace until they got to the edge of the tree line. Harry paused, taking her arm to draw her off the road to the closest tree.

"What are we doing?" she asked.

"We're waiting."

"For?"

There was a small single-story house up ahead. With a short porch and a pick-up parked outside, there didn't seem to be anything threatening about it.

"He's a man of science and a doctor," Harry murmured, his lips barely moving. "But he is Olympus."

Using his body to push her aside, he made sure she was behind the tree, unable to see the house, while he tucked his side against it. His arm curled around to his back toward the gun, though he didn't take it out.

"Meaning?" she whispered.

It was still daylight. The trees were cover, though she didn't relish the idea of losing herself in them if anything went wrong. The Beast was within running distance, but it would take some kind of expert move to turn the vehicle and its trailer around on such a narrow road flanked by trees. A get away wouldn't be easy, it definitely wouldn't be fast.

They stood in silence, waiting, listening to the distant sound of the occasional vehicle on the road they'd left behind not so long ago. She heard a bird, the burrow of some creature scratching around, wildlife, nature, nothing unexpected.

"Harry?" she said after a good two or three minutes.

"Shh," he said, holding a hand in front of her. "Just wait."

For something, she didn't know what. His focus was intent on the house, unflinching, never wavering. Another minute passed. Then another. Eventually, just as she was giving up hope of them ever moving, the creak and slide of a door opening piqued her interest. A smile slowly crept to Harry's lips.

"Got yourself in some trouble, Hades?" a voice called out. "Didn't think you'd be darkening my door any time soon… The girl a present?"

Her mouth opened in outrage, but Harry laughed. "Your gift was your life, remember? You wouldn't have it if it wasn't for me."

"This is no safe haven for you," the man called back. "He's looking for you."

"He'll find me when I want him to," Harry said, still half behind the tree. "Your work will continue… If you tell me what I need to know."

There was a pause.

A score of seconds went by, she waited, sensing Harry's anticipation. If that was Asclepius, they needed him to acquiesce, to let them in. It all depended on how much the man trusted Harry. Hence why she wasn't holding her breath.

"Then I guess you better get inside."

Harry's shoulders dropped, maybe in relief, and then he glanced at her. "Don't tell him who you are."

She frowned. "What?"

"No matter what happens, don't offer anything. You're an asset. That's it."

"But what if—"

"We want to learn information, not offer it. If he knows, he knows. If he figures it out, fine. But we don't tip our hand until it suits us."

Withhold until the optimum moment, no surprise that was Harry's attitude. She didn't feel like being exploited again anyway so nodded.

"All clear!"

The call came from the direction of the house again, she hadn't expected that Asclepius was still up there or that they needed to wait for anything to be clear. Her ignorance was another example of how far removed she was from the eminent Olympus agents.

Harry took her arm to pull her out from her hiding place. Asclepius had known she was there, even though she wasn't in view. Her father kept her tucked in close, his head moved as he took in their environment. Asclepius had given them the all clear, but apparently Harry wasn't too trusting of the doctor.

They passed the pick-up and went up the wooden stairs to cross the porch. What would they find inside? Her heart hammered so hard in her chest that the bass of it vibrated her eardrums.

Using his foot, Harry pushed open the door. The long hall ahead had a wooden floor with a frayed runner down the middle. There were knickknacks on the walls, nothing significant or particularly interesting. They crept inside, slowly, Harry absorbing everything. Three doors, one to the left, one at the end of the hall and another further along to the right. The last was open and it was the one Asclepius appeared from.

"In here."

With lingering trepidation, she let Harry lead her into the living room where Asclepius was waiting. The light space stretched from the front of the property to the back with a dining area to the rear. Asclepius opened a hand at the couch next to the door and went over to seat himself in an armchair by the fireplace.

Harry took his time about moving, probably still building a plan for escape, in case anything went wrong. Eventually, they were there, at the couch, and her father pushed her down to sit while he stayed on his feet.

"You're on edge, Harry," Asclepius said.

There was no hint of sympathy or even of annoyance.

The doctor stated fact, made an observation not meant to put Harry at ease or to aggravate him. Not that she could tell anyway.

"You know what's going on?" Harry asked.

"I've heard," Asclepius said, picking up a pipe from the rickety table at his side. "I always said his own arrogance would be enough to kill him."

"I remember him saying the same thing about you."

"No," Asclepius said, curling his fingers around the bowl of the pipe. "He said my arrogance would drive others to kill me... Something he tried himself."

"Yeah," Harry said. "And I don't have to tell you that if he gets Olympus back on its feet, you'll be on his hit list."

"I've survived on that list for a long time."

"Because you had me standing between you, diverting his attention to other things. Only way he gets back into power is if he eliminates the enemies in his way... that includes me."

Asclepius sat up straighter to twist away from them. She heard the pipe tap on something but couldn't see what he was doing. "This is not a safe haven," the doctor said. "If you came here hoping for shelter—"

"I would never come to you for shelter. You're no soldier."

"No," Asclepius said, raising his attention from what he was doing for just long enough to glance at Harry. "And I don't doubt yours is nearby."

His... soldier? Daire. Asclepius assumed that Daire was nearby. That was a good safety net for them. Hopefully, the invisible threat would keep the doctor from hurting them. If he knew what was good for him anyway... Unless he was trying to draw Daire out... She shook her head. Was that a valid suspicion or paranoia? Something about being there made her uneasy. It didn't seem right that the unassuming man sitting there putting his pipe back together was some evil Olympus agent. Except just that very fact was enough to pique her paranoia.

"Who else has been through here?"

Asclepius stopped pushing the stem of the pipe into

the bowl to look at Harry by the window. Between her and the window she noted, though couldn't quite believe he was doing that to protect her or provide cover. If anyone out there wanted to take a shot, Harry being put down wouldn't help her position in any way. She'd just be left there. Alone.

Suddenly, it seemed insane to have gone there without leaving Daire a hint. He'd track them eventually, but by then it could be too late.

"If I won't offer you shelter, why'd do you think I'd do it for Garrick?"

"Because he's more useful to you," Harry said. "Your passion relies on his... And I don't think you'd offer him shelter. Like you said, you're no soldier. The two of you together could never take down Zeus alone."

Still clutching the pipe, although it wasn't lit, Asclepius sank back in his chair. "You think we need you."

"I know you need me."

"Your pet would be more useful."

"Exactly why he's not here," Harry said. "Only one person comes out of this alive, me or Z. That's it. The rest of you might come or go, but if there's a battle, no way both of us walk out of it."

"What do you want, Hades?" Asclepius lost some of his ease. "You came here for a reason."

The doctor's attention crossed to her. She tried not to tense or squirm under the scrutiny, but it was difficult to be still while being examined.

"What does she have that I need?" Asclepius asked.

"Nothing," Harry said, stepping in front of her to interrupt the inspection.

"Then what does she have that you need," the doctor asked. "You don't take prisoners unless they're of use to you. She's not Olympus."

"She's here to hear a story, same reason I'm here."

"A story," Asclepius said with intrigue.

She couldn't see past Harry and didn't mind. There shouldn't be anything more innocuous than an isolated man in his humble home, separated from the masses of civilization. Yet, the place reminded her of horror movies. The simple home dweller offering their hospitality to the unsuspecting travelers. It was all too… easy. Her ears pricked, listening for sounds of scrabbling or screaming from the basement.

"You know what he wants, what Z wants. What he needs to pick up at Gamma."

"Yes," Asclepius said, surprising her with the warmth of his voice, though the laugh that followed was unsettling. "Oh, I should've known…" There was a long exhale and a pause. "Garrick has the answers too… Is there a reason you're not getting them from him?"

"He's in the wind."

"In the wind?" Asclepius asked. "Is that all? Should I assume he is with Z? If he hasn't offered his allegiance, you know he's already dead. Z has no patience and Garrick knows the buttons to push."

"So do I," Harry said in a growling promise that startled her. "Like I said, he's in the wind."

"Minotaur isn't your problem. Do you have the keys?" Harry didn't answer. Asclepius exhaled again. "You never think about what it took from you, Harry. Never stop to wonder if it maybe isn't just a better idea to let the whole thing go to shit."

"Walking away doesn't mean freedom."

"To which I can attest," Asclepius said. "Taking Z down would be a relief for us all. Is that your plan?"

"Talk to me about JARR."

Harry wasn't going to give away any of his plans, probably because the next major one would involve allowing Daire to execute Six. She didn't know if Asclepius had any love for the Six or what his relationship to them was. If he'd heard about the current issues in Olympus, that meant he had some kind of link to someone on the inside. Warning Six of what was coming could endanger Daire. She wouldn't let anyone put her Heart at risk.

TWENTY-THREE

"RELEASING JARR MEANS FREEING THE DATA," Asclepius said.

Harry moved aside to reverse and sit at her side, up close, forward in his seat, apparently ready to jump if it became necessary.

"I didn't come here to be told why I shouldn't do it," Harry said. "Even if I chose not to, Z would. Someone will gain control of it."

"The program that's running…? It's dangerous. Don't believe for a second you know everything it's been collecting all this time. For years, it's been searching for information, compiling data. The plan was always to wait until an algorithm could be written and hardware built to weaponize what it contained."

"Weaponize data," Harry said like he really hadn't known that.

She stayed on alert, choosing not to accept anything at face value.

Asclepius stared into the empty fireplace. "It was twenty-five years ago… It was only just becoming clear to everyone what Olympus truly was. None of us wanted to believe it."

She didn't know why he sounded so wistful or why the doctor was telling Harry who should've been around at the time.

"None of you believed what I said about Z," Harry said. "About the lengths he would go to."

"You were living it. You were the first one to face his determination... What he wanted, that control, it was impossible. No one could wield that much power. No one did. There was always someone out there somewhere ready to steal it away."

"JARR was developed without my input."

"JARR was developed while you were AWOL. Life with Helen might have been a great bliss for you, the rest of us suffered the consequences."

"Believe me, I suffered them to."

"Zeus wanted a way to control everyone and everything. Not just politics and business, he wanted to control the underworld, the terrorists, the greater population. Even if he collected every weapon there was, every nuke, there would always be a resistance. To control planet Earth, he'd have to destroy it. The easiest way to control people is to eliminate them. All of them. Except he needed a workforce, soldiers, breeders, anyone who could be of use to him. He couldn't have complete control without a method of manipulation."

"JARR was that method," she murmured.

The words came out of her mouth of their own accord and were enough to tear Asclepius's stare from the fireplace. "It knows something about everyone. It could know. We don't know what's in there. We don't know how much data it has collected or how much of it is of use. Its primary goal was to collect international data, anything that could help Z take control in a specific region. Any imminent threat would be sent to Minotaur, so agents could take care of it."

She knew that. Daire told her about the links between Minotaur and JARR.

"It wasn't supposed to be a weapon."

"Garrick had limited input. We had outside

contractors, agencies providing resources, even if they didn't know it. What started as a simple data storage solution soon became something else. The reach of it was unparalleled. With so many different people working on so many different parts without each knowing what the other was doing, it became impossible to track exactly what JARR was capable of. It became even harder when those resources were erased."

"Resources," she said. "People. You mean the people who worked on it were killed."

He nodded once. "That was Z's way. People need to breathe to share what's in their minds. They need blood and oxygen. Without them, no one is capable of revealing anything."

"What was the fuck up?" she asked. "Something went wrong, didn't it?"

"Yes," he said, his eyes narrowing. "The error came later. The error came in a test phase when we were attempting to secure the device to limit access. The concept harked back to Zeus's philosophy on sharing and death. JARR, though collecting data, is essentially dead. It can't share its data. It can't share what it knows."

"You have to give it life," Harry said. "It needs blood and oxygen."

The doctor smiled. "Exactly. Living blood. Developing a mechanism for testing was difficult. The access system tests not only genetic markers, it tests the enzymes in the blood to ensure it's living. It's not only interested in the oxygen, but in other factors that wouldn't be present in deceased blood."

"So that's what it is. Blood. Just blood?"

She'd known about the blood for a while. They were supposed to be there for details.

"Yes," Asclepius said, becoming confused though only for a moment. Clarity crept onto his expression, relaxing his features. Though she tried to avoid looking at him, she worried that only made her more conspicuous. "I am sitting here trying to figure out why Harry would so closely ally himself with a civilian. He hasn't brought his men here, to save their lives as much as mine."

Because if Zeus wanted to know where the doctor was and Harry wouldn't give it up, he'd turn his attention to the Olympus agents. If they didn't know the location, they couldn't reveal it. Maybe they hadn't known it at the time, but that decision was smart. Zeus had proven in Vegas that the agents were expendable as far as he was concerned.

"You know about compartmentalizing," Harry said. "How Olympus likes to divide information so no one person knows everything."

"Yes," Asclepius said on an inhale. "I do know about that. I know how it frustrated the principals. The agents were accustomed to it." There was a pause, a long one, before the doctor began stuffing his pipe. "No one person should know everything. I always thought that was an interesting distinction."

"That no one person should know everything while we developed a system to harvest information from global services?"

"Yes," Asclepius said. "There was a reason we chose the subject that we did. There was a level of irony in it or meant to be. No one person would have access to JARR providing the principals maintained control of their individual keys. Those need to be used too, just like for Minotaur. There is a precise procedure, the keys must be entered and turned in a specific sequence."

"What sequence?" Harry asked.

Asclepius continued without answering the question. "But those don't matter. They won't be accepted, nothing will, until after the system analyzes the blood of the gatekeeper. The one person who could, in theory, take and keep JARR… Of course, it would never work. The gatekeeper would be far too weak to extract JARR. They would need an accomplice."

"Too weak," Harry said. "Why? How much blood does this system of yours need?"

The frown on the doctor's face seemed incredulous. "I can't possibly take the risk of allowing it to fall into the hands of someone who could misuse it."

From what she had heard, there was no way to use JARR in the right way either. If it wasn't destroyed, there would always be the risk of it causing serious harm.

"If I can't get there to extract it before Z—"

"Zeus can't extract it," Asclepius said. "Even if he got there first, even if he has all the keys, he cannot extract JARR. If he attempts to, if anyone attempts to and doesn't use the right sequence or the right blood, the site will be destroyed entirely in under a minute. Obliterated. There would be no chance of escape. Zero."

Sinking back on the couch, Harry breathed out as his hand rose to his forehead. "It's tapped into the failsafes."

"Of course it is," the doctor said.

Daire had only told her pieces of what Olympus Beta was capable of. Outside, by the gate, explosives were buried beneath the ground. If anyone put in the wrong code requesting access, they'd be blown up. Something she hadn't known at the time, but he'd told her after. If there were explosives there, it stood to reason that they could be planted anywhere.

"Walk me through it," Harry said, sitting up again. "The JARR control room is accessible. We've all been in there. We need access to the coded panel by the operator station." Asclepius nodded, lighting a match to raise it to the pipe between his lips. "We don't know the code for that panel. Are the failsafes triggered if we input the wrong code?"

Asclepius took his time puffing on his pipe, lighting the thing, only then did he lower it. "Garrick has the code," he said. "I don't have it… Ares will know." That got the attention of both her and Harry. "He chose it."

"When he was eight years old?" she asked.

"That's right."

"How will he remember something from when he was eight years old?"

"He'll remember," Harry mumbled. It seemed his patience was thinning. "Why did you bring him into it?"

"He was supposed to be the subject," Asclepius said. "It was his blood that was supposed to grant access. Zeus agreed knowing that Ares was always likely to be with us. We didn't dream the system would go untouched for twenty-five years. I don't know about the delay, why there was a delay. I assumed that Zeus would have attempted to access it years ago. Of course, if he'd had Ares on site, it could've been accessed any time."

"You said supposed to be," she said. "That means it wasn't him. Ares wasn't the subject."

Settling deeper into his chair, the doctor puffed on his pipe. She didn't like the smell. Cigarette smoke would be worse, one small mercy. The voluminous smoke clouded their shared air. Anyone who smoked inside without asking the others in the room if they minded was rude as far as she was concerned. Though the house was his and it wasn't like they'd been invited.

"No," he said, fixating on her. "You have your mother's eyes, Pandora."

Horrified, her attention flew around to Harry, but he didn't flinch. The doctor was his target. "You used my daughter."

"Not on purpose," the doctor said. "She was a test subject, meant to be used to test the system we'd built. Ares was with her that day. We wanted to be sure that everything worked before using him as the final subject. We wouldn't have been able to tell if it worked if we'd used him for both the test and the finalization. We made it into a game for them."

"Where was Carrie?"

"This was before she was allowed access. You were on a mission, maybe you went to retrieve her, I can't remember now. Your daughter was under Ares's jurisdiction. We told him to bring her to the control room and he did. The whole process was monitored closely. The intention was always to test the system with her and finalize with Ares."

"You said that already," Harry growled. "Either way you were using my charges. What gave you the right—"

"Zeus gave us the right. We couldn't trust an agent and there would always be the chance of losing that individual on a mission in the field. Pandora and Ares were children. Yes, Ares was being trained, but like I said, JARR was never supposed to be sealed off for so long. I assume Zeus planned to use Ares to access it before he was sent overseas. Domestic missions, local, those were never as dangerous for him, not with you watching him so closely."

But with her and her mom on the run after they left Olympus, Zeus didn't have instant access to her. Therefore, he wouldn't have access to JARR.

"Why did he let us leave?" she asked. "If Zeus knew that I was tied in to JARR, why did he let Harry make the deal to—"

"He didn't know," Asclepius said, switching his focus to Harry. "It was years before Garrick told him about the mix-up."

"You still haven't told me how it happened."

The doctor took another hit from his pipe. "I don't know exactly. Garrick was on the workstation; I was dealing with the biology. She was hooked up to the system, we went through the steps, and then JARR was suddenly locked down, out of reach. Whatever the test protocol, it somehow got mixed up with the final execute and… that's what happened."

"I was tied to this, put in this position… by accident?" she asked.

Asclepius was slow to lower his pipe. "I am sorry. I'd say there was no excuse, but the whole thing was new. We were figuring it out as we went along. It was a mistake."

"Why not undo it?" she asked. "Just open the system up and do it over again."

"The three principals were set up to receive alerts when JARR was accessed. We couldn't do it there and then because frankly, you didn't have enough blood. We would've needed to wait weeks for you to regain your previous levels before taking another swing. By that time, your mother was on site and wouldn't let you out of her sight."

"And because Zeus didn't know, you couldn't demand that he force Carrie to give her up."

"It was a tense time," Asclepius said. "Zeus was on a knife edge. The situation between the two of you shortened his fuse. We didn't know there was ever a deal in the works. By the time we did, you'd taken Helen and Pandora away."

So because they'd fucked up, she'd become JARR's gatekeeper without either of her parents' knowledge or consent. Zeus couldn't be told about the fuck up or he might've blown a gasket… or ended someone. Asclepius and Garrick had feared him. They were too scared to stand up and admit a mistake, too scared to open the system knowing Zeus would get a notification.

It was possible, if Zeus was so unhinged, he wouldn't have believed his men about the why. Sure, JARR being closed for such a short period of time meant it couldn't have gathered much in the way of intelligence. Maybe he'd have thought his men were putting in some kind of back door so they could get in whenever they wanted.

She didn't know. A mistake made two and a half decades ago put her right in the middle of the principals, each with their own motivations and level of concern for her safety.

"Did Ares know?" she asked, reminding herself to use his code name. "About the screw up?"

"At the time, no," Asclepius said. "He was on a need to know. We told him to bring you to us, but nothing else about what we were doing."

"He probably thought it was a drill," Harry mumbled. "Or for the vault."

"Well, we had already taken her blood for the DNA analysis. Daire's is on record too. But you know what he's like, what he was like, he didn't ask questions, only did as he was told."

When she'd told her Heart about the blood, he hadn't seemed to instantly know about it. Though he had been the one to mention JARR, so it was possible he'd put the pieces together without telling her exactly how he'd come to that conclusion. If he remembered them using her blood, she'd like to think he'd have told her.

But he'd been eight years old. In a restrictive environment. How many weird and wonderful—and horrifying—things might he have seen at that age and younger? No one could remember every detail of being a child. Having been only two when Zeus first took her to Olympus, she had no memory of being there at all.

Sometimes when she heard the stories from that place, even when they included her, it felt like another world, like another person. Her mom hadn't given her any hints about what they'd gone through or her father's identity. JARR was beyond her mother's orbit. Even Harry didn't seem to know the details and he was an Olympus principal, at the top of the tree. Considering that, what chance did she and her mother have of being clued in? None.

"I have plenty of stores, I can make some food," the doctor said. "And you should stay the night. I can't offer shelter beyond that. It's too dangerous. You won't be protected here."

"If Zeus has Garrick, he won't need you."

"No. If he doesn't, then we should all be worried," Asclepius said. "Though, like you said, he will come for me once he regains control."

"We won't allow him to regain control," Harry said. "It's too dangerous for all of us."

"Not just us in Olympus," Asclepius said, taking another draw from his pipe then setting it down on the little table. "Excuse me."

He got up and strode to, she guessed, the kitchen, going through the back dining space and disappearing into another room.

"I don't want to stay," she murmured. "It's too dangerous."

"If we go to Beta, without knowing how to extract JARR, we're all as good as dead."

"Garrick knows," she said, keeping her volume low. "Asclepius said so."

Harry twisted to make eye contact. "He could be dead or already working with Zeus. We don't know."

"Why didn't you talk about this with him?" she asked, frustrated by the missed opportunity. "You had the chance. In Vegas. Are you telling me that you and he didn't—"

"The only power he has is information," he hissed in response. "I did try to talk to him, about this and other things, but he's smart. Too smart. He won't tell me, and he won't tell Zeus. As soon as he's no longer useful, his life is at risk. Z doesn't know where Asclepius is, at least he didn't, I don't know what he knows now. Garrick is an easier mark for him."

"If we don't know where Garrick is, Zeus doesn't know."

"All of us are heading towards the same objective right now," Harry said. "The finish line is at the beta site. We get there first, make the extraction, and maybe we'll be safe. If we get there after…"

"I can't," she said, accepting the new intelligence. "I can't be there after because apparently he needs me to bleed into this machine to get what he wants."

Harry hooked a hand around the side of her face. "I won't let him use you."

No, because if he did, Z would have one up on him. Daire had promised no one would hurt her while he was around, her father was less specific about her wellbeing.

"What do you want to do with it?" she asked, needing some reassurance for the human race beyond what might happen to her. "If you get your hands on JARR, what are you going to do with it?"

He didn't reply. Gamma was setup, presumably, to accept the device. That would mean allowing Harry, and anyone else in his faction, to access the data. If Zeus got hold of JARR, Gamma would be his goal for sure.

If Harry went there to install it, not only would he have access, but unless Zeus was dead, he could always come and take over.

"We can't take the risk that it could be used to hurt people."

All along, she'd said she didn't trust her father. Sitting there, looking into him, she couldn't work out if she wanted him to get his hands on JARR anymore than she wanted Zeus to have control of it.

"Let's just take this slow," Harry said, giving her knee a condescending pat as he slid off the couch to go after Asclepius.

Her eye was drawn to the smoke rising from the pipe propped in a little stand on the table by Asclepius's chair. She wasn't safe, but knowing the determination of the players, would she be safe anywhere?

TWENTY-FOUR

HARRY SEEMED DETERMINED to stay the night with the doctor. The two men remained in the kitchen until after the pipe stopped smoking and the sky darkened.

There were medical books piled behind Asclepius's chair. She didn't look much closer than that. Both because understanding them would be beyond her and because if she snooped, she didn't place much faith in her ability to put everything back how it had been. Daire would know how to do it; she needed to ask for lessons in super-sleuthing the next time they were together.

Seconds after she went out onto the porch for some air, Harry appeared in the front doorway to tell her dinner was ready. He also chastised her for wandering without permission. His permission, not their host's. It had been on the tip of her tongue to tell him not to wander off and leave her on her own if he wanted her to stay put. But by the time he was done nagging at her, they were at the dining table and Asclepius was serving some sort of casserole.

While the men discussed previous missions between long silences, she wondered if their meal was Omega friendly. The men were still guarded. Even though Harry apparently saved Asclepius from Zeus's displeasure, there wasn't a burning loyalty. It was odd. She almost felt as though they liked each other, maybe they wanted to trust, but it just wasn't there.

In the beta control room, Daire had been about as mad with Harry as she'd seen anyone. Except it hadn't taken long for their camaraderie to return. The respect was always there.

The two men breaking bread with her treated each other with respect, guarded respect. Whether that was rooted in a place of genuine comradeship or dubious wariness, she didn't know.

After dinner, they had coffee. Night had descended. Another night away from her Heart.

The only way to stomach it was to make it worth it. If she didn't do something, she'd give into her urge to flee. The Beast was close. Her home was right there, she wanted to be ensconced in it. In the Beast, she was closest to Daire. In his bed. Their bed. That was the only place she wanted to be if she didn't have the sanctuary of his arms.

"Why did Zeus want to kill you, doctor?" she asked, breaking another of the protracted silences.

Harry and Asclepius both looked at her, but she wasn't for budging and kept her focus on the man opposite her father.

Asclepius glanced at the man next to her. "I suppose there was a lot to catch up on. Some things must have slipped through the net. How much does she know about Olympus history?"

"*She* is sitting here," she said. "It doesn't matter what I already know, please answer the question."

The doctor waited for the nod from Harry. Even without checking, she could tell that her father was reluctant. If he hadn't been so clear in telling her not to mention Daire in relation to her, she'd remind Harry that her Heart would tell her if he was around.

Withholding was just crazy when they had the opportunity to probe into Asclepius's nature and perspective. Finding out from Daire in a couple of days was great for her curiosity, but it wouldn't benefit her Heart. She wanted to be of benefit to him always.

"She's tenacious," Harry said on a sigh, a parent at the end of his rope.

"Like her father," Asclepius said with amusement. "It's interesting to learn how many of her traits are genetic. She didn't grow up with you, eliminating nurture."

"I spent eighteen months with her before she was taken."

"Yes," Asclepius said, becoming more discerning. "Is it genetics or do they imprint that young and adopt qualities that continue for a lifetime?"

"My mother was determined," she said, unsure if she wanted to be compared to her father or share qualities with him. "She taught me that I have value. I don't need anyone else to give it to me. My questions are as valid as anyone else's."

"They may be," the doctor said. "But you have to be careful about asking questions you don't want the answers to."

Harry laughed. "I've given her that speech. She never listens, she doesn't get it."

"I can be patronized from all corners," she said. "It doesn't daunt me. I know what I want. So talk over me, dismiss me, try to pretend I don't exist, whatever you want. But I will continue to rise. I won't be marginalized just because you both think you're older and wiser."

It took a score of seconds, but eventually Harry gave a brief, subtle nod.

The doctor took his time about relaxing his posture. "I worked with Olympus for years. I did as I was told. Our breakthroughs were incredible. To have access to resources and capital like that… it's seductive. It didn't help that we lived so far off the grid. Our isolation gave us great latitude, but it also skewed our perspectives."

"Fascinating, but it's not an answer to my question."

"No," he said, laying a smile on Harry that suggested he was impressed. "Over the years, I built an extensive archive of data. Useful data. Money and resources may not have been in short supply, but to advance my research I needed test subjects. A larger scale project that would allow me to examine the effects of different variables."

She didn't understand. That could be because she hadn't processed much beyond the words "test subjects." Shocking as it was, she couldn't figure out why Zeus would have a problem with it. Anything that would enrich Olympus sounded like it would be right up his alley, regardless of who it hurt.

"Doesn't seem like you're doing that here." Something passed between him and Harry. "Keep your secrets if you want, but don't be surprised when I tell you to go to hell if you need something from me in the future." She paused to let that sink in. "And if you remember our conversation this afternoon, my compliance is going to be important to someone soon."

"There's something we didn't discuss," Asclepius said. "Your compliance is optional. Your blood has to be living, that doesn't mean you have to be conscious."

"But she can't have drugs in her system surely? The system would be able to detect them."

"There are... options. Specific options. Some markers are allowed, others would lead to an instant fail," the doctor said. "The thinking was that even if someone was injured or ill, they could be kept alive to..."

"Be used to access JARR," she said outraged for her Heart. She flipped around to glare at Harry. "You know who he's talking about? Who his subject was supposed to be?" Her father's reaction was subdued. No, it was invisible. Which only infuriated her further. "Do you care about him at all?"

"Clearly you do," Asclepius said. "Or are you so compassionate about all humankind?"

As Harry reminded her before they entered, they weren't there to give out intel. "I don't like anyone who disregards human life. You knew there was a chance of your subject being hurt and rather than worry about combatting that, you found a solution that would allow you access to your ones and zeros. Can't you see that's sick? The technology was more important. The data more important than a living, breathing human being."

"Seems you have a problem with the greater good."

The damn greater good, which had caused her to step aside for Daire so he could be with Olympus. That greater good might be more important than one person or relationship, that was undeniable, but it wasn't what Olympus was fighting for anymore. Olympus was fighting an internal battle that benefited no one except the victor.

"Do you know who doesn't have a problem with the greater good?" she asked, thinking it was better to get the conversation away from Daire as quickly as possible. She'd never be able to hold her tongue if it continued. "Zeus. If you had some evil plan to use your work to make upgrades or improve the Olympus situation, there's no way I believe Zeus had a problem with it."

"Zeus has a problem with the greatest threat to Olympus," Harry said in a drawl that made her think she should know what he was talking about.

It took her a minute, but she got there eventually. "Exposure."

"That's right," Asclepius said. "He believed scaling up the trials would increase the chances of being discovered."

"He wasn't wrong," Harry said. "Building a facility, you'd need staff, and it would have to be near a population center if you wanted people from across the social and medical spectrum."

"What I was doing," Asclepius said, his jaw tightening. "It was important to more than just Olympus. My work had the potential to help the human race ease suffering."

"Yeah, and it would've been a great money train. You start your own medical company, make progress and, eventually, you'd make money."

"Which the Six wouldn't like," she said, seeking confirmation from both men. "They didn't want you to do it either."

"If Olympus created its own profit, we'd have more autonomy."

It was something. Zeus didn't want Olympus to be exposed because he liked being king of his own empire. Even if Asclepius's plan did risk exposure, she had a feeling that was a risk Zeus might have balanced if it meant increasing the size of his empire.

But everything had to be cleared through the Six. They liked their positions of power too much to risk the monster they'd created becoming independent. The whole mess of an organization was built by power-hungry egomaniacs who believed they had the right to not only play God, but to, apparently, improve on his original design.

"What you're suggesting is that you made revelations in your work that could combat human disease," she said, receiving a slow nod from the doctor. "Why not go public? I mean now you're out here in the middle of nowhere, living a simple life, what do you have to lose?"

"My life," Asclepius said. "It's not selfish either. If I try to fly above Olympus and reveal what I know, my wings will melt." And he'd plummet to his death. "Then what happens to my work?"

"Garrick must know where it is… You must have kept records."

"Some, yes. But Olympus teaches us that intel is—"

"The key to survival, I know."

So he hadn't committed his secrets to paper because as long as they only existed in his head, he had value. Smart. Most people might assume that the key to saving people from suffering should be worth more than an individual life.

"What I know, if it were to fall into the wrong hands, it could be very dangerous."

"I've heard that before," she mumbled, curving a hand around her coffee cup while looking over her shoulder at her father. "You accused me of making a mess. Yours has been in the making for decades."

"It's a dangerous balance," Harry said. "We have all made sacrifices… and we make decisions based on what we think is best. It's not an exact science."

"If it was, I would've conquered it by now and I'd be the one in charge," Asclepius said, maybe in an attempt at a joke. Another silence stretched for a minute or two before the doctor broke it. "Since I answered your question, it seems only fair that you should answer one of mine, Pandora."

He was looking at her. Right at her. "What?"

She wouldn't make any promises about answering but was curious what he wanted to know.

"Where is your mother?"

She tensed. Questions about her mother weren't her favorite to field. With a stranger, who she didn't trust, and her father at her side, she wasn't sure her mood would hold up to reasoned discussion.

"Not here," she said.

His attention switched to Harry. "The only reason you would be alone with your daughter is if Helen is dead." He didn't wait for confirmation. "Whoever is responsible for that wanted to weaken your daughter."

"It was an accident," she said, though the possibility of her mother's death being caused by a deliberate act was never far from her psyche.

"If that is true, it was the most fortuitous timing. With Zulu and the demise of the beta site, anyone who knew anything about Olympus had to be aware that Minotaur would have to be extracted. Most of the agents are aware of JARR, few of them would know Pandora's blood was required to remove it."

"Who knew?" Harry asked.

Asclepius sank back in his chair, sucking in a breath through his teeth. "We did. Garrick. Zeus."

"If Garrick and Zeus knew where she was at the time of Carrie's accident, they would've taken Pandora immediately."

Or they would've followed her and Daire across the country and back. It wouldn't surprise her if someone was too afraid to approach her while Daire was in her periphery. It would surprise her to learn that Daire didn't notice someone following them for thousands and thousands of miles over the course of a month.

Even after that, she'd been with her father and Daire. Since they joined up with Garrick, people had been around her almost all the time. Olympus-trained people. Trying to abduct her or tempt her away from the Vegas house would've been dangerous. Daire's security should've picked up on them being monitored too. As far as she knew, there hadn't been any imminent threats like that.

Perhaps Zeus having her brought to London was the move. Maybe he'd been monitoring her and hadn't approached because he could have her delivered. That would mean both Three and One were involved. Except there was a major flaw in that theory: her trip to London was a long time after her mother was lost.

"The Six..." she said, thinking about how she'd learned of the requirement for her blood. "Some of them are aware of what's required for JARR. I don't know exactly who or precisely what they know, but I heard Zeus discussing it with them."

"If the Six know then it could be anyone," Asclepius said. "They have access to all kinds of people. If they hired someone or recruited a private team... mercs wouldn't have to know the why, only the who."

The idea of a private team watching her and her mother and subsequently being responsible for her mother's death was unnerving. Except she couldn't get past the same obstacle. Daire. There was no way he'd have missed someone, or several someones, on their tail. The sex had been distracting, but not that distracting.

There were opportunities for people to approach her too. Since her mom's death, she'd been alone a bunch of times. Though, Daire had shown that she wasn't always as alone as she thought. Her date with Patrick being a prime example. Maybe Daire had noticed and hadn't said anything because he didn't want to scare her. Maybe he'd been tailing her, watching her, all those times she thought she was by herself.

"Watch your back, that's all I'm saying," Asclepius said. "Whoever reaches JARR first, whoever gets there first, they're the new leader. That's not a role many people would refuse."

"Would you?" she asked, still suspicious of the doctor. "Out here all alone, it must be frustrating to know what you'd be capable of, what you might achieve if you were given free rein. The kind of free rein you could give yourself if you were in charge."

"Tess—"

"No, Harry, it's okay," the doctor said. "I can only imagine what you've been through. I don't know what your mother told you about Olympus and your father, but I'd suppose that recently you'll have learned a lot that you didn't know before."

"More condescension," she said, keeping her shoulders straight.

"No," he said, shaking his head. "I admire you being suspicious. It's only right that you should be wary. We don't know each other and what you learned today won't have put you at ease about what kind of person I am. You shouldn't trust anyone right now. Though, I'm sorry to say, it's unlikely you'll survive what's coming. You'll be put at risk for JARR and once that's free, you'll be of no more use." She swallowed because some part of her knew he was right. "Unfortunately for you, you don't have any intel that's worth keeping you alive for."

"That won't happen," Harry said. "Zeus is the only one who'd think about hurting her and that won't happen as long as I'm around."

Asclepius smiled. "Sweet of you to say. I know better than most what you're capable of. You've protected your daughter all her life, but without Carrie around to keep her on the move, she'll have to stay still and that target on her back isn't going anywhere any time soon. Even if you take Z down, you'll still have the Six to deal with. I am assuming you plan to resume Olympus's work if you triumph… How else could you offer me the chance to continue my work?"

So that was the deal they'd struck? The doctor's help for guarantees he'd be allowed to do what he wanted when Olympus was back on its feet. Her father had made vague reference to that outside. The doctor wouldn't hang his hat on something so undefined. All that time they'd spent alone in the kitchen took on new meaning.

Maybe she should've followed them to find out exactly what had been promised in exchange for their meal and conversation.

"It's getting late," Asclepius said, rising from the

table. "Let me show you to your rooms."

She didn't know the exact time. Under normal circumstances, she'd offer to help with the clean-up in the kitchen. She waited to hear Harry say that they wouldn't be staying. Instead, he stood up. Expectation hung in the air as both men lingered for her to follow suit.

As she stood, she thought about Daire. Four days. That's what he'd said. If she didn't see him the following day when the four days were up, she'd go after him herself. Not because she thought he was in trouble, but because she had a lot to say. Some of it he'd want to hear, some of it would be less palatable. But he was her sounding board and her compass, she had to share with him. He'd give her some much needed perspective.

TWENTY-FIVE

SLEEP WAS SUCH A FICKLE THING. Though her bones tingled and her mind spun, she wanted to sleep. But it wouldn't come. Lying in the dark, staring at the ceiling, her Heart wouldn't leave her head. Where was he? Close to being at her side? He better be close. She didn't like it when they were apart. Without him, a piece of her was missing.

The hallway off Asclepius's dining area led to the bedrooms and a bathroom. The Beast was so close. Right there. It didn't make sense that Harry wanted them to sleep in the doctor's house when they had their own base on wheels not so far away.

She'd tuned out external noises a while ago and instead focused on the rhythm of her own heart. The house was silent. It had been, probably for hours. The darkness, the thick, uncomfortable air, everything built to an unnerving combination. Even the twin bed wasn't comfortable. The mattress springs prodded her spine and the thin, dusty comforter had seen better days.

In hope of getting at least some sleep, she considered going to the Beast. Harry had the keys, and she guessed he was in a room off the same hallway as her, so she could sneak in and look for them. While building herself up to move, a creaking floorboard distracted her attention. She waited, braced to hear another creak, wondering whether it would be further away or closer.

She waited so long that she started to think it was maybe just the house. It could be old, it sure wasn't new. That could mean old pipes, animals scurrying around under the house, or maybe even in the house. Her speculation at least put a smile on her face. Only because it led her to thinking about Daire. Being in an old house, filled with suspect noises would drive him batty.

In the Beast, sometimes he'd go check out the noises from the wilderness around them. At least in their home, he could basically see the whole interior from the bed. So he could wake up, look around, and be able to tell whether they were safe. It was tough to sneak into an Airstream. Especially one that was always locked up tight and she was sure he had his own custom locks on the windows.

Her mind wandered until she heard something else. Not so much heard as saw. The handle on the door at the other side of the room moved. She had a split second to decide: fake sleep or sit up? She went with the latter. It was likely Harry coming in to tell her she'd done something wrong. With the comforter pooled around her hips, she watched the handle continue down one tiny increment at a time.

Once it stopped, it stayed there for what seemed like a lifetime. Awareness prickled the back of her neck. It was wrong. Whoever that was, whatever was happening, it didn't feel right. No one who had nothing to hide would loiter before walking into a room.

She held her breath as the door began to open. Just like she'd thought, it was a damn horror movie house. Some stupid part of her wanted it to be Daire. Wanted to believe he'd found her and somehow known where she was. Except it couldn't be. He had the skill to find her, sure, but when her love was near, she felt him. Daire's presence wouldn't put her so on edge.

The door kept moving and she waited. Tempted to call out, she fought to stay quiet. If Harry wanted them to sneak out for some reason, she didn't want to be the one to foil the plan. Especially when it was one she'd embrace. The sooner they got out of the creepy place, the better.

Waiting, hoping for a positive, her hopes were dashed when the doctor came into view. Her lips parted, taking in a silent breath. He stopped, probably startled to see her sitting up.

"What's going on?" she asked, without quietening her voice at all. "What are you doing here?"

"I thought you would be asleep," he said, leaving the door open, but coming deeper into the room.

"Stay there," she said, tossing the comforter aside to throw her legs off the edge of the bed. "You shouldn't be in here. What kind of host creeps into a female guest's room at night?"

"You're valuable, Pandora."

He snuck closer, raising his arm. He was subduing his voice, which screamed his intention.

Thrusting to her feet, she opened her mouth wide to shout. "Harry!"

"He can't hear you," Asclepius said. "We had a nightcap before bed. His contained a little something extra… takes a while to work, but I checked on him just now. He won't be bothering us."

A chill of fear went through her. "You killed him."

For some reason that bothered her more, felt more real, than what she'd experienced on learning of the Vegas explosion.

Asclepius laughed. "No. Unlike some, I value my life. Killing him would immediately mobilize Ares. Harry has enough pull with his men already, we don't need to make a martyr of him."

"We?" she asked, trying to figure out if making a run for it was feasible. "Who is we?"

Jumping out the window or even getting to the front door wouldn't be much help. Until the trees there was no cover. She didn't know how good a shot he was or who else might be on the property ready to take her down.

"I don't want to cause trouble," he said, edging nearer. "I don't want to hurt you. This is necessary. You understand, don't you? My work is important."

Backing off, she was cornered with the bed and nightstand at her back. The nearby window was closed. She rushed over to try opening it, figuring an attempt was better than giving in.

The doctor ran up behind her and before she could even turn around, something pricked the back of her shoulder. Damnit.

"Relax," Asclepius said as she flung herself around, throwing both fists into his body. "Just let it work."

Her head was spinning. "Let what work?" she asked, her mouth drying out.

Albany shot her with a tranquilizer once. It had worked fast. Right then, she couldn't see straight, her blurred eyes and dizziness caused her to grab for something steadying. But she was upright, still on her feet, not out like she'd been after Albany's shot.

"Just something that will help you relax," he said. "It won't knock you out, you'll stay conscious."

Which could be a blessing or a curse. Did she want to be awake while God knew what was done to her?

"You'll regret this," she said, kind of hearing the slur in her words.

It was like being drunk, slower and heavier, but drunk. Very drunk. Someone took her arm, she guessed the doctor, but her thoughts were beginning to merge and swirl.

"You're the only chance I have," he said, his grip tightening on her forearms. "Harry is capable, but he won't go as far as Ulysses. The victor has to want it more than anything. They have to love the power more than anything else in the world."

Her feet were moving. Dragging and slow, they took her forward, out of the room, she thought. Following their progress was difficult when her eyes were still unfocused.

"You're taking me to… Harry will win."

"No," Asclepius said. "He can't win. Not while he loves you. You're his weakness. Even if he comes close, he won't have the instinct needed to sacrifice everything, to give up everything for Olympus. That's why he cannot be in charge. He cannot win. Even if he takes down Zeus, do you think the Six will let Harry run things? He has too much humanity, too much compassion. Ares has yet to prove himself to them. It's possible they will give it to him."

It took some effort to force words from her tightening throat. "Then take me to… to Ares… Take me to him."

She couldn't keep going, couldn't let the spinning continue. Closing her eyes, she dropped to the side, grateful that there was a wall there to hold her up.

"I can't. I don't know where he is and will never find him."

That wasn't true. The doctor would find him in a snap… rather her love would find him. As soon as Daire heard who had her, what happened, he'd dedicate his life to tracking her down.

"You know… Zeus, you're taking me to… to Zeus."

"I'll get a message to him. Let him know I have you. Don't you see it's the only way? I trade you for my work. A chance to return to what was and to explore what could be. Zeus wants the world now. When he gets JARR, when he has access to all that it can offer, exposure will be the least of his worries. Anyone who even thinks to cross him, to go after him, he'll use JARR against them. JARR gives him the power, which means I can have it too."

"He'll never…" Tugging on her arm, she couldn't find any of her strength. Dropping her shoulder from the wall to give it the weight of her back, she couldn't get her arms out of the doctor's grasp. "Z will never let you have it… He won't want to… It's blackmail."

"It's business. Business that he understands," Asclepius said. "A trade. You for my work, it's as simple as that."

Licking her lips, her head lolled on the wall, trying to combat the spinning. "You said yours…yourself… he… he'll kill me when he's done with me."

"He'll kill you anyway, Pandora. With this trade, your death won't be meaningless. I'll be able to save humanity. Cure disease. Ease suffering. All because of you. Because your sacrifice—"

"I don't wanna sacrifice!"

Her exclamation came out more petulant than she'd intended. Given that she didn't have complete control of herself, that was forgivable.

"Would you rather he kill you for nothing? That your death should mean nothing?"

She forced herself to open her eyes, intending to look into his. The shadows around them and the fuzziness of her gaze, it just wasn't possible.

"It doesn't matter how many people you save, how much progress you make," she said, using every ounce of her breath to get the words out, though it felt like her heart was about to burst out of her chest. "He'll kill twice as many as you save, torture as many people as you protect… You'll never win."

"Maybe," he said, wrenching her hard to force her off the wall. "But it's what I live for… I need to do it. I need to finish my work."

"It's never finished," she said, unable to resist when he yanked and tugged, pulling her through the house.

There was something of a breeze and then her legs disappeared from under her. Collapsing as they crumpled, she bumped and rolled down something hard only to land on loose dirt. It was nice. Being on the ground. It was still spinning, but at least her head didn't hurt down there.

Her eyes began to close. He'd said that she wouldn't pass out. Sickness welled in her throat. Passing out didn't sound like such a bad prospect. With the tingling in her skin and the nausea roiling her belly, she would rather sleep through whatever was about to happen.

Just another sign that she wasn't in her right mind. She should want to be aware and ready to fight back. Trouble was, her body ached, pins and needles trembled in her fingertips and toes, she wanted to sleep. To curl up right there and give in to the abyss of slumber.

"Up," Asclepius hissed.

She only knew it was him because he was about the only person she could remember. He'd been there with her, and for a second, she couldn't remember that anyone else existed.

Her arm began to ache, though it took some time to realize that was because he was tugging on her. His grip bit into her upper arm. She tried to pull away, tried even to turn over. It was ridiculous, she couldn't even tell which way was up.

The yanking, the dragging of his flesh on hers, burned. If she was thinking, she would kick out. As it was, all she could do was be moved when he fought to get her on her knees.

He wanted her up because he wanted to move. Were they going somewhere in his truck? That would mean driving by the Beast. Her Beast.

"No," she grumbled. "No, I can't… I won't."

Her home gave her hope. She couldn't kid herself there was any hope of her making a run for it. If she could get there, the Beast would keep her safe. Somehow. But she couldn't even get her feet under her. Running was a pipe dream.

"You've gotta move. You don't move, I'll drag you."

The doctor wasn't as calm and benign as he'd probably want her to believe. Like she'd thought when they were approaching the house. He was Olympus. Apparently, he hadn't missed the course on how to hoodwink people.

Her palm cut on the loose grit beneath them. Pushing up, she ignored the quaking of her arms.

"Move!" Asclepius called.

He might think he was dialing up the scary. He wasn't. Not compared to some of what she'd faced. Or that could be the drugs.

He hauled her up to her feet, showing that he did have some physical strength. Against her will, she clung to him, seeking a steadying force.

Everything was fuzzy. Everything confused. Where were her hands? Where were his? What was holding her up? Was she in pain or hurt? Focusing was impossible.

"Let her go."

The sudden sound of a deep voice brought her head

swinging around. After a few blinks and through a few speckling stars, she made out a shape over the back of the truck parked a few feet away. Someone was standing on the opposite side of the truck-bed. Someone…

"Harry," she whispered.

A jolt went through her. Something solid smacked into her back… or she smacked into it.

"How did you… I checked you were out."

"You think I'd be stupid enough to drink anything I didn't see you pour? Anything you didn't share? Not when my daughter's life is on the line. You fucker, I gave you your life."

"Yeah, and what is it worth without my work? You saved me so I could do this. So I could do good."

"This isn't good. This isn't why I gave you your life."

She stumbled when her captor tugged her sideways. His forearm closed around her throat, stalling her breath.

"Let her fucking go or I'll take what I gave you."

"You can't," Asclepius said. "You need me. You need me and I need her."

"I need her more than I need you."

"No," Asclepius said, some hope in his voice. "Think this through, I take her to Z, we get JARR and then if you get a chance to take him down, do it."

"And you think I'd let you fall back into ranks after this? You want to take my daughter, hand her to the enemy who plans to use and kill her. And you think I won't skin you alive first chance I get?"

"You can't do it without me," Asclepius said. Though there was a thread of desperation, she was sure—though her head was whirling—that his confidence was almost optimistic. "We can work together. We can do this together… Think about it, think about how this could work, what we could build."

"If you think I'd agree to any strategy that involved anyone handing my daughter over to Z, you're fucking crazy. But you do fucking know it… You wouldn't have tried drugging me and taking her from me if you thought you had any chance of convincing me."

"You're emotional, Harry," Asclepius said, his voice

deeper. "Emotions make you weak. You never understood it. Always got yourself attached."

Was he berating her father? Her eyes were closing, her blinks lengthening, Tess pulled in a long breath and tried to push away. If she passed out, anything could happen. She needed to fight for herself. Fight for her freedom.

"No," she said, pushing her shoulders back, using her elbows to put some distance between their bodies.

He was behind her. Holding her. She didn't want to be his prey or anyone's weakness. Her father's, Daire's, no one. If struggling ended her life, at least she would leave the Earth a fighter.

"Stop," Asclepius hissed. "Stop it!"

He tugged her hard and as her form hit his again, something jagged into the side of her neck.

"No!" Harry barked, seeing more than she could. "Another dose could kill her."

"Yeah," Asclepius snarled. "Or it could waste her brain. A vegetable is just fine, as long as she's alive."

The pressure on her neck grew until something pierced her skin. Just like inside, the feeling was the same. Another dose. That's what they were talking about, he was going to inject her with whatever was sending her kooky, again.

"You're crazy," Harry growled, side-stepping toward the end of the truck that provided him cover. "You've lost your goddamn mind."

"No, I'm alive. Invigorated. Excited about the future. If your daughter is the price for—"

A single bang startled her. For a second, her mind was alert. Asclepius was silent, she guessed the sound had surprised him too. Except the pressure on her neck lessened, something dragged and then there was another sound. Like one she'd heard before... when Daire came upon her and Leonard in the desert house garage.

No one was holding her anymore. Her arms were free, her body loose. Confused, trying to figure out what was going on and what had happened, she swung one way and then the other. The wobble of her clumsy movement almost threatened to bring up some of the sickness roiling in her gut. All of that was forgotten when she saw the body on the ground. Asclepius's body... blood darkening the dry, pale ground around him. Moonlight, spotlighting his form.

"Oh my God," she whispered.

"Light-Sprite."

The close voice brought her around fast, too fast, she grabbed for him before she was even sure he was there. The sting on her neck ebbed to a buzz just a fraction of a second before she fell forward. Rather than hit the dirt, something hard dug into her gut and then she was lifted off her feet.

"Harry," she murmured, the ground bouncing... or maybe that was her. "I... I..."

"Don't talk," he said, his voice coming from an angle she couldn't understand. "You're safe. Close your eyes... I'm getting us out of here."

Whether it was following orders or giving in to the heaviness consuming her, she did as he suggested and closed her eyes. Asclepius... she didn't understand what had happened or where they were going, but Harry had her, he said they were safe. In her current state, not trusting him just wasn't an option.

TWENTY-SIX

THERE WERE VOICES. What day was it? Where was she? Not that it mattered. Her safety was guaranteed. She hadn't opened her eyes but didn't need to. Certainty of her safety was absolute. Why? Because the scent filling her senses and the soft comfort beneath her body told her one thing: she was in bed in the Beast.

She let herself just breathe. Let her muscles stay loose and breathed. The reason for her need to relax took her a minute to remember. The house... Asclepius's house. The night. The drug. She tried to move only for a pain to shoot through her head.

Rolling onto her back, she cupped her temple. What had happened? Hoping it would give her some more clarity, she opened her eyes. She stared at the ceiling, ignoring the light from the covered windows and the voices that had to originate somewhere.

They were quiet, muffled, almost inaudible. Their words were so distant she couldn't make them out. Only the rumble of deep intonations carried to her ears.

But she couldn't... not yet. Somehow, she knew

without trying that sitting up would be too much. Before she could move or pursue whoever was talking, she needed to replay her memories. Going to the doctor's, she remembered that. She remembered talking with him by the fireplace and even dinner.

After that, everything was hazy… She couldn't remember him coming to her room or drugging her. Yet, her mind told her it had happened. The fogginess, the confusion, she remembered some of that. Remembered the sensation of her limbs dragging and her balance wavering. She wasn't supposed to waver.

What had happened? How had she gotten free…? She couldn't remember. She couldn't remember that or how she'd come to be in the Beast. The safe space reassured her. It was possible she'd be happy to lay there for the rest of time. That satisfaction was obliterated when another thought came to mind.

"Daire."

Saying his name aloud clenched her core muscles and she sat up. Her hands flew out at her sides to grab for support as her balance wasn't quite all the way back yet.

The voices. The sound.

She frowned at the empty space before her. From her place in the middle of the bed, she could see right down the central passageway. No one was there. There was no sound from the shower or the bathroom opposite. No smells that suggested anything was cooking. No music. No TV.

"Daire," she said again, her voice louder.

Wherever she was, whatever was happening, Tess could only think of her Heart and her need to be with him, near him. That was her goal. Her only purpose.

The mission. Her memories were coming back slowly rather than in a rush. A trickle of information like a slow drip was increasing her urgency with every new detail she remembered.

Harry had been with her at the doctor's. He must have taken her from there. Maybe he hadn't. Maybe the whole thing had been a ruse meant to get her to Asclepius. She froze for a moment, trying to remember. When nothing came to mind, she pushed her knuckles into the center of her infuriating head.

"Remember," she whispered. "Please."

Heat and pressure began to build in her sinuses. She didn't want to break down. She didn't even know where she was or if she was someone's prisoner. Even her father was a potential suspect; she'd never trusted him.

Grabbing for the covers over her, she fought to free herself and wriggled to the edge of the bed. Adrenaline was beginning to warm her veins. She encouraged it, coveted it, because it could give her strength to free herself.

Pushing off the bed, she ignored the weakness of her limbs and forced herself to stand, to walk, to move. She forged down the trailer. Sickness hit her hard, stopping her dead. The weakness became instability and she grabbed for the kitchen counter, her eyes closing, her stomach churning.

"Daire," she whispered, reminding herself of her purpose.

Getting to him was all that mattered. Although she didn't know where he was, or even if she should know, her determination burned.

"You can do this," she said, her hands opening on the counter, flattening out to give herself a solid anchor point.

While she didn't have Daire, the Beast was the closest thing she had to family. The only thing she could rely on.

That reassurance was dented when a noise brought her head up. Before she could even breathe out, the trailer door flew open.

"Get the hell out of there!" a man yelled just a fraction of a second before someone planted a foot on the threshold to boost themselves inside.

Her wide eyes fixated and focused to identify him. The moment they did, a long, relieved breath escaped her lips.

"Daire."

Stepping away from the counter, she intended to go to him, but her balance wasn't back. She wobbled, not that it mattered, Daire was right there scooping her up off her feet to carry her to the back of the trailer again.

When he laid her down on the bed and tried to slide

his arms away, she grabbed for him. "Don't go," she whispered. "Don't leave me."

"I'm not going anywhere, I'm staying right here."

Her hold didn't stop him from twisting around to lean off the edge of their bed. As long as he was still near to her, she wouldn't complain. One heavy boot hit the floor and then the other. He raised his legs onto the bed and reached over to pull the covers back across her body.

Enamored by his care and still sluggish, she didn't even notice there was anyone else around until her father spoke up.

"You have to let her rest." Her attention swung from her love to the man standing at the end of the bed. Harry. "You have to give her privacy."

"Rest she gets," Daire said, his fingers sliding from the side of her neck to her cleavage. His touch redirected her focus again, but the moment she looked at him, his fierce gaze leaped around to Harry. "Privacy is what you're going to give us. Now."

"Son—"

"Don't even try it. A scratch I said. I told you what would happen if she was hurt. Now you've got one chance to keep your life and that's if she lets you, old man. You don't give me the chance to talk to her, I won't take any chances with her safety, not again. Get out of here or I'll kill you here and now."

Harry's stern look landed on her for a heartbeat before he turned to stride out, slamming the door so hard the whole trailer shook.

Her Heart's expression softened as he watched his fingertips glide across her skin. He didn't ask a question, didn't probe her with a stare, he just... appreciated her.

"Did you get the processor?" she asked, recalling what had taken him from her. "The Titan processor, did you get it?"

He frowned, his caress pausing on the mound of her breast. "I don't care about the processor. You need to tell me what happened."

The clench of his jaw betrayed why he was avoiding

her gaze. It wasn't because he'd forgotten her body or even because he wanted to enjoy it. Sliding a hand over the stubble on his jaw, she drew his attention to hers.

"I love you," she murmured.

"I'm sorry, baby," he said, the truth of his painful guilt apparent in his tone. "I should never have left you. I can't trust anyone, not even Harry. Goddamnit, I told you my primary mission was keeping you safe and I failed. I keep failing you."

"I'm here," she said, stroking his face. "We're together. You didn't fail."

Curling his fingers around hers, he took her hand from his face. "Tell me what happened," he said. "Everything you remember."

She shook her head in the cradle of the pillow. "I can't… I don't…" Searching her memory, she pieced together what was still in there. "I remember Miami and you saying goodbye. Harry woke me up the next morning, said we were leaving. We packed up the truck and the Beast and got on the road."

"He took you to Asclepius?"

She licked her lips, still concentrating. "I remember we got there. The doctor let us in, we talked, we ate dinner, and then we went to bed."

"Why did you stay the night?" he asked on an incredulous rush of breath. "Why did you think that was a good idea? Where was the Beast?"

"I didn't think it was a good idea. Harry decided to stay, so we stayed… I don't know why, he didn't tell me. I went to bed and they stayed up a while… I think… I don't remember much after that. I remember I couldn't sleep and thought about going to the Beast, thought about you and how much I missed you."

"Little Red…" he whispered, pressing her hand to his chest. "He drugged you."

"I think so… For some reason, I think he came into my room and drugged me, but I… I can't remember. The details are… they aren't there."

"The Whist. It's a drug we've used for years. A drug

Olympus used for years. It's a sort of variation on a date-rape drug," he said, but quickly followed up. "Not that we ever used it for that."

She could believe Daire didn't. The idea of sex without consent would be abhorrent to him. Knowing what she did of Zeus and the lengths Olympus had gone to before, she wasn't so confident the idea hadn't at least occurred to other agents or the principals.

"Is it the same thing Albany used?"

He shook his head. "Not exactly. They're both derived from the same compound. Harry said Asclepius used the Whist," he said, then seemed to doubt himself. "Do you want me to draw your blood? We can get it tested if—"

"No," she said. "It doesn't matter. I just... whatever Albany shot into me, I slept for like almost a whole day... I don't know where we are or how long—"

"Styx and I contacted Harry early, he told us you were on the road. We haven't been here long; I haven't got all the details... He was telling us what happened, where he'd taken you, I heard you say my name. I needed to get to you. Needed to see you."

"Oh, baby," she said, sliding her hands up his body to fumble for his neck. "I missed you so much."

Though her mind was still sluggish, her body was coming around. She managed to sit up enough to link her hands at the back of his neck to pull up. Except as she went up, he came down and so she ended up lying down, nestled against him.

"I should fucking learn not to trust anyone else to keep you safe. Why did you go there? Huh? Why did you let him walk you into danger?"

"For you," she said, closing her eyes to press her face against him. "For us. We needed to know what my blood was for."

"And did you find out?"

"Yes," she said, loathed to push away, but she needed to see him while she said it. "In the JARR control room, he said there's a coded panel by the operator station... There's a code, he said you and Garrick were the only other two who knew it… If the wrong one is used, failsafes are triggered."

His brow lowered. "A code? That I'll know?"

She nodded. "You picked it… when you were eight." He blinked in surprise. "You were supposed to be the subject. I was meant to be the test subject. They wanted to make sure everything worked before locking it down for good. Only… something went wrong, they followed the wrong procedure by mistake. So I became the subject."

"When was this? When they had you?" She nodded. "What about your mom? Why didn't they tell Zeus?"

Licking her lips, she relaxed, preparing herself to talk. She told him everything that she could remember about the conversation in front of the fireplace and at the dinner table. Anything that came after was still fuzzy.

"All of the principals are notified," he said in a curious way.

Knowing him and his history, she could only assume one thing. "You want to use JARR to draw Zeus out." Like he had with the Echo entrance code and Harry. "You need to remember the code… and we'd have to find out the right order of the keys. You can't get payback if you're dead."

While it was her Heart's demise that she feared the most, she hadn't quite reached the end of the story yet.

"I'll remember," he muttered, his mind still working.

Tucking herself against him again, she absorbed his heat. "Once JARR is liberated, I won't be of use anymore."

"What does that mean?" he snapped, no longer distracted. He grabbed her shoulder to push her back. The scowl he wore definitely couldn't be attributed to patience or strategizing. "Tess?"

"No one will kill me while they need my blood for JARR. Afterwards, they won't need me alive anymore."

"You don't have to worry about that," he said, his determination set. "Z will be gone long before he gets anywhere near the beta site."

"That wasn't the deal," she said. "You only asked for Lowell."

"Harry knows Z needs to die."

"And then what?" she asked, thinking of the deal he'd

made with the doctor. "The way he and Asclepius were talking, it was like… Harry plans to pick up right where Zeus left off."

"We'll build something new," he said. Losing the scowl, he ran the back of his fingers down her cheek. "Asclepius and Garrick are the only two who know the procedure for extracting JARR, right?" She nodded. "Harry had to keep the doc sweet. Promising he'd get a chance to return to work was just Harry's way of getting what he needed."

Her Heart was sure. As she tried to doubt her father, something niggled at her. Something had happened. Something she was forgetting.

"Everything's getting more dangerous," she whispered. "With every day that goes by, we get closer to the possibility that…"

"What? We'll clean up this mess and be able to get on with our lives? Personally, I can't wait."

Dread moved her head in a shake. "Don't be eager. Don't look past right now. Please, my Heart. Please don't underestimate Zeus's desire to win… don't underestimate the Six."

Bowing lower, he brushed his nose across hers. "Don't underestimate how much I want us to be free. I'll do anything to keep you safe, anything to guarantee our future." His mouth touched hers, but she was still distracted by what they were facing. As if sensing her reluctance, Daire rose to meet her eye. "I meant what I said in the bar. Say the word and we're gone. If you want to run—"

"I don't want anything to happen to you," she said, opening a hand on his chest.

Something happening to her would end him. It would destroy him. She might put his value and safety above her own, but losing her, if she was killed, it would be the same to him as losing his own life.

"You know what I want?" he asked, the edge of his mouth ascending.

"Me, the Beast, and the open road."

He exhaled a laugh. "Got it first time, Little Red."

Daire kissed her again and squeezed her waist. "We're in bed and you're not trying to seduce me, Temptress… What are you not telling me?"

About his father. She hadn't been thinking about Richard Merrill, her mind had been on Olympus and the Six and what was to come. But when he'd posed that question, in that way, suddenly her omission came rushing back.

"There is something we have to talk about," she said, drawing a fingertip down his arm. "And I want to talk about my mom, about whether there was a chance what happened to her wasn't an accident."

Which she'd tried to raise with him in the Beast before Harry interrupted and took them out for burgers.

"There's a chance," he said. "Finding any responsible parties won't be easy."

"I am right though, right?" she asked. "You would've noticed if someone was tailing us back when you were Danny, wouldn't you? Or did you notice and just not tell me?"

There wasn't a chance for him to answer. The door opened and Daire sat up, sliding in one swift move to the end of the bed, putting her behind him. His whole form blocked the entrance to the bedroom when he stood up.

She heard her father's voice. "We got word from Garrick."

TWENTY-SEVEN

"WORD?" DAIRE ASKED. "What word? Where is he? Who's he got?"

"They were south of the border. Hit some trouble of their own," Harry said. "I didn't get the details."

Sitting up, she pushed her fists into the mattress to boost herself toward the foot of the bed.

"At least we know he's alive," Styx said.

She stopped. It wasn't Styx's presence… it was… something else. Focusing on Daire's back, she tuned out the men's conversation, trying to figure out what was still niggling at her.

In a flash, a memory hit her. Hard. So hard that she gasped.

Daire stopped talking to turn around and look at her. "Babe?"

Quickly scooching down the bed, she grabbed for him to pull herself onto her feet. But her love was just her steady support, it was her father's eyes she sought.

"You killed him," she said, the words quiet and disbelieving. "You killed Asclepius."

Her father didn't say anything. The silent invasion of a crackling tension wormed its way into the air around them.

The brothers seemed to be waiting for a response, a confirmation or denial, something she would like too. Her memory of the doctor sprawled on the dark ground was just a snapshot. A still image. One that she'd possibly invented during her slumber.

When her father did eventually draw in breath to speak, it wasn't to satisfy their interest. "How are you feeling, Light-Sprite? Took you a while to settle in the truck. Once you were out, you slept for about ten hours."

"Harry," Daire said, somehow encroaching further on her even though he didn't move. "Is Asclepius dead?"

"I did what I had to do," Harry asserted.

"Shit," Styx exhaled. "Now Garrick's our only shot."

He turned his back on Harry who was in front of the sink. "There's always another way," her father said. "His life was not worth more than my child's."

She was so dazed that she didn't even react to Daire's arm going around her shoulders to pull her close. Harry had killed for her. To protect her. More than that, he'd killed someone who could've been a useful ally. At the very least, he was someone with information they needed. Though he'd been more explicit about what was required of her and how her position had come about, there were still things they didn't know.

Like the order of the keys.

If they didn't get that right, the failsafe would kill them before they got the chance to do anything else.

She couldn't wrap her head around it, couldn't figure out why her father had done something so final, something that weakened their position, just to protect her from Zeus.

"He was taking me to him," she said. "To Zeus, wasn't he?"

"That was his plan," Harry said, more somber, yet still apologetic. "He tried to sell me some bullcrap about working him from the inside, but Landyn was never that guy. He didn't have it in him."

Landyn was Asclepius's real last name.

"He stood up to you," she said, still trying to come to terms with what her father had done and what it meant.

"Yeah, 'cause I caught him at it… He tried to take me out of the running first."

But Harry had been there for her. When she needed help. If it wasn't for him, if he hadn't confronted Asclepius for taking her or if he'd agreed to the doctor's plan, she could be on her way to Zeus, moving further away from her Heart.

Her fingers curled into the fabric of his tee-shirt. Daire was beside her, just in front of her, yet angled to keep an arm around her.

"You saved her life," Daire said. She shared his incredulity. "You actually came through for her."

And that was it. Although Daire was talking to Harry, he was giving her thoughts definition. Her father, a man she'd thought didn't care for her. One who put Olympus first. He'd put himself at a disadvantage, lessened his chance of learning what he needed to know, because of her.

"I'm her father," Harry said. "I'd do the same for any of you three. There's nothing more important than family… Just took me a few decades to realize there's more than one way to protect the people I love."

That was sort of an admission that he loved his boys too and it put a smile on her face. Harry wasn't looking at her, he wasn't looking at any of them, not in the eye. Baby steps. Saving her to the detriment of the mission, admitting his affection for the boys he'd raised to be good men, he was making a lot of progress. She couldn't expect him to go all the way out the gate.

"What's next?" she asked, choosing to help the three men out. If it wasn't for her, they'd probably have stood there awkwardly avoiding eye contact for the rest of the day. "We go to Garrick?"

"No," Daire said. "Six is next."

His frown landed on her father. Determination replaced discomfort; at least they were moving on.

Harry shook his head. "No, Tess is right. We have to join with the rest of our faction."

"We don't know if they're our faction," Daire said. "We don't know that we can trust Garrick."

Everyone had presumed Garrick was too passive to

make moves on his own. It had been a surprise when he was the one to begin gathering up Olympus agents. The surprise gave them some more insight, gave her insight anyway. Garrick wasn't all he made himself out to be. Standing back, loitering in the shadows, allowing people to believe he was meek and unthreatening… it was excellent cover.

Yet, she heard herself say. "We can't take the chance that he sneaks up behind us," she said. "We should wait to join him. Yes, he might be working for Zeus, but if we find out that's true, you'll have both targets there to take down. You won't risk him running and hiding, you can take him out there and then."

A smile crept onto Styx's face. "I love this attitude. If you weren't screwing my brother, I'd definitely marry you."

"Hey," Daire snapped.

She laid a soothing hand on his abdomen while addressing his brother. "It will be their attitude. We have to match it."

Those on Zeus's side may want Daire to join them. When it became clear he had no interest in hurting Harry, their patience would wear thin and wouldn't last forever.

If Daire wasn't with them, he'd be against them. No one refuted his capability; no one would want to oppose his skill.

"We can take them out before they know we're coming," Daire said, glaring at Harry. "I got your titan, and we had a deal… Six for Titan."

"You also agreed to follow his command," she said before Harry could retort. Having the men at odds would weaken their side. The last thing she wanted was a fight. Stepping in closer, his surprise wasn't unexpected. "I want you to take him down too. All of them. Harry remembers the deal. He doesn't plan to go back on it, do you, Harry?"

Keeping her eyes on Daire's, she knew he'd be less confrontational if she was the one in his sights.

"No," Harry said, his voice flat. "You'll get Lowell when the time is right. We must be smart. Letting yourself be driven by emotion is never smart."

As Daire's fingertips met her cheekbone, she smiled.

He adored her, loved her, not as much as she loved him because that just wasn't possible. Turning her head up, she brushed her lips across his caress.

For as long as they were against Zeus and whoever else he'd recruited, she wasn't sure Daire would be able to ignore his emotion or not let it drive him. Now that he understood the power it could give him, and what he was fighting for, it wouldn't be easily ignored.

"Your something," she whispered, catching his hand by twining their fingers.

"Right back attcha."

"You know that's like a magic power," Styx said, his voice closer than before.

She and Daire were still entranced by each other. Being apart, even for a few days, left them starved for each other. They'd want to gobble up as much of each other as possible for a while.

"Styx," Harry warned.

"The way she subdued him like that," Styx said. "I thought he was ramping up to something and then she just… takes it away."

Was that what she did? Take something from him? Daire must have seen her alarm because he caught her chin to raise it higher.

"You make everything possible. You give me strength and power and focus."

"Do you know how much I missed you?"

He bowed lower until their lips were only an inch apart. "Not half as much as I missed you."

"Okay, yeah, no time for mushy," Harry said. "We've gotta get this rig on the road. Ares, you're up front. Styx, you're in the rear with Pandora."

"Yeah," Styx said.

Harry went out first. She only just saw him go as she coiled both her arms around one of Daire's. Styx was just a meter away.

"How come you're always Styx?" she asked.

He started down the trailer; she and Daire followed.

"Who'd you want me to be, Lady?"

"I don't know your real name."

"Styx is it," he said, almost cold in his finality.

He left and Daire held her back. "He doesn't want to be associated with what came before," he murmured. "He says his life started at Olympus. That what came before was a different life."

Extracting his arm from her grip, he jumped onto the asphalt under the Beast, but turned to reach for her waist. The steps weren't out and they were about to take off, so she was happy to drop her hands onto his shoulders to let him lift her out.

"Okay," she said, nuzzling his mouth when he hesitated to put her down. "Then Styx it is. I take my lead from you, my Heart."

He kissed her, finishing with a smile on his face. "My lead after you give the orders." He set her on her feet, turning her toward the truck. "Settle in, Harry will have Styx and I tag in and out until we get to where we're going."

"Where is that?" she asked, sliding her hands over his when he squeezed her shoulders to guide her path from behind.

He kept their pace slow. "Don't know. You said we follow orders, so we follow orders."

Stopping at the back passenger door, she tipped her head all the way back. "Sounds like I'm not going to get laid for a while."

After a pause, he came closer, she only knew how close because his mouth warmed the hair over her ear. "All you have to do is say the word, Temptress."

Yeah, right. With her father in charge, it wouldn't be that straight forward.

TWENTY-EIGHT

SOMETIMES BEING RIGHT WAS NO FUN. For the last day and a half, they'd been on the road. With both Styx and Daire on hand, Harry switched them out every eight hours, so there was no need to stop for more than food and bathroom breaks.

She didn't doubt either man's stamina. Though she did doubt the quality of sleep they got squashed into the back next to her. She hadn't enjoyed being cooped up in the truck and she was much smaller. Plus, when Daire was in the back, she could stretch herself out and sleep with her head in her Heart's lap.

In the darkness around them, they drove across uneven ground. Daire was in the driving seat again and had been for the last four hours or so. She had no idea where they were going. Occasionally, Harry would mutter something to the man at his side. Sometimes it sounded like directions, but they had a shorthand she hadn't quite figured out.

As they bumped over uneven ground, she blinked into the landscape being lit up by the truck headlights. They were going down a hill, surrounded by trees, toward a lake with a backdrop of hills and mountains. If it wasn't the middle of nowhere and they weren't possibly being pursued by a nefarious posse or two, the colors and terrain may be considered picturesque… not that it was at its best in the artificial lighting.

"This doesn't look like a place it's easy to run from," she said to everyone.

The man at her side answered. "Which is what our enemies will think too."

His eyes were closed; she'd thought he was asleep. Apparently not. Shifting her shoulder to the back of the seat, she focused on Styx, the fake sleeper.

"You don't even know where we are."

"I know where we are," he said, without opening his eyes. "Life was missions and Olympus, sure, but training could happen anywhere."

She didn't like the idea they were somewhere the Olympus agents had been before. "If this is Olympus, won't Zeus know where we are?"

Styx's lips twitched. "Zeus didn't train with us."

"We need to be somewhere the guys can find us," Daire said from the front, concentrating on taking them down the slope. Thankfully, it was beginning to level off. "Somewhere Lowe knows."

"I thought it was Garrick you spoke to," she said, directing her question to her father.

"Harry spoke to Garrick," Daire said. "I spoke to Lowe."

Because they still trusted their men more than the principal whose loyalty could go either way.

"Do you know who they found?" she asked. "Who is with them?"

"Would it matter if we told you?" Styx asked. "You don't know anyone."

"It would be nice to know just how many big, scary, highly-trained men I'll be sharing this new horror movie location with."

Somehow these sinister settings were becoming a part of her everyday life.

"Think the Whist caused permanent damage," Styx said, sinking lower in his seat. "Your father and boyfriend own their asses. If you think you have anything to fear, you haven't been paying attention."

Raising her eyes to the rearview, she wasn't surprised to find Daire looking back. Every once in a while, he'd glance back at her, probably for longer than he should considering he was meant to be concentrating on what was ahead.

She wasn't afraid, not really. Intimidated? Maybe. Styx also seemed to forget that the men hadn't been made aware of her relationship with Daire yet. Not that the news would mean she had something to be afraid of. But Harry's words kept trickling into her thoughts. *"Daire, you'll have to be ready for the men to doubt you."* That was what her father had said. Daire hadn't seemed worried. But she was. Those men had to have her Heart's back when they were in the field. She didn't want any doubts. Even in training, she didn't want to be the cause of tension in the ranks.

They got to the bottom of the hill and parked the truck in front of the trees, parallel to the water, a good thirty feet away.

When Daire turned off the engine, relief rose.

"Thank God," she groaned in a long rush of breath and grabbed for the door release, ready to jump out.

Styx grabbed hold of her, pulling her to the center of the backseat before she could get out. Surprised he'd lunged across for her like that, she planned to glare at him, but her expression snagged on the scowling Daire who was twisted around fixating on her.

"I taught you better than that," Daire said.

Her jaw swung loose. What had she done wrong? No one seemed interested in enlightening her.

"She's impulsive," her father said.

"Think maybe that's why she fell into bed with you, bro," Styx asked, lacing his voice with teasing.

"Yes," Harry said. "Which is why we expect you to have restraint."

He wasn't talking to her; his judgment was reserved for Daire.

Her Heart ignored both men. "Stay here until we come back and let you out."

"Are you serious?" she called as the three men got out in sync.

She got no response except the electronic thud of the doors being locked, trapping her inside. Exhaling, she tried to remind herself that them leaving her behind was their way of protecting her. She understood that. Appreciated it. They were the key to her survival.

Lying down on the backseat, she tried to stretch her cramped muscles. Somewhere along the way, somehow, she'd dampened some of the spirit that compelled her to make a nuisance of herself. The men didn't consult her. They didn't include her.

Harry had saved her life; there was no denying that. Judging him was easy because he'd been absent her whole life. She made allowances for Daire being the man he was trained to be. Yet, all along, she'd failed to make those allowances for her father. Why did she expect more from him?

Daire had admitted to spending a portion of his life hating her. He'd come around. Faster than her father. She didn't feel the love from him, couldn't see any indication in his gaze that he valued her, not for more than the occasional flash of a second or two.

Styx was a complex guy as well. If he rejected the name he'd been born with, his upbringing must have been awful. He'd killed his own father, that was proof enough. Knowing what she did of Olympus and the hints of what they'd been asked to do on missions, it was tough to believe how awful his childhood must have been in comparison.

Her father had saved her life.

Lost in that thought, she tried to figure out how what had happened with the doctor had changed things between her and Harry. They didn't have trust. They hadn't had trust. But he'd saved her life.

Curling her fingers around the bullet on her cleavage, she wished her mother was there to guide her. She was so lost in her thoughts that she didn't hear anyone approach. The door behind her head opened.

She tipped her chin up to see Daire standing there. "We haven't had sex since Harry arrived," she said.

That hadn't been close to what was in her head. Just seeing him brought the words out of her. It didn't seem he'd expected her to be so abrupt. Whatever had been on his lips stayed in his mouth as he sealed them. They began to curl, but her Heart had no chance to come up with a response.

Her father got there first. "Don't expect to any time soon."

She couldn't even see him. Drawing in a breath, she sat up.

Sliding herself to the end of the seat, she dangled her legs out of the door. Her father was striding over toward them.

"Is this you making up for missing my teen years?" she asked. "Or do you like to see a man ragged on the edge of his control?"

Just before he stopped, Harry gave Daire the once over. "He looks fine to me."

She grinned, curling her fingers into the edge of the seat. "That's because I haven't started yet."

"And you won't," Harry said to her, then turned to his ward. "It's hands off, soldier. Your dick stays in your pants."

"Wait a second," she said, quick to lose her humor. "That wasn't part of the deal."

"The deal was to follow my orders," Harry said without equivocating. Sometimes she envied how sure he was of everything all the time. "Until the guys get here, we train. Both of these guys need to be in top form for what's to come."

She shrugged. "I don't mind if he does all the work. He usually takes over anyway. That's Omega. Working up a sweat... He can be pretty energetic when he wants to be."

"LR," Daire said on an exhale.

"What? He started it, he said training."

"Is your relationship only as strong as the frequency of your intimacy?" Harry asked. "If you don't get laid, you don't love him, is that it?"

"No," she said, not appreciating him twisting her words. "Fine, no sex." Keeping her grip on the seat, she leaned back to stretch out a straight leg to run a foot up the inside of Daire's thigh. "There's plenty of other stuff he's good at."

"No," Harry said, stepping between them, using his own leg to push hers down. "He's at work now. There is no play."

"None," she said, frowning. "How do you plan to police that? Are you going to put a camera over our bed?"

"There won't be an '*our*' bed."

That sent a chill through her. By the time her hands loosened and her head began to shake, her frustration had already become dread.

"You can't," she said. "You can't stop us from sleeping together. It's sleep."

"If that's all it is, what does it matter where it happens? Together or apart?"

Again, her father was sure. Always so damn sure. She didn't want to admit how much comfort and security her Heart provided. It seemed weak to give voice to her vulnerability. The last thing they needed to do was talk about how their proximity gave them strength. Anything could lie ahead, and it could involve being apart. She didn't want to weaken Daire, which was what Harry said she did any time she mentioned her Heart's name. And she didn't want him to doubt that Daire was any less than at his peak without her.

They could function apart. They'd proved that over the last few days. But being separated gave her such an appreciation for the time that they had together. Why should they waste any of it? She got so much from him just sharing the same sheets. His physical presence gave her safety sure, but her emotions could take a break from the negative when he was around. Her mind didn't have to work and race. Even if something was bothering her, all she had to do was kiss him and he'd wake up enough that she'd tempt him into talking.

"Babe?" Jolted from her thoughts, she found her eyes on his. Harry had stepped aside at some point. "Say the word."

She couldn't. As much as she loved being intimate with him, sharing the night with her Heart, sleeping together wasn't more important than what they were facing. Besides, they were all the way out there now. If she told Daire that she wanted to leave, would they just abandon Styx and Harry? The others would get there… eventually. Though she didn't have a clue when.

"Guess you'll have to live without me for a while," she said, doing her best to tease him though it was trepidation that quickened her pulse.

"Whatever you say," Daire said, offering her a hand.

Instead of taking it or getting out, she leaned back again. "Can I sleep in here?"

"You sleep in the bed," Harry said. "In the trailer."

That was Daire's bed.

"Then where does he sleep?" she asked.

A clatter behind Harry made him step aside, opening the moonlit view. Styx was standing there, twenty feet from the water, a lump on the ground in front of him, presumably the cause of the noise. Hunkering down, he opened it up and began to pull something out. A tent. Camping gear.

She scowled at the back of her father's head. "You knew you were going to pull this since the beginning. Since you found out about Daire and me."

"He told us to source the camping equipment before he knew about us, babe."

"She's not wrong," Harry said. "Why do you think I said you'd have a problem following orders?"

"Oh, so you knew he'd follow you just fine, unless I was shaking my tail in his face."

"Policing your relationship was not a job I wanted," Harry said. "I offered to walk away. Gave you the chance to call it off."

She folded her arms. "I told you we would respect the hierarchy and we will."

"Providing you don't exploit our agreement," Daire said. "Tess and I are together. Nothing changes that. Sex or not. Sleep or not. We're in it together. Once this is over—"

"Once this is over, what?" Harry asked.

Though she was interested in the men's conversation and wanted to ensure it didn't become an argument, she kept an eye on Styx too. The guy was just over there, doing his job, probably listening, though it didn't look like he cared what they were doing or saying to each other.

"Just don't forget Tess is my home. She's my primary mission."

"You have to get this attitude in check before the guys get here," Harry said with a hint of anger and a whisper of disappointment. "You're too defensive when it comes to her."

Facing his father, Daire strengthened his stance. "You want to talk about why? About the fuck who took her to another continent or the bastard who took her to a guy who tried to abduct her?"

"Don't you fucking dare—"

"Hey!" Leaping from the truck, she put herself between the two men. Laying a hand on both of them. "We're allies. Friends… Harry, Daire is serious about his relationship with me. He only gets emotional about it when you minimize it. How would you feel if someone questioned your love for mom?"

Startling him was a good way to get Daire out of his sights. "No one would dare."

"Exactly," she said. "That's how Daire feels." She turned to look at her love, keeping a hand on each man. "Daire, Harry is worried for your safety. There is a lot of pressure on his shoulders right now. He wants to get his men out of this situation in one piece. Zeus has already proved personnel are expendable. You have to be focused, at the top of your game. He doesn't want you to relax. Being with me splits your focus… Anything could happen any second. We don't know who to trust. He needs to know you're strong because we need you. All of us need you. I gave you to Olympus once. Now I have to give you to this… Nothing is more important than protecting the world from Zeus. I'll always be yours and you'll always belong to me. We don't need sex to prove that to each other."

"You know what we are, Little Red," Daire said, curling a finger under her chin to run his thumb across her lower lip.

"Yes, I do. You know I do."

She wasn't just talking about what they were

anymore.

Daire picked up on her meaning and smiled. "Right back attacha."

"Right, now can we get on with this?" Harry asked but didn't manage to break their trance. That was probably why he grabbed her arm to drag her away from the truck. "Ares, get to work."

Her father was in charge, she had given him that right. Even if she wanted to rebel, she couldn't. Daire might take that as a sign she was unhappy or a sign she wanted to leave. They could be together without being together. Whatever they had to do to bring Zeus down, to protect the people they cared about, they'd do it. No questions asked… which was going to be a mammoth task.

TWENTY-NINE

REFRAINING FROM ASKING questions wasn't easy. While they were in their serene little spot, that felt a million miles from the Olympus war, she did her best to be helpful. For ten days they'd lived there, being polite, no one starting arguments.

Each night, Harry occupied the dinette bed, while she slept in the main bed. Either he didn't like camping or he didn't trust her inside alone. He'd never given her a reason for his choice, but it didn't really matter.

Both Daire and Styx slept outside. They weren't allowed in the Beast at all, as a matter of fact. Their training exercises kept them busy outside. Sometimes she wouldn't see them all day. They'd collect wood for the fire outside and for the most part, they hunted and fished, providing a lot of what they ate. Any of the three men could be responsible for any gutting and skinning that was required. When it came to cooking, Harry had been coaching her.

It was odd taking lessons from her father. On the days when she did see Daire and Styx, she would watch Harry train them. Watch them push their bodies to the height of their ability or spar together, practicing different fighting techniques.

The man who trained the agents was tough, unapologetic, punishing. Yes, they could relax and mess around when the work was done, but while they were in training, Harry expected complete focus. He'd bark orders and command them to do tasks many would find impossible.

Yet, in the Beast, when he was teaching her about cuts of meat or seasoning and cooking times, he spoke in a slower, more patient way. Sometimes he reminded her of Daire. Learning from him gave her an insight into Daire's respect for him and into why Daire did things the way he did.

She was nowhere near an expert in the kitchen, but even she could tell there had been an improvement.

The guys had been on some run that kept them away all day. Somehow, Harry had known when they were coming back, and he'd gone outside to greet them. That meant serving had been left to her.

The brothers weren't allowed in the trailer. That didn't mean she and Harry weren't allowed outside. Of course they were. So usually, they'd all eat together around the campfire. Fall was drawing in, so the sun set earlier, though it wasn't completely dark, not when they started to eat anyway.

Waiting for her timer to go off, she retrieved water from the fridge and smiled when the music changed to something familiar. While she gulped down her drink, she went to the panel on the wall to turn it up. She didn't know exactly where Daire was, but if he was within earshot, he'd know what was on her mind.

Her bubble was quickly burst when the door opened and her father leaped inside. "Turn it down, Tess."

Although she wanted to whine at him, the timer went off, saving either of them from taking a stand. She shut the music off and went over to serve food onto each of the plates. Her father was a traditional man when it came to food. Though not even he could find everything they needed in nature. Styx was allowed to go into town on his own, Harry and Daire never did.

Daire and Styx were by the trailer door, waiting for their plates and bottles of water like eager schoolboys waiting in the cafeteria line. That was about the closest they came to alone time. She always gave Styx his food first, so that he was turning to leave when she handed Daire his. Each night he'd smile and wink. Although she appreciated that acknowledgement of them, surviving in a drought was getting more difficult with each minute that passed.

The men went to their fire. She went back to retrieve her own plate and bottle as Harry went out. Alone in the Beast, she closed her eyes and set both hands on the counter. It wasn't the sex. Sure, there were times she had an itch that needed to be scratched and with her father sharing the trailer, she couldn't even take care of that herself.

But it was his voice, his arms, the scent of him surrounding her. Her sleep was suffering, her appetite dwindling. Most days she woke up in a good mood until she rolled over in their bed to find herself alone. Again. Every day the same torture.

It ate at her like an acid chewing its way through her guts. Her love, the remedy to her ails, was so close. Lying in her bed in the dark, listening to her father's breathing as he slept, she always struggled to chase away thoughts of how easy it would be to sneak out and into Daire's tent.

Maybe it wouldn't be so easy to sneak in because as soon as he heard anyone at the entrance, he'd wake up and go on high alert. But would he chase her away? She didn't like to think so. It wasn't like she'd go to him demanding sex. All she wanted was to appreciate him for just a few minutes, to be alone with him.

Except she'd promised not to compromise him. The mission had him. That was where his focus had to be. It wasn't right that she dreamed of compromising his integrity with such alarming frequency.

Standing there all night, or even going to bed, were more appealing options than going outside to sit with the men and pretend everything was a-okay. She had to act that way. To smile through like everything was okay. Her torture was her own, no one else's.

Picking up her plate and water, she went to the door and took a deep breath. The fresh air was good, it felt good. Opening the door and breathing in nature was about the only thing she looked forward to anymore.

Going outside, she was aware the men were talking, but she didn't even try to listen in. She just went over and dropped down onto the grass, leaning back on the stump that had been brought over as a seat. She preferred the grass to the hard wood and resting on something meant less effort than holding herself upright.

They were talking about a hike. Picking at her food, she didn't eat much and eventually decided to cast it aside. It didn't matter if she ate. With a full stomach, she'd have to stay up for at least a couple of hours. If it was empty, she'd be more likely to pass out in bed faster. Sleep was the only time she got to be with him, the only time they enjoyed each other.

"Shouldn't take more than two or three days," Harry said.

She squeezed her open water bottle in two hands, watching the water inside rise and fall as she applied and released the pressure.

"And if Garrick shows up while we're gone?" Styx asked.

"I'll send the guys to retrieve you. An exercise for them, it'll be fun."

"It'll be wasting time," Daire said. "As soon as they get here, we should hit the road."

"No," Harry said, firm in his conviction, as always. "We'll need at least a few days, maybe a few weeks, to bring you back together. For this mission we need a cohesive unit. It's more important than ever."

"You really think any of the guys would flip on you?"

"It's been more than a year," Harry said. "We don't know what they've been through or what they've assumed happened before and after Exodus. For all we know, Zeus has been in their ears."

"How?" Styx asked. "If it took Garrick all this time to track them down, how could Zeus have gotten to them when he's spent most of the last year overseas?"

"I don't know. It doesn't matter. If we're going after him, the guys could come face to face with him any time. They might not even realize they're open to it, but Zeus has a way of knowing exactly how to appeal to what a man wants most. He promises you the world until he has you on the hook and then…"

"He stabs you in the back," Styx said. "The guys know that."

Sending Styx and Daire away was a good idea, in her opinion. At least then she wouldn't have to yearn for him while he was so close. Being apart might make it easier. Maybe it wouldn't. In the past, when they'd been apart, she'd had purpose. In that place, all she could do was wait.

"Wouldn't be so bad for me and Garrick to have some time alone."

"Are you going to tell him about Asclepius?" Styx asked.

Harry drew in a long breath. "I don't know. I'll have to judge his attitude when he gets here. If he's with us, all the way, I'll be more likely to trust him. If not, if he doesn't want to play ball and share what he knows—"

"Why should he?" Daire asked. "I wouldn't. None of us would. Zeus wants to put Olympus back together. If that's what Garrick wants, he probably won't like the idea we're tearing it down."

"We plan to replace it," Harry said. "With something better. Something more efficient and less bogged down by internal politics."

"Do we?" Daire asked. "How will that work out after I take down the Six?"

Her gaze ascended from the water bottle that was still in her fists, propped against her thighs, as her knees were drawn up. Her eyes flicked between Harry and Daire, much the same as Styx's were doing as they assessed how far the men's confrontation would go. They'd done so well being civil over the last ten days, all of them, but nothing could last forever.

"Lowell," Harry said. "You wanted him. I said you could have him. We don't want a guy like that behind us, a man we can't trust."

"We can't trust any of them," Daire said. "One and Three stole Tess away to London behind our backs. Two and

Five are brand fucking new and probably don't have a clue what they signed up for."

"We don't hurt the innocent for no reason."

"If they're still in fourteen, which we're hoping they are, but don't know for sure, Zeus knows where they are. Whether he's with them or not, he'll be communicating with them. That means he's been dripping nectar into their ears since the explosion… They belong to him."

Her father shook his head. "And once he's dead, then what? They'll reconsider, shift their loyalty?"

"Or they'll back out and leave us vulnerable to exposure. We don't know enough about them to trust them. We don't know the full story about their politics or their approach to risk. If they run, and we leave them out there, can you promise they won't have an attack of conscience and go to the cops?"

"We can take on law enforcement," Harry said, dismissing Daire's concern. "There's no way Zeus tells them everything. No way he gives them enough about the messier missions over brandy and cigars."

"That's a helluva risk you're willing to take, old man."

"Isn't it better than murdering them?" Harry asked. "You risk exposing us by taking down high-profile individuals with families. The Six are not easy to just disappear. None of them."

"Zeus did it," Daire said. "He had the balls to take the last Two out because the guy betrayed him."

"I thought we were doing things a different way?" Harry said. "We're supposed to be better than Z, right?"

"Better than him? I don't lay awake at night wondering about whose morality is more righteous and I bet he doesn't either. He did what needed to be done. We have to be willing to do the same or we're dead in the water already."

"You're too hasty. You need to breathe. You should be calm… The whole damn point of the last ten days was to get you back on form for this battle." Her father's eyes narrowed on Daire. "What happened to you? You never used to be like this."

No, he didn't. She happened to him. That was the

only explanation. The Daire he'd been in the control room, after… Hell, even before that when he was Danny. He was calm, calculated, patient. Right then, around that fire, while they were supposed to be eating, he was none of those things. Daire was tense and edgy and definitely not patient.

"JARR will fix this," Styx said, injecting something before Daire would be forced to respond to Harry's question. "Keeping the Six on the reservation will be easy with JARR. It will know something about them, maybe a lot about them. No one will expose us if we're sitting on a way to expose them in return."

"You support this?" Daire said. "Support letting them live?"

"You know me, brother," Styx said, scooping up some food onto his fork. "I'll always vote for a body count. Always seems cleaner to me." He smiled, a goofy sort of grin that showed his teeth. "Despite all the blood."

Shoving his fork in his mouth, he cleaned it off and began to chew, completely at ease with what he'd just said.

"Both of you need to look at this from a wider perspective," Harry said. "Taking the Six out, all of them, is too risky. We want to rebuild something and we'll need them behind us to do it."

"I don't trust them," Daire said. "They don't deserve to live."

Frustrated, Harry tossed his plate down. "Based on what? Because they screwed with Z? Because a couple of them kidnapped your girlfriend? Hell, if we're measuring a man's right to live on the criminal acts he's committed, all three of us should've been in the ground long ago."

Usually, she would be the one to step in and calm them down. It didn't seem to matter anymore. Nothing mattered. The hollow weight in her belly was about all she could feel. Her knees dropped to the side as she stared into the flames of the fire.

Harry and Daire had argued since the minute she'd first seen them together. There was so much history, so much had gone on between them that their relationship would never be straightforward. They loved each other like father and son, but they also had the frustration and impatience that came with a parent, child relationship too.

"You're not usually so quiet."

Someone else must have noticed that she wasn't jumping in, though it took a few seconds for the words to percolate into her psyche. When they did and she realized they were aimed at her, she sought out the speaker: Styx.

Opposite her at the fire, his curious stare was almost a glare. She didn't blame him for wondering why she was so indifferent. In fact, she was grateful that if anyone was going to question her on it, that it was the brother and not her father or her Heart.

She shrugged. "What do you want me to say?"

"Have an opinion."

There was a time when she wouldn't have hesitated to offer her opinion. Instead of taking a stand, she went with a more diplomatic approach. "Both make good points."

"What's the matter with you?" Styx asked like he didn't recognize her.

"Nothing."

"Yeah, right," Styx scoffed.

"She's been sleeping a lot," Harry said. "Nauseous too, which has put her off her food. The Whist may have had an adverse effect on her, it's happened once or twice."

"I'm fine," she said, descending onto her side, keeping the curve of her back to the log, which meant she had to shift just a tiny bit closer to Daire. "There's nothing wrong with me."

"Could be pregnant," Styx said. "That makes women tired and sick, right?"

"They used protection," Harry said, picking up his food again, "would be irresponsible not to."

She only knew that her father was eating because she heard the fork on the plate. The flames were drawing her into a trance.

"I didn't see condoms in Miami," Styx said. "You use rubbers, bro?"

Something touched her ankle, startling her into pulling away and lifting her head. When she processed that it was Daire, she looked anywhere except in his eyes and curled her legs higher, taking them further from him. He couldn't tease her like that. Shouldn't be allowed to touch her for such a fleeting moment. Reminding her of what they were was cruel when they couldn't be them there.

"Babe?"

"I'm not pregnant," she said, curling an arm under her head and settling back down. "I'm bored and I'm frustrated."

"Sexually frustrated," Styx said on a snicker.

"You didn't answer his question."

The depth of Harry's slow, unimpressed voice wasn't encouraging. She didn't care that he was annoyed about something. Daire was more affected.

"'Cause it's none of his damn business," Daire said. "Like it's none of your damn business."

"I shouldn't have to tell you how insane you would be to take the risk of being unprotected," Harry said, his voice almost crackling with rage though somehow he subdued it.

Putting that kind of anger under pressure probably wasn't a good idea. Not when, at some point, it would inevitably overwhelm the suppression and burst out.

"Neither of you are in this relationship," Daire said, doing his best to dampen his own irritation. "Unless you're in it, our methods of birth control are none of your business."

"It is my business," Harry said, the sound of his plate being tossed aside was more forceful than before. "She's my daughter. It is my duty to protect—"

"*My* duty to protect," Daire interrupted him. It was only then she realized he hadn't been holding his own dinner when she was looking at him before. Appeared she wasn't the only one off her food. "Tess is mine, old man. Not yours."

"You gonna let them fight over you like you're chattel?" Styx asked, his smirk seemed to be more about trying to cheer her up and lighten the mood than being antagonistic.

"I tried to do the traditional thing," Harry said. "I thought I could have it all. What I went through… didn't that teach you anything? Do you want Tess to become Carrie? To live a life like that? Would you want your child to live like that?"

"These are conversations that happen between me and Tess, no one else needs to know our thoughts on it."

"Why? Because you're ashamed of your thoughts," Harry said. "There's nothing I want more than for Tess to be happy." Which so far wasn't working out. "But even if she told me that meant carrying your child, I couldn't condone it."

"Condone it?" Daire snarled, fury bubbling up, becoming much more sinister. "I don't need you dictating the life of my woman or my child."

Still mesmerized by the fire, it was only because Styx was on the other side of it that she noticed him putting his plate down and shifting, apparently preparing himself to move fast.

"You have to trust my experience," Harry said. "It's not possible to have both. It's not possible to do what we do and have love… a life beyond the job."

"The whole damn point of what we're doing is to free ourselves from that shit," Daire said. "Zeus was the one who put that pressure on you. He threatened Carrie and Tess. We get rid of him, we don't have to worry about that anymore."

"And you think that you can be the first? You can balance the job and a traditional home life? It won't happen. You will always have enemies. We don't know how much the Six were involved in Zeus's decisions on the Accord. They may have been party to the deal that saw Carrie and Tess freed from Olympus."

"They were never free," Daire said. "But I'll do what you wouldn't, what you were too scared to do. I'll take 'em all down, every single one. I'll slaughter anyone who even thinks about hurting the woman I love."

Breathing out a sort of snicker, Harry didn't sound impressed. "You think you can do it. You think you can protect them. It's bullshit. I was you. Don't you get it? Thirty years ago, I said exactly the same thing. You can spill all the blood you want, it will never be enough. You can't kill everyone that wants to hurt you, who wants to control you. Your position is worse than mine ever was because your reputation is bigger. You were trained to be what you are from the second you were born. There are people who've never even heard of Olympus, but they've heard of you… You just don't get it."

"No, you don't get it," Daire said, pouncing to his feet. The moment he was up, Harry was too, and Styx wasn't far behind. "I don't want to be a soldier for hire, not for sport, not for money. Tess is the only thing I want. The only thing I value."

"If you valued her, you'd let her go," Harry snapped. "You'd let her live her life free of any ties to Olympus. That's all you are, a weight, holding her back, pulling her down. She has a chance. After we get through with Zeus and JARR, when we're set up at Gamma, Tess has a chance to be free. She can live a real life, one that doesn't have to be about running and hiding."

"She can have a normal life, but I can't?"

Some of the anger was replaced by pity when Harry next spoke. "Once JARR has been liberated, they won't need her. She won't be a playing piece on the board anymore. She'll be a regular citizen. Sure, she knows some things about Olympus, but she won't reveal them. She doesn't know enough or have the credibility to do damage where it counts. We won't pursue her, Garrick won't, and the Six won't care as long as we're doing the work."

A long silence followed. Maybe Daire was considering Harry's words. Was he right? She didn't know. Maybe. A normal life. That's what she'd told her father she wanted back when they first met. It's what she'd told Danny, that she just wanted to be free of what was chasing her. But did she want that if it meant sacrificing Daire?

THIRTY

WITHOUT SAYING ANYTHING ELSE, Daire turned and strode away. It annoyed her when people said they didn't have to worry about him because he could take care of himself. Except it was the first thing that came to mind when he disappeared into the night.

Sitting up, she looked over her shoulder to see him striding toward the trees, far from the Beast… far from safety.

"That was harsh," Styx said, though she didn't look at him. "You know what he's going through right now. He didn't need to be told the prize he was waiting to win was never going to be his. Not now."

"Better that than to lie to him," Harry muttered.

"I get that you want Tess to be safe," Styx said. "We all do. But if she's going to be with someone, who better than a guy trained to protect and serve? You can't doubt that Daire would do anything for her. He's more bloodthirsty than me these days and that's saying something."

"He's a danger to her," Harry said. "He doesn't know it because he's always had the protection of Olympus. Soon he won't have that anymore and then what? Yeah, we'll have more freedom to do things our way, but we'll be more vulnerable too. And that vulnerability only grows with every member of the Six he goes after."

Rising to her feet, back to the fire, she brushed the ground debris from her legs.

"Leave him, Tess," Harry said. "Have heart. He needs his space. He can cope with whatever's out there."

In the scary dark woods, maybe. What was in his own mind? That wouldn't be so easy to shrug off or fight.

"I've lost my appetite," she muttered, stepping around the log to go after Daire.

"Let her go," Styx said, though she barely heard the words.

Her appetite hadn't been typical since they'd arrived there. It probably hadn't been right for longer than that. Both of them had coped with being apart before, but their current situation was different. She needed to know what it was doing to Daire's head.

It had to be in the right place if he was going to get through the mission. She needed to know he could do it, as much for her own sanity as for his.

She didn't see him as she crossed the tree line and went into the darkness, but it didn't matter. In a few meters, she'd be lost and wouldn't have any hope of finding her way out in the dark. Yet, she wasn't worried. Daire was somewhere, close by. With every step she took, that sense of his proximity grew. She could feel it.

Though it was insane and made no sense, she'd always been able to feel him watching her. It wasn't a sinister, creepy sensation as someone might assume. His gaze warmed her, it encircled her, shielding her with a ring of faithful protection.

All she could hear was the crack and rustle of strewn leaves and twigs beneath her feet. He was close but wasn't making himself known. He'd have his reasons, so she kept on going, waiting for him to approach or call out to tell her to go back

Another few meters passed. She didn't want to hesitate. The cold and dark were closing in, the warmth of his protection was waning. He'd never leave her there. Never abandon her.

Trusting her instinct, she stopped walking. She didn't look around, there was no point. If her Heart didn't want to be seen, he wouldn't be.

"Is this hide and seek?" she asked, raising her voice, though not by much. "I think your thirty years of training give you an unfair advantage." No response. For the first time in quite a while, a smile flirted with her lips. "The big, bad wolf doesn't want to come out to play? You go, I go, remember? I can stay here all night."

And she would. She'd freeze her ass off, but she'd stay out there and wait for him. He wouldn't go back without her because he loved her and because Harry would chew him out for leaving her in potential danger. There was enough tension between the men, they didn't need another thing to add to the list.

Waiting, breathing into the night, she closed her eyes, anticipating him. He'd be somewhere. Close… And that moment was the closest they'd had to being alone since… she could barely remember when. They'd shared their bed in the Beast for too short a time after she woke up from the Whist. She'd been so out of it then and hadn't known Harry's intention for their relationship. Sometimes she cursed herself for not taking advantage of those seconds. Though they seemed so distant.

Her whole body relaxed when she next felt him. At her back. Right there. So close. She didn't need to open her eyes or turn around to know he was there. The ache in her chest was eased by the heat of his body near hers. They weren't touching. They didn't need to.

Something touched her hair. Him. It had to be him. The feeling wasn't physical, it was visceral. His digits moved down over her locks, never making contact with her skin. She needed him. More then than maybe she ever had.

"Say something," she begged in a desperate whisper, terrified to break the intimacy of the moment.

She felt the weakness without him. His words were the only hope she had of restoring any semblance of strength.

"Don't worry," he murmured, sending an electric shock through her whole body. "Your warm is right here…

My Something."

"Baby," she whispered, relaxing her muscles to sway back and lean against his solid support. "You belong only to me."

"Only to you." His hand slithered onto her hip, around to her abdomen. In a single abrupt move, he yanked her back hard against him. "I would never walk away from my family."

Pressing her palm over the back of his hand, she slid her fingers between his when they opened. "I'm not pregnant."

His lips moved in her hair. "Are you sure?"

How could she be? A tear slid from the corner of her closed eyes. Her body hurt everywhere, exhaustion was her constant companion, and nausea accompanied her every morning. She wanted to assure him of her certainty... but she couldn't lie to him.

Without opening her eyes, she let his hand slide away from beneath hers and allowed herself to be turned around. His fingers drove into her hair, holding it back from her face as he tipped it upward to brush his lips across hers.

"We'll be okay," he said against her. "Always. As long as we're together, I can get us through anything."

Curling her fingers around his wrists, she used her grip to gather strength from him. "We can't have a baby," she breathed, another tear joining the first. "Harry's right. It's too dangerous."

"I can keep you safe. I will keep you safe," he said, his voice only just loud enough to rouse the air between their lips that still moved together as they spoke. His resolve was sincere. It wasn't possible to doubt his honor. He pulled back, though her eyes remained closed. "Or do you mean he was right that it's too dangerous for us to be together? You want to end us to give yourself and our child a chance?"

She didn't even know if they were pregnant. She hadn't meant that. Harry was right, about their safety as a couple, about the life their child would have if they had one. There were no guarantees that taking Zeus down would be easy. It could take years. They didn't know how the Six would respond to the new concept of Olympus that Harry, Styx, and Daire spoke about building. The danger was far from over and it may never be.

"My Heart," she exhaled, releasing his wrists to pull his mouth to hers again.

Anytime he withdrew, she chilled. Out there, in the black woods surrounding them, the cold was more potent than ever. Right up until the second his mouth responded to hers. It grabbed for control, his tongue plunging deep against hers, reminding her of exactly what they'd been starving for. Throwing her arms around him, she jumped up when he snatched her ass, picking her up only to drop to his knees and lay her down in the glorious dirt.

"Are we putting platonic on pause?" she asked, arching up against him as his mouth trailed down her throat to her cleavage.

"Fuck platonic," he growled, tugging at the button on her shorts to give himself space to shove a hand down into her panties.

Those long, rough digits were at home in their warm playground. Massaging her clit, he was skilled in heating her core, putting her whole being on ready alert. She knew what he wanted; it was what she wanted too.

Using his teeth, he dragged her top away from the swell of her breast. Catching her bra cup too, he was forceful about pulling it aside to catch her nipple in his mouth. That was what he wanted. The deep dormant desire that had hidden behind the hollowness for so long suddenly broke free in a snap of sensation so raw and stinging that she shoved Daire away.

Though he tensed to spurn her rejection, he did plant a hand on the ground to rise high over her. "You don't want this?"

"I want this too much," she panted. "I want you too much... It's against the rules and I always swore I'd never compromise—"

"I love you, Little Red... That's the only thing I'll never compromise."

Raising a hand to his cheek, she took advantage of

the opportunity to appreciate him. "I've missed you," she said, the words cracking. "I don't feel whole without you."

"I'm here," he said, laying a hand over hers to bring her palm around to his mouth. "Your orders will always override his. Say the word, I'll always be yours first."

Losing herself in his fierce gaze, she could only admit the truth. "I don't know if I'm pregnant," she whispered. "But if I am… Baby, I couldn't—"

"I would never ask you to." Dropping his forearms to the ground on either side of her head, he aligned their eyes. "You already told me you would never get rid of our child. That's what you mean, right?" She nodded, shaking a few tears loose. Breathing out a faint laugh, he smiled. "I would never ask you to… I want you and our children. I will never stop until you are safe."

She laid a hand over his heart. "Here. I'll always be safe here. Inside you."

He lowered to press his lips onto hers. "Works the other way around, Temptress."

Boosting away from her, the blanket of his body disappeared, leaving her open to the chilling elements. Blinking into the branches above them, she was dazed by the sudden cold until she felt her shorts being drawn down her legs and her shoes slipped from her feet.

"No way," she said, clamping her legs closed when he tried to part them. Raising her head from the ground, she smiled at the man poised in a crouch by her feet. "If we are breaking the rules, we're doing it the whole way."

Rolling over to rise onto her knees, she crawled around to him, ignoring the scrape of the undergrowth on her legs.

Daire descended to his knees in front of her, their bodies swaying closer, sharing their heat. "The whole way?" he asked, watching her fingers work to open his pants.

Shoving them from his hips, she was so happy Danny had come to play: he wasn't wearing underwear.

"The whole way," she whispered, wrapping her arms around his neck to pull him down into another kiss.

It wouldn't stop at a kiss, but that was exactly what she wanted. All of him. While they had the chance.

THIRTY-ONE

"HAVE YOU EVER DISOBEYED A DIRECT ORDER?" Tess asked, without lifting her head from his chest.

"Yeah, right then, two minutes ago."

She smiled. "Before the sex."

"Not since I was six years old."

When Harry ordered him out of Olympus? She didn't know if that was what he meant, but the memory of it changed her mood.

Despite the volume of things they had to talk about, their intimacy had taken priority. Maybe it had been wrong, but at the time it felt vital to their existence.

"Baby," she said, trailing a fingertip down his arm that was relaxed on the ground at his side. "I know things."

"What things? That Asclepius told you?"

She'd been about as honest as she could about what the doctor told her before his demise.

As they were outdoors and the ground was rough, after they were both sexually satisfied, Daire had lay down and pulled her whole body on top of his. Her ass and lower back were already beginning to sting. At the time, she hadn't noticed how the undergrowth cut and scratched her, she'd been too busy appreciating the man screwing her into the ground. It was okay though, she didn't mind the injuries. In the days to come, when they were separated again, she'd probably appreciate her battle scars as a reminder of their passion.

Inhaling, she planted her hands on his chest to sit up, straddling his hips. "There are things I know that I want to share with you."

"So share them."

Moistening her lips, she stroked his tee-shirt covered chest and considered her words. Planning them seemed better than just talking and hoping she'd hit the mark without angering or hurting him.

"Now isn't the right time. I promise I want to share everything with you. But while we're out here, on this mission, and with what's up ahead, I don't think it would be right to share them."

The tension between Daire and Harry was stretched to almost breaking point. Having sex with Daire was, at the time, a completely selfish act. She was coming to realize it had the unexpected side-effect of calming her Heart. He'd vented some of his pent-up frustration, which should top up his stores of patience… for a while anyway.

"Then why are you bringing it up?" he asked, rising onto his elbows, a frown creasing his brow. "You say you have things to tell me, but won't tell me? What's that designed to do? Piss me off?"

"I'm still feeling my way with this stuff," she said, touching his face, trying to soothe his tense brow. "I trust you, but I'm trying to protect you too. To make this easier for you."

If she told him about his father and he went on a rampage or turned his back on Harry, they'd be weakened. She wanted her love to be as strong as he could be because it maximized his chance of winning. When the victor's prize was living, and the loser's death, she definitely wanted her man to triumph, whatever the cost.

"You just did," he said, sitting straighter to rub his palms up her arms. "I was going crazy without you."

Smiling, she leaned in so close that her nose bumped his. "I kept thinking about the escape route. You know you told me to climb out the back window… I thought if I did that, I could sneak into your tent—"

He groaned. "Temptress, I would never have let you go."

She flopped her arms onto his shoulders. "I'd be okay with that."

Using his head to move most of her hair out of his way, he kissed her neck. "You tell me what you have to tell me when the time is right. I trust you to know that," he murmured, teasing her with his mouth.

"Why did you storm off from the fire?" she asked, running her fingers through his hair. "Is this what you were hoping? That I'd come after you and we'd…"

"I'm always hoping that," he said, slipping both hands under the hem of her top to spread them on her lower back. Her bra was still unhooked, trapped inside her top. No doubt his hands would find their way inside it again. "I walked away because I realized Harry's not wrong."

Again with the refusal to just say someone else was right. These men were flat stubborn. She doubted they even knew they did it, which put a smile on her face.

"He's not wrong about what? Bringing us here? The training?"

"You'd be safer without ties to me and Olympus."

She did not want to go down that path with him. "You should rename it," she said, paying little attention to what he was trying to tell her. "Whatever comes next needs a new name. It's not going to be the same as Olympus, is it? So we shouldn't call it that."

"Little Red—"

"What about Elysium?" she asked, cutting him off before he could suggest something that would upset them both. "That's like the afterlife and Hades' jurisdiction, right?"

"I love you, but—"

"No buts," she said, grabbing his shoulders to push him back. "We were just saying that you might've knocked me up and now you're trying to dump me? What happened to never leaving your family?"

"If you're pregnant, there's not a chance in hell we're splitting up. We're getting married and then I'll find somewhere safe for you to stay while we finish things with Zeus."

"You want me to run and hide?" she said, shoving away from him to climb off his lap. "I said I wouldn't do it. Everyone agreed it wasn't safe for me to be separated from the group in—"

"That was before," he said. "If you're pregnant, we have to consider the baby."

Snagging her shorts, she was still sitting in the dirt when she pulled them on. "Yeah, and it will be my responsibility to protect that baby. Staying with the child's father and his band of highly-trained professional super-agents is smarter than holing myself away in some dingy apartment."

"There are options," Daire said. She heard him getting to his feet and fastening his pants. "You wouldn't be left alone. We'd make sure you were protected."

"Who's we?" she asked, tossing her hair from her face as she stood up and hooked her bra. "Harry doesn't think it's a good idea for us to have a kid at all. He thinks we should abort."

Daire's expression hardened in a flash. "And I said I would never ask you to do that."

That was hardly a soaring, heart-lifting declaration of his desire to father a child with her. "Would you want me to do it?"

"No!"

"You just said that you wouldn't ask me to do it. What if *I* said I was going to abort, would you support me?"

She would never do that. She just couldn't imagine sitting in a gynecologist's chair, legs spread, doing nothing while some doctor killed the child she'd created with the man she loved. It would be like killing a part of them, a part of their love. Maybe it made no sense to anyone else, but the thought just broke her heart.

"Tess..." he started, approaching her with his hands out like he intended to take her shoulders.

She backed away, shaking her head. "The last thing I ever wanted was to weaken you. I know that the vulnerability of a child does that. I have the implant. I was sure it would work. I didn't do this on purpose. I can't command my body to release an egg for you to fertilize."

"I know that."

She only stopped retreating when her back came up against a tree. "I could say it's someone else's… No one can know for sure. We're not common knowledge. Harry and Styx can keep a secret. If you're suggesting we break up because you don't want the responsibility of a child—"

"Hey," he said, cupping her jaw to brush his thumb back and forth on her cheek. "Would you stop talking? There are so many things wrong with what you just said, I don't know where to start. We don't even know if you're pregnant."

So they shouldn't worry about how to handle it until they knew for sure? She hadn't considered it a possibility, she'd just thought she was depressed about the distance in their relationship. A child would change everything. For them, for the future of whatever Olympus became, in the relationship between Harry and Daire. Just being together had caused so many problems she wondered why he'd choose to keep putting himself through the stress.

Maybe that was why he was open to Harry's suggestion. Maybe Daire was beginning to see that their relationship was more trouble than it was worth. That would lead to his reluctance to have a child too. Everything she did weakened him. When he'd been free of her, part of Olympus, his life had been straightforward. Yes, the danger still existed, but he had more control over it and how he responded to it.

She was a difficult variable to handle. A child would add a whole other layer of uncertainty.

He began to lower like he intended to kiss her. Before his mouth got to hers, he paused. For a few seconds, he just stood there, a frown beginning to take shape on his face.

"What?" she asked. "What is it?"

"Listen," he murmured.

She did but didn't pick up on whatever he was hearing. Maybe half a minute later, the rumble reached her ears. "What is that?"

Whatever it was, it sounded like it was coming from

above. But it wasn't a helicopter or plane, it was something else.

"Vehicles," he said, grabbing her hand. "Come on."

Pulling her away from the tree, he built up their pace with each new step until they were in a run. "Vehicles? How can that...? It sounds like it's coming from the sky."

"Not the sky, the ridge above us," he said. "They'll be coming down the same way we did."

She remembered leaving the road and driving across wilderness before turning to come slowly down the curving hill that hugged the forest and took them to where they'd made camp.

Her shoes were back at their fuck-site, her panties too; she hadn't found them before putting on her shorts.

They broke through the tree line. Daire didn't slow down. Pulling her across the grass, his urgency sent some signal to Harry and Styx. They both leaped up from their places around the fire and rushed over to meet them.

"What is it?"

"We've got company," Daire said.

"Garrick?" Harry asked.

Daire shook his head. "I didn't get eyes on."

Harry slapped a hand to his upper arm. "Go."

Her Heart didn't even look at her, he dropped her hand and sprinted away, past the Beast, presumably to check who was coming to join them.

She was still looking in the direction he'd disappeared when Harry stepped into her eyeline. "Go with Styx, do what he says." Her father looked her up and down. "Get long pants and sturdy footwear from inside. Don't change, just grab them. You have twenty seconds."

No time to argue or ask questions. While Harry gave Styx his orders, they dowsed the fire, and she ran inside to do as her father said. Getting pants, boots, and a pair of panties from the closet, she also grabbed one of Daire's hoodies and a pair of his thick socks. They could be out there for a while, depending on who was coming, and she didn't want to get cold.

The hoodie only took a second to pull on as it was so

big. She snagged a couple of bottles of water from the fridge and a handful of power bars, stuffing both into the long pocket at the front of the sweater. Her panties and socks went in there too. Her lover's brother did not need to know about her lost underwear; if he knew, he wouldn't miss the chance to tease her about it.

Styx was waiting for her, pack on his back, when she jumped down from the Beast. "We've gotta get out of here, fast."

Again, her hand was stolen from her side. Styx wasn't taking her to camp though, he was taking her away from it. From the Beast, from safety, from her Heart. Someone was coming. Daire ran towards the danger while his brother took her away from it. If anything happened to either of them, their stolen moment in the forest could end up being their last.

TO BE CONTINUED...

Thank you for reading this tale!
If you can, please take the time to review.

~

Ask your local library for more Scarlett Finn
novels!

~

For all things Scarlett Finn
check out:

www.scarlettfinn.com

BOOK FOUR

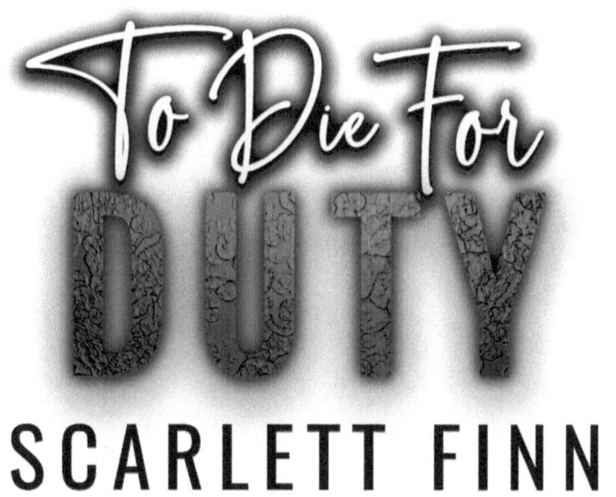

SCARLETT FINN

OUT NOW!

www.ingramcontent.com/pod-product-compliance
Lightning Source LLC
Chambersburg PA
CBHW060759190726
48285CB00002B/487